C000148535

The Road to Agincourt

Book 5 in the Struggle for a Crown Series

By

Griff Hosker

Contents

The Road to Agincourt

Published by Sword Books Ltd 2019

Copyright ©Griff Hosker First Edition

Cover by Design for Writers

List of important characters in the novel

(Fictional characters are italicized)

- *Sir William Strongstaff*
- King Henry IV formerly Henry Bolingbroke
- Henry of Monmouth (Prince of Wales and Henry's son)
- Ralph Neville, 4th Baron Neville of Raby, and 1st Earl of Westmorland
- Henry Percy, the Earl of Northumberland
- Sir Thomas Fitzalan, Earl of Arundel
- Thomas Arundel-Archbishop of Canterbury
- Sir Edmund Mortimer
- Edmund Mortimer, 5th Earl of March (Nephew of Sir Edmund Mortimer and claimant to the English crown)
- Thomas Bardolf, 5th Earl of Bardolf
- Owain Glyndŵr (Glendower), Rebel and pretender to the Welsh crown

Royal Family Tree of England

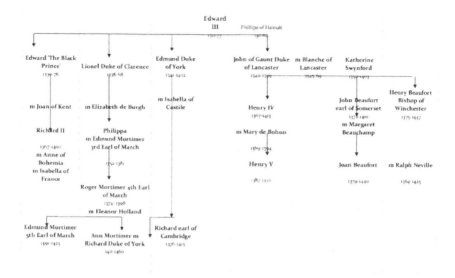

Edward III 1312-77 — Phillipa of Hainalt 1311-69

Edward 'The Black Prince' 1330-76 — m Joan of Kent — Richard II 1367-1400 — m Anne of Bohemia — m Isabella of France

Lionel Duke of Clarence 1338-68 — m Elizabeth de Burgh — Philippa m Edmund Mortimer 3rd Earl of March 1352-1381 — Roger Mortimer 4th Earl of March 1374-1398 m Eleanor Holland

Edmund Duke of York 1341-1402 — m Isabella of Castile

John of Gaunt Duke of Lancaster 1340-1399 — m Blanche of Lancaster 1345-69 — Henry IV 1367-1413 — m Mary de Bohun 1369-1394 — Henry V 1387-1422

Katherine Swynford 1350-1403 — John Beaufort earl of Somerset 1373-1410 — m Margaret Beauchamp — Joan Beaufort 1379-1440

Henry Beaufort Bishop of Winchester 1375-1447

m Ralph Neville 1364-1425

Edmund Mortimer 5th Earl of March 1391-1425

Ann Mortimer m Richard Duke of York 1430-1460

Richard earl of Cambridge 1376-1415

North

60 Miles

Chapter 1

Henry of Monmouth, King Henry's eldest son, Prince Henry, took his first steps to become a warrior in the mould of Edward, The Black Prince, on the field of Shrewsbury. The battle had been hard-fought and we had come close to defeat for Hotspur and our enemies had employed the archers of Cheshire. Attempts had been made on the King's life and the battle had hung by a thread until Hotspur was slain. He was killed by me. I am Will Strongstaff brought up by common soldiers, the Blue Company who served The Black Prince. I was not born a noble but I became one and I am a warrior and I know how to fight; I know how to kill and I know when I see a leader. I saw one that day when Henry Monmouth fought for the whole battle with an arrow lodged in his skull. I know of no other man who could have done as he did and yet, at that battle, he had been a mere callow youth. But I saw, in him, a leader who could lead our knights, men at arms and, most importantly, our longbowmen, to victory.

Although we had won the battle of Shrewsbury, we had lost many men and the Welsh were still to be defeated and Owain Glendower was still at large. The northern barons, despite the loss of Harry Hotspur, were still in a rebellious mood for their earl, Hotspur's father, had not been at the battle and having lost his son and his brother was not in a mood for reconciliation. I had lost men from my retinue, men who had fought with me for years and others had been wounded, but we could not go home for King Henry was forced to keep his army in the field. The Welsh, as cunning as ever, had sent few men to aid their allies and they had taken many English castles in Wales. We were still at Shrewsbury for it had been a bloody battle and many men had been hurt. The Prince of Wales had been taken to Kenilworth Castle where his doctor, John Bradmore, was still trying to ensure that the King would not lose his eldest son!

I was summoned, in my new role as Sherriff of Northampton, to a meeting with the King and his senior advisors in Shrewsbury. I was in elevated company for there were nobles there, such as Richard Beauchamp, Earl of Warwick who had claims to the throne as well as newly-promoted men like the Earl of Arundel. However, I was not intimidated by my presence in such an august body for I had been the bodyguard to two kings, Richard and Henry and every man at the meeting was younger than I was. I had proved myself on battlefields more times than enough. I had been on crusade with King Henry and although I had earned my place, I did wonder why I was present for all those assembled knew that I had little to do with politics and this meeting had a political undercurrent.

There were just ten of us in the chamber in Shrewsbury Castle and the doors were closely guarded by loyal knights. The rebellion had unnerved Henry Bolingbroke as some of those who had fought against us at Shrewsbury had been, apparently, loyal men. Thomas Percy had been one of those who had changed sides at the last moment. Everyone, it seemed, was now under scrutiny. I think that the council of war was the first time I noticed the illness which soon came to define Henry Bolingbroke in his later years. I do not think any other would have noticed; indeed, they did not but I had been caring for the King since before he had even had aspirations to be one. As the other lords were speaking amongst each other and not to the camp follower elevated far beyond his expectations, I had the opportunity to study the King. I knew that it was not only the rebellion which played on his mind but the terrible injury sustained by his son. That was not the reason for my concern. I noticed that his skin had begun to flake a little. I knew that it was little enough for wearing a mail coif and helmet was always an irritation but the King had always enjoyed robust health. Even when we were on crusade in Latvia, he had been healthy. I wondered what had caused his skin to blister and redden. I put it down to the mail he wore and the battle. I know that my wife had had a salve made up for me to prevent the chafing which came from wearing a mail coif for long periods. I decided, erroneously, to ascribe the skin complaint to that even though I noticed that he also appeared to be wearier than he should for a man who was not even forty summers old.

"My lords, your attention." Sir Roger was his pursuivant and his mace, banged on the table, made all silent.

The King had a monk who was scribing for him. King Henry liked everything in its proper place and ordered. He liked to have records of who was present and what was said. It was not only his face which showed the King's condition, but it was also his voice which sounded weaker and more tremulous than I remembered. "We have won the battle but the war is far from over. We have enemies all around us. Glendower and Mortimer are still free in Wales and I have lost castles to them. The Earl of Northumberland, too, is at large and I have heard that the French are eagerly anticipating our downfall so that they can attack us as they did in the reign of King John."

He allowed that to sink in but I do not think it came as a surprise to any of us.

"Tomorrow, I will be heading north with half of the army and the Earl of Warwick to deal with the rebels who have still to accept my authority. I have already asked Sir Ralph Neville to raise an army of the loyal men of the north and to apprehend the Earl of Northumberland. I leave the Earl of Arundel here, with my son when he is recovered, to face the threat of the Welsh." He looked specifically at me, "I know that the protector of kings, Baron William Strongstaff, will watch over my son for he is the future of England and there is none better than the Sherriff of Northampton to guard him. God willing, we shall overcome the threats of our enemies and England will emerge triumphant." We all nodded. "I will write to the Lord Lieutenant of Ireland. It may well be that our forces there can attack the Welsh from across the seas. If so, then that might aid our cause. We will depart on the morrow but we will not hold a feast this day for until my son is recovered from his wound and England is once again free from threat then there is nothing to celebrate. Until that time, we would be alone."

We rose to leave and each lord bowed as he did so. I was the most junior of all the lords and I waited to the end. King Henry said as I passed him, "Will, I would have a word in private with you. Clerk, finish that elsewhere and when it is done place it next to my bed and I shall read if before I sleep." When he had gone and the door had closed King Henry said, "Sit."

4

I knew that something bothered him and I asked, "What ails you, Your Majesty?"

He laughed, "Ails me? How long is there, Will, for I seemed to be plagued by every ague known to man?" He shook his head, "I am well enough but I am not the warrior I once was. When you trained me, as a young man, then was I strong and healthy but I now sit and talk when I should be at the pel."

"You are the King, and that is a heavy responsibility."

"And it weighs like an anvil upon my shoulders. Do you know that there are rumours that my cousin Richard lives?"

I had heard such rumours. "Aye, King Henry, but we both know that he is dead."

"Yet when he was alive all men wished his death. Ironically, I was not one of them and yet as soon as he died men beat their chests and tore their clothes saying that he was a saintly man and that I had murdered him! You know that was not true!" His voice showed his state of mind and he was pleading with me almost as though I was a priest and could give absolution. He had not killed the King but he had usurped him and I knew that Henry Bolingbroke felt guilt. Could that be the cause of his ailment?

"King Henry, I was a common man as you know and I have grown into this world of lords and nobles. It seems to me that as soon as you give most men power it changes them. They become politicians and, as such, are self-serving. Sir Edward Mortimer was one such good example. He was a supporter and now sees the opportunity to claim one-third of England. I would not envy you your crown for it must be hard to see into men's hearts and know what they truly feel and not what they wish "

"You are right and yet what you say is not true of you. I see the same warrior who treated my cousin and me equally and has served this royal house well." I said nothing. "It is for that reason that I would have you watch over my son. Hotspur had control of him and it almost proved ill. You, I can trust to watch him and guide him as you did with me. I confess that there were times when I was younger where I did not always choose to take the advice you offered and I have paid the price for that arrogance. I am learning to be a better king but I pray that it is not too late. I see in Prince Henry something much greater than is in me or was in poor Richard. I would have you nurture it."

"I will do so."

"It means, of course, that you will have to stay close by him and that means abandoning your family."

"I will never abandon my family but I can still watch over the Prince and my family."

"Then you are a better man than I am, Will Strongstaff. But if any can do it then it is you. I will now go to pray. I do this more and more. Perhaps I should have been a priest."

We left the room together and he went to his quarters almost bent double as though he was Atlas carrying the world upon his shoulders and I returned to the chamber to gather my thoughts. We both knew that this sudden concern was because his world had been rocked by the treachery of those around him and the closeness of the blades in the battle. Knights dressed as the King had been brutally butchered in the battle. Hotspur had not just wanted victory he had wanted the King dead! Prince Henry should have died by that arrow but he had been saved and would be healed. Such encounters with the spectre of death made every man closer to God. When I had been with the Blue Company, those hard men alongside whom I had fought had prayed to God each time they went into battle! The clerk had left some parchment, spare quills and ink. I sat and wrote a letter to my wife. She would understand why I did that which I did. When I had finished, I sealed the letter with my signet ring. I went to seek my quarters and my son.

My son, Harry, was my squire and he had food ready for me when I entered the house we had commandeered. He knew me well and saw that I wished to be alone. He left me with the jug of wine, the bread and the cheese. I sat and thought about the Kings words and the implications for me. I was Sherriff of Northampton and that title brought me the castle of Northampton as well as the protection of the King. I doubted that my wife would wish to live there and so I needed a constable. I smiled as the question popped into my head for there was an easy answer. My son Sir Thomas could learn to be a mighty lord there. He and his family would be safe and he would be close to my wife. Prince Henry had many of his own knights and I would not need my own. Sir Wilfred could return to his manor along with those men who had been wounded in battle. I would keep my youngest son, Harry, and retain the unmarried men from my retinue.

Shrewsbury Castle was a large one but it had been damaged in the fighting and my retinue had taken over the house of a disgraced knight who had fought against the King. So far, King Henry had not decided who would reap the rewards of the fine house. Until that time, it suited us. All had known that I was in a meeting with the King and the lords who advised him. As I left the castle I was seen and by the time I reached the timber and stone house my men had begun to gather in the yard at the rear while I sat and ate. King Henry was right, I had not changed. At least, in my mind I had not changed and I had always told my men, all. They were expecting to go home for they knew not of the impending campaign.

I stepped out of the door into the yard and I looked at their faces as they stared expectantly at me. "You have all done well and the King told me to tell you so." He had not but I took his praise for me as implied praise for my men. "We did well from the battle for although there was little ransom there was armour, horses and weapons. Know that my share will be divided equally between those who died for the King and for me." I turned to Abelard, Alan of the Woods' son and the squire of Sir Roger. Sir Roger had died at Shrewsbury. "Abelard, I had a mind to send you back to Weedon with your father and the other wounded men but, if you choose, then you can stay at my side and help my son Harry for I need another squire." It was in my mind to give Harry his spurs sometime soon.

I saw him glance briefly at his father who gave a nod and he replied, "My lord, I had set my feet on the path to knighthood, I know that I lost my lord and I mourn him but I would carry on and I will follow you if you will have me."

"Then you shall become my second squire. The King wishes me to stay here in the Welsh Marches and I shall obey him. As for the rest, you can leave on the morrow. The King and a mighty host will be on the road and my advice would be to leave early. My son, Sir Thomas, shall lead you. Tonight, we feast and we will speak of the dead for they deserve to be honoured."

Sir John and the newly knighted son of Red Ralph, Ralph, came over to speak with me. "Do you have need of us lord?"

It was Sir John who spoke and I smiled for I knew that he wished to be home with his family. "No, John, go to your family." We both looked at Ralph, "But Ralph, you are newly knighted. There is a manor for you if you wish it as Sir Roger had no family."

Ralph shook his head, "And that is both kind and thoughtful but this bloody battle has shown me that the north is full of traitors. I know that Sir Ralph Neville is not one of them and he has a castle at Middleham. I would return to my mother's farm at Middleham Tyas and offer my services to Sir Ralph. I am my father's son and I believe that I can train men to follow my banner." He looked at me nervously, "Have I offended you, my lord?"

"Quite the opposite for it is what I might have said. You are your father's son and there will always be a place for you in my household."

As they left Thomas and Harry, my sons, came over and Thomas said, "I am to lead the men home. What of you, father? You did not tell the men what task has been entrusted to you."

I gestured towards the River Severn which flowed close by the town, "Come, let us sit beneath the trees for I have much to say." When we were seated beneath the willows, I handed Thomas the letter I had written to Eleanor, "Give this to your mother, it will explain much to her. As for you, I would have you become the constable at Northampton and act as Sherriff in my absence."

"You have yet to say what your tasks are to be, father." My son was persistent.

"I am to be with Prince Henry, to guard and to guide him in his efforts to retake his birthright back from the Welsh. We have the Welsh to bring to heel. This may take some time but I need a strong hand in Northampton for the King goes north with Sir Ralph Neville and there is a rumour that the French think to invade. When Prince Louis did that he landed in London and we know how unpredictable are the people there. They do not think of England, only of themselves. Even if London were to fall then Northampton could be held by doughty men. The task I give you is a hard one but I know that you can do it."

Thomas was clever and he smiled, "And the fact that my family and your grandchildren will be safe is another factor. You never change, father, and I will discharge my duty although I will not do it half so well as you,"

I laughed, "I am a warrior, Tom, pure and simple!"

The feast was a good one and better than I would have enjoyed had there been a royal feast. My men and I were all equal and my sons had continued that tradition. We felt more like a company than a lord and his men. There was all the banter one might expect from a company of warriors and no one became upset because they were mocked. I was awoken early as a third of my men prepared to leave. It made me sad for it meant I had just seventeen men left. That they were better than any who followed a mightier and richer lord was a comfort to me but they were a smaller number than I was used to. They had heeded my words and my son knew that if he followed the King and his army then his pace would be slower and there would be little in the way of food or grazing for them. They would be many miles down the road before the King had even risen.

I sought out Sir Thomas Fitzalan once the King and his army had left. The Earl of Arundel was a loyal supporter of the King and that was why, despite his youth, he had been given such a responsible position. His father had been executed by King Richard and Sir Thomas seemed to have learned from that. He and I had not always got on for he had been instrumental in deposing King Richard but I respected him for his loyalty to King Henry and he was a good soldier. He also had connections which helped for his uncle, Thomas Arundel, was the Archbishop of Canterbury and the most powerful priest in the land. The Earl was a young man, barely twenty-three, with much experience for one so young but he also knew that I had far more and when I spoke with him, I realised that he would heed my words and my advice. We sat in the Great Hall with his closest knights.

"The King, Sir William, has given me a hard task. This is a long border and the Welsh could strike at us anywhere."

I nodded, "And until Prince Henry rejoins us it would not be prudent to be too aggressive for he is the Prince of Wales and I know that he will want to be part of this campaign, despite his wounds."

"Then we have a little time and I would use it to good effect. If we are to campaign then we need a good base from which to operate. We have made Shrewsbury stronger and as Worcester strikes me as also being key to that defence, I will fortify this castle and garrison it well." I nodded for that made sense. "I would have you ride to Kenilworth to speak with the Prince. You know him as well as any and you are a warrior who understands wounds. I would know if he is ready to campaign. I am anxious to press Glendower into the north. If the Lord Lieutenant of Ireland is able to aid us then it cannot be this campaign season and until we have pressure from two sides then we will be limited to punitive raids."

"And yet that can hurt the Welsh, Sir Thomas, for if they are fighting us then they cannot produce food."

Sir Thomas laughed, "You are a true warrior, Sir William. I will await your return."

It took a day or so to prepare for the ride as we did not know if we would be returning to Shrewsbury and so we took all of our war gear with us. My men were pleased to be on the road again as idleness, even though enforced, did not sit well with them. We had won the battle but rebellion was still in the air and we rode with archers as scouts and prepared for war. I let Harry ride with Abelard. My son was the same age as Prince Henry and like the Prince had grown up with war. He had seen men die and he would know what to say to the squire who had served a knight so briefly.

We had over sixty miles to travel but our horses were in good condition as they had not been used in the battle. With just one overnight stop we reached the castle well before dark for these were the long days of summer. While my men were accommodated, I was admitted to the Prince in his chambers. His face was heavily bandaged and I saw that his features, beneath the bandages, appeared to be badly swollen. Despite the pain he was obviously in he seemed in good spirits and greeted me warmly.

"If I do not say much, old friend and teacher, it is because to speak overmuch causes me pain and not from any rudeness. Tell me all!"

As his servants brought us wine, I told him everything which had happened both in the battle and in the aftermath. I saw from his animated eyes that he had been starved of such news. I came to the meeting I had had with his father and then he truly became excited and began banging the arms of the padded chair upon which he sat. I smiled for this was Henry of Monmouth the way I had always remembered him. He had lived with my wife and me briefly and he had shown us then that he was nothing like his father or his father's predecessor, King Richard. He was as close to a common man as one could be.

"Then I am ready to ride!"

I shook my head, "Prince Henry, your father charged me with your care and, until your doctor, John Bradmore, tells me that you are ready and fit to travel then we will stay here."

He nodded and waved to his servant, "Peter, fetch the doctor!"

John Bradmore looked more like a blacksmith than a doctor but I had heard that it was a device he had invented which had saved the life of Prince Henry.

"Doctor, tell Sir William that I am fit!"

I shook my head, "Doctor, I would know the Prince's true condition as I have been charged by his father with his care."

"And that is my primary concern, too, Sir William. The arrowhead has been removed and, so far as we can tell, there is no putrefaction. The wound needs to be bathed each day with a mixture of white bread, barley, flour, honey and turpentine oil. This needs to continue for a further three days. Then the wound on his face will need an application of my special ointment to reduce the scarring."

"And you must administer these treatments?"

He looked at Prince Henry and smiled, "His servant, Peter, has watched me each day and with a little training and instructions then he could administer them but I would advise him to stay here and to rest."

Prince Henry said, triumphantly, "See!"

It was my turn to smile, "And that will fit in with our plans perfectly. I will send a rider back to Worcester where Sir Thomas is strengthening the defences and we will arrange to meet him in Shrewsbury in five days' time. That will allow the treatment to be finished and we can still make the journey and meet with your army."

The answer pleased both the doctor and the patient. I was learning to be a diplomat.

King Henry sent a constant stream of riders to both Kenilworth and thence to Shrewsbury and Worcester so that we had an accurate report of his progress against the northern rebels. Henry Percy had fled with his army to Newcastle, where the good burghers refused him entry and he was ensconced in Warkworth Castle which was a powerful castle. The King was racing north to York and the messages filled both the Prince and me with hope.

"If the north is secure then we only have the Welsh as a thorn in our side."

"And that thorn is the size of a battering ram, my lord! Glendower has Aberystwyth, Beaumaris and Harlech under siege and the land is in rebellion. I know not how many men we will take with us but it cannot be the flower of England as many are already with your father and we suffered grievous hurts in the battle."

I saw him taking that in. I had been with him for two days and already the swelling had gone down somewhat so that talking was easier. Of course, he was still heavily bandaged but England owed a debt to John Bradmore which it could never fully repay. The Prince showed that the battle had had an effect on him and he was more thoughtful. "When I go to France to reclaim the lands which are ours by right then I may not be able to take a large army. Perhaps I should learn to fight with a smaller army but fight in a cleverer manner." He did not smile with his mouth, for it caused him pain, but I saw him smile with his eyes. "The Free Companies are the model I should use. I can see that my grandsire showed great foresight when he appointed you to train King Richard and my father. How many archers do you bring with you?"

"Not as many as you might expect, Prince. I lost archers and others were wounded. I had almost thirty but now I just bring nine to war. When the others are recovered, they will swell my numbers."

"Then I need to hire more archers from my purse. I am Prince of Wales and the Welsh are good archers. I will hire those who are loyal to me and I will offer an inducement for those archers which fought against us, the men of Cheshire. We cannot be petty if we are to win back Wales and France."

He was showing maturity beyond his years and before we left Kenilworth, he had already hired ten archers. Until he had a captain for them, they joined my archers and served under Owen the Welshman. The Prince of Wales had with him ten young knights who chose to follow his banner. That was a great compliment for he was just sixteen years old but as he had demonstrated at Shrewsbury, he was a fearless and courageous leader who had fought most of the battle with an arrow lodged in his skull. The ten knights would act as men at arms when we fought. Wales, and especially North Wales, was not the country for mounted horsemen. Once you left the Clwyd valley you were amongst the foothills and rocks of Snowdonia.

I do not think that we left too soon but what we could not know was that there were still groups of rebels who had fled the battlefield but not yet returned home. The Earl of Northumberland was still at large while Sir Edward Mortimer and Glendower were free and threatening the borders. Despite King Henry's leniency, they had not availed themselves of the opportunity to make peace with the King. Instead, they became wolves who waited for the chance to take from the King and his son.

I had sent a rider to tell the Earl of Arundel that we would meet him at Shrewsbury and another to warn the constable that the Prince would require accommodation. I did not swear the two riders to secrecy and that may have been a mistake for men knew that we were riding the road to Shrewsbury and not everyone was loyal. We stayed at the small manor of Wolveren Hampton. We stayed for the simple reason that one of the young knights who followed Prince Henry, Sir Giles Jenyns came from the small market town and his father was a prosperous woollen merchant. We were feted and well treated but that, ironically, ill-prepared us for the next day for some of the young knights had enjoyed the hospitality of the Jenyns family just a little too much!

Apart from sheep, Staffordshire had many forests and, inevitably, we passed through some of them. The young knights who accompanied the Prince were just that, young knights, and to them it was a ride in the country. Luckily my men at arms and my archers were alert. Even Abelard and Harry were more vigilant than Prince Henry's knights and it was their vigilance, allied to my horse, Hart, which gave us warning of the attack.

We were close to some trees when she pricked her ears and stamped the ground. At the same time, Walter of Sheffield suddenly nocked an arrow and the other archers followed suit. I drew my sword as did my men at arms and my two squires. We just reacted to Hart and Walter. I always trusted the instincts of my men and my horses. The Prince and his knights were too engaged in some discussion or other. I could have shouted but I was too concerned with spotting the threat and when I saw the movement in the trees, I knew whence it came. It was then I shouted, "Guard the Prince!" The command was for his knights. My men knew what to do without being ordered. They would slay whoever came to do us harm. Even as my last word echoed back from the trees an arrow flew from Walter's bow. The other archers let fly. Then the forty or so men who had been in the woods burst forth. I recognised, on some, the livery they wore, and knew them for what they were. They were Northumbrians.

When Hotspur had been killed the archers he had led from Cheshire went home. Without a paymaster, they had no income. The men at arms, however, that he brought from Northumberland and the young men who thought to come south and make mischief, had not returned home. It was they who launched the attack. They burst from the trees which were just thirty paces from the road. Some wore mail and all had a helmet and a weapon of some description. I saw pole weapons as well as axes and swords. Even before they had reached us six had been struck by arrows and I led my men at arms and squires at them using our horses, as well as our swords as a weapon. Hart was not a warhorse but she was clever and as I neared the first wild man, who had a long poleaxe which he swung at me, I pulled back on the reins and stood in the stirrups so that Hart reared and flailed her hooves. It made the warrior from the wild north swing his poleaxe in panic missing both me and my horse and I brought down my sword to hack off the end. He turned and ran. I urged Hart, not to follow him but to head for the next ambusher. We had to keep them as far away from the Prince as we could. He had still to recover from his wound.

Abelard and Harry were close to me and it was Harry who drew first blood. As a swordsman armed with a shield as well as a sword raced at my side, Harry leaned from his saddle and brought it across the back of the warrior. His back was protected by a mail hauberk but that did not stop my son's sword which tore through the mail links of the hauberk and not only tore flesh but broke

14

bones. I swung my sword in a scything sweep and hit a spearman in the throat. My sword sliced first through his spear and came upwards to find his unprotected neck. As we reached the edge of the wood, I saw that the attackers were fleeing. More for the Prince's knights than my men I shouted, "Hold! Find me a prisoner!"

Seeing there was no apparent danger, now that the attackers had fled, I rode back to the Prince and was pleased to see a wall of chastened knights around him. My helmet was an open-faced sallet and my eyes bored into them as I approached. None could bear my gaze for they knew they had been remiss. Prince Henry knew it too, "Blame me, Sir William, for I have served with you and know that vigilance is all. I forgot and for that, I apologise."

No other member of the royal family would ever have apologised and I nodded as I sheathed my bloody sword. "Had my horse and archers not been alert then they might have closed with you and you, Prince Henry, are not yet well enough to defend yourself."

"Who were they?"

"From their livery, weapons and the words I heard them use, they are from Northumberland. The folk there are loyal to their chiefs and they are more akin to the Scots than to the English. I think they saw the horses and wanted those. They made a mistake and many men have paid the price."

I turned as Stephen of Morpeth and Dick Dickson half carried a wounded man towards me, "My lord, we have a prisoner!" I dismounted. "He is from the Wear, my lord, and they are all treacherous bastards there. Watch him!" Stephen of Morpeth was a Northumbrian but loyal to me.

"What is your name?"

In answer, the prisoner spat at me and snapped, "Go to, go to, you whoreson!"

I saw Stephen raise his arm but I said, "Hold! The man is dying although he knows it not yet and if we know not his name then we will throw him with the other beggars in a ditch. He does not wish to be buried in a churchyard."

The man had a stomach wound and while he was a big man he would succumb eventually. He seemed to realise the dilemma he was in and his attitude changed. "You would bury me in a churchyard, lord?"

"If you told me what I need to know then aye but I cannot guarantee that you would get to heaven for I am no priest."

"We are men who served Lord Percy, Harry Hotspur. We swore vengeance on the King and all of his supporters." He pointed at the Prince's livery, "When we saw that yon lord was related to the King, we thought to have our revenge."

"I shook my head, "That is Prince Henry, the son of the King and you and all the others are fools. How many of you are there?"

"There were a hundred but some headed home." He winced as pain coursed through his body and had not my two men been holding him he would have fallen. As he opened his eyes, he suddenly seemed to see me, "It is you, you were the one killed our master!" In a flash, he had reached into his buskin for a bodkin dagger. Even as it came for my throat Stephen of Morpeth's knife had driven into his ear and his brain. The bodkin fell from dead hands.

As he wiped the knife on the dead man's tunic he stood and said, "As I told you, lord, they are all treacherous bastards and I knew he would try something!"

We buried the bodies in shallow graves and we headed, this time with vigilance from all, towards Shrewsbury. It was not until we neared the castle that we began to relax. I rode next to the Prince for the last few miles. We were not silent for Prince Henry was a clever and thoughtful young man. "There will be other such bands roaming the land."

"Aye, Prince Henry, and when your father quells the northern rebels there will be more. I know from my time at Middleham that the north has an independent spirit. For some reason, they like not your father. It may be the death of Richard as they seemed to like him. Your father needs a strong Sherriff of York and a strong Archbishop of York."

"And I am not sure Archbishop Scrope is such a loyal man." As we spied the gatehouse of Shrewsbury, he sat straighter in the saddle. "Then it is all the more urgent that I rid the border of the threat of Glendower." He looked at me, "With your help, we shall do this."

16

I nodded my agreement but my heart would not be in the venture. I had grandchildren and, selfishly, I wished to see them but a promise made to a long-dead Black Prince meant that I would continue to put the crown of England above the wishes and desires of William Strongstaff. I could not help it, loyalty and service were in my blood.

Chapter 2

It was September when Sir Thomas Fitzalan and the rest of the army arrived to head north. We were not a huge army, indeed, by the standards of Shrewsbury, we were not even as strong as one of the wings which had fought so valiantly that day. With just two hundred knights and two hundred men at arms, it could be said that we were little more than a chevauchée but the men of Shropshire who followed us were in determined mood for they had suffered Welsh raids and wished to end the threat. It helped that they were all good archers. We would pick up another group of men, archers this time, from Chester but the fact that the men of Cheshire had risen against the King meant that it would be a shadow of the men who followed Hotspur. They would, however, give us more archers and they would be under my direction.

I was the oldest of all of the knights and nobles who headed towards the Clwyd and I was also the most experienced. The young Sir Thomas deferred to me for the others with my experience, like Sir Ralph Neville and Sir John Talbot were either with the King or had fallen at the bloodbath which had been Shrewsbury. They listened to my advice as we sat in the Great Hall at Chester and decided our strategy for the campaign. I knew the castle well for when King Richard had returned from Ireland this northern stronghold had played a crucial role in his downfall and, ultimately, his demise. I put him from my mind as I spoke for I was a professional soldier and I had been asked for my advice and I gave it.

"We have, at most, two months to campaign. After that, the snows will come and the passes will be blocked. Our army will starve and men will desert. You have brought, my lord, the Shropshire levies and that is good for they are sound warriors but they are also farmers and when the snows come and the wolves howl in the mountains then they will yearn for home. I say we strike down the Clwyd and make for Conwy. That castle is still in our hands but all around is under threat. We cannot reach Harlech and they must perforce try to hold out."

Prince Henry said, "But you think that they will fail to do so?"

"Fail is the wrong word, Prince Henry, for it suggests a lack of will or effort. The garrison is less than fifty men all told. They have been isolated for too long with no hope of supplies from the sea or land. It will finally fall but if Conwy and Caernarfon are strengthened and reinforced then those who escape Harlech will find a refuge."

Sir Thomas said, "But that does not bring us any closer to capturing Glendower."

I smiled, "And where is he, Sir Thomas? The Prince and I have been fighting him since this rebellion began and we have yet to get close to him. I have never seen him on a battlefield and he remains undefeated. The closest I came was when Sir Edward was taken and that was in the heart of Wales. The man is clever and so long as he is free, he will continue to be a symbol of freedom from English rule. When winter is over, we begin once more and, hopefully, the north and Scotland shall be secure and we will have more men available."

Prince Henry seemed satisfied and he nodded, "Then that is what we shall do and when winter comes, I will return to London and lick my wounds!" He smiled. Now that the bandage had been taken from his face, we could see the terrible, disfiguring wound. The Prince knew how to be self-deprecating and it endeared him to his men both low and high. "We will try to make London a royal stronghold once more. I may not always be in Wales, Sir Thomas, but the plans which we have will be mine and I charge you with being the instrument which keeps the blade in Glendower and Mortimer's back."

"I will, Prince Henry but…"

"There is a but?" I noticed that, since Shrewsbury, there was steel in the Prince's voice.

"It costs coins to keep men in the field and many of the knights have yet to be paid." He added, hurriedly, "They are loyal but they have families. Sir William here is lucky for he has lands which garner him money and means he can have men serving him who are the envy of the rest of us."

He was right of course but that was nothing to do with me. That was my wife and her skill as a manager of land, commerce and coin!

Prince Henry said, "I hear what you are saying, Sir Thomas." He turned to the clerk who always attended our meetings. "I will sell some of my jewels and plate, make a note of it. Others have given more to England than I have. Money and coin are nothing and England is all. See that it is so. There, Sir Thomas, you shall have the funds to prosecute this war and I will try, in my father's absence, to ensure that more money is available. Parliament and London must provide!"

Looking back, while Shrewsbury was the making of the warrior king he would become, Chester was the start of the creation of the perfect king and I was privileged to be at both.

Flint was in royal hands but Rhuddlan, once again, had fallen to the Welsh. We headed there first and I impressed upon Sir Thomas the need for speed. We found horses for all of the archers and he placed Sir Richard de Lacey, a Shropshire knight, to command the levy. They would follow, on foot, our rapid ride down the Clwyd. The Prince's wound still looked angry and hideous but John Bradmore's salve seemed to work and the Prince acted as though he had never been wounded. With twenty Cheshire archers and Owen the Welshman, we raced down the Clwyd. Prince Henry took priests with us and at each farm and village we had the men swear allegiance to King Henry of England and to Henry of Monmouth, Prince of Wales. Some might call it draconian for those who did not so swear, on the Bible, we took with us after they were evicted from their lands and their property confiscated. We did not have to do this often for word spread and the illusion of freedom evaporated. The farmers were realists and knew that Glendower and Mortimer were more concerned with the heartland of Wales and the rich marches of the Gower than the northern mountains.

We reached Rhuddlan Castle which was one of the many castles built by King Edward, Longshanks, the hammer of the Scots. It should never have fallen but then none of the others should have. Sir Thomas was keen to besiege it but I counselled against it for word had come to us that Beaumaris and Caernarfon were also now under siege. "We wait for the Shropshire levy and leave them to besiege Rhuddlan. If we can get to Caernarfon quickly then we can break their siege before it is begun."

Prince Henry asked, "And Beaumaris?"

"Will have to wait, Prince Henry, for we have a sea to cross to relieve that one and if we have little enough money for men then we have none to spare for ships."

Once more my words were heeded and, two days later, we galloped towards the coast and hurried down the road to Caernarfon. Pausing only to pick up some more archers and knights from Conwy, we raced through increasingly autumnal weather to reach the siege lines at Caernarfon. That we reached there unseen was vital and we halted our small army five miles from their walls. I rode with four of my men at arms and my archers to spy out the defences. Prince Henry was loath to let me go but of all the knights and men we had, I was the one best qualified for this. Sir Wilfred could have done this but I had sent him home. Sir Roger would have been perfect but his body lay buried at Shrewsbury. I took my squires too but we did not wear plate nor even mail, we were scouts and had to move silently.

I knew Caernarfon, not well but well enough for I had been there with King Richard. Attackers had to attack from the north and east for the river and the sea protected the other side. Nor were the Welsh particularly well endowed with siege weapons and knights. As we crept through a damp evening towards their siege lines, we saw their fires, spluttering in the rain. That we were unexpected was obvious by the lack of sentries facing the land. The twenty-one miles from Conwy might as well have been a hundred for the garrison at Conwy had been beleaguered and the land betwixt the castles surrendered to us immediately; the Welsh who lived there had expected no relief to come to Conwy Castle. Prince Henry was already anticipating how he would strengthen his hold on the land once Glendower was defeated.

I had taken Abelard and Harry because they needed to know how to do this. It was not the normal work of knights but I knew its value. Red Ralph had taken me on such scouting expeditions many times and being a lonely scout held no fear for me. We managed to get within five hundred paces of the walls and the rain-soaked fires helped us to see their defences. I had not intended to take so many men but my men were mindful of the danger the scout might face and Owen insisted upon bringing all of my archers. Their bows were carried like staffs in their leather sheaths and their strings were under their hats but my men could string a bow so quickly that we would be protected. Wearing just our coifs and arming caps we moved down the line of the camps of the Welsh besiegers. The rain and the night meant that we were, to all intents and purposes, invisible. I moved easily for I knew that I was protected. The Welsh knights had a camp, as I had expected, away from the levy and the archers. King Henry and his knights would probably do the same. I also saw more than a sprinkling of men at arms. These were not nobles but they had the money to buy mail and plate. In addition, they had been trained to use their weapons well. They could not compare with my men at arms but then few could. We returned to our own camp an hour before dawn.

Sir Thomas and the Prince were awake and waiting for us although the bulk of the army was still resting and sheltering from the rain. They looked at me expectantly. I said, "If we could go inside a tent, for although I am soaked being under shelter might make these old bones feel warmer."

"Of course."

Once inside I took off my cloak, coif and arming cap. "They outnumber us, not necessarily in knights but in all other aspects." While Sir Thomas looked worried Prince Henry merely nodded. "However, we have arrived at the right time for they have not prepared ditches to prevent their camp from being attacked. It may well be they are overconfident or, perhaps, that they have not yet had time to do so. I propose that we use our archers to rain death upon their lines while the mounted men at arms and knights attack the camp of their knights. It is close by the coast and the only place they have to retreat is through their own lines or across the River Seiont."

Prince Henry nodded, "And when do we attack?"

"Late afternoon for Snowdon and the mountains make the east darker and the arrows flying through the air will be harder to see. They will have been busy all day either building war machines or fighting and they will not expect an attack."

Sir Thomas said, "On horseback? But at Shrewsbury, we fought on foot."

I nodded, "For that suited the battlefield but here we use our strongest weapon, horsemen."

Prince Henry was in support and when he said, "It is good!" then it was decided.

I was unsure what Sir Roger had taught Abelard and so Harry and I spent some time explaining how the two of them would ride behind the last knight with a spare spear in case I needed it and to watch in case I was unhorsed. If I was then the nearest to me would give me their horse. I did not think it would come to that but it was important that he knew his role and what he had to do. I always preferred a spear to a lance. For one thing, they were easier for squires to carry and for another, I found them more effective for they were slightly shorter and I could aim the broader, sharper steel head more accurately. Now that most enemies wore plate it was harder to make a telling blow with a lance. My spearhead, like all the spears I used, was tapered and had a narrow point and then broadened out to tear terrible wounds. It could find narrow gaps in the plate and could even break mail. Not everyone could use such a weapon but I had grown up as a boy in a Free Company and I had to make do with whatever I had to hand. I had learned with the tapered spear and I had stuck with it.

Owen led the archers off first. When we had scouted, we had seen a line of trees which, in addition to the town of Caernarfon, could be used to mask our approach. My men at arms went with them and would fight on foot although they would have their horses with them. and he would order Will of Corby to sound three blasts on the horn when the first flight of arrows was released. The young Earl of Arundel had questioned my use of the horn as he thought it would alert the Welsh. I was keenly aware that I was training the young noble and so I patiently explained my thinking to him.

"The arrows will be in the air when the horn is sounded. True the Welsh will know that an attack is imminent but they will not know from whence it comes. Some men will look up for it is in their nature to do so and plunging arrows are deadly. More importantly, although the Welsh attacking the walls will be wearing mail and helmets, those toiling behind will not and the Prince will attest to the efficacy of an arrow which is released at flesh uncovered by plate. Their uncertainty will allow us to get closer to them. We will be charging, Sir Thomas, from less than four hundred paces range. We have chosen the side closest to the straits to attack for there the ground is flat and is perfect for horses. It is why we spent so long scouting. If the two of you take one thing from this then it should be that scouting is never wasted!"

We moved into position not long after noon. The ground was wet but the overnight rain had stopped and a chill wind blew from the north. It was a lazy wind for it did not go around you but came straight through you! I trusted my men and that came as a surprise to some of the other knights but I knew that they would make the correct decisions. The first flight of arrows would be released when the light was the best. The rain might have stopped but there were still dark scudding clouds which threatened more. Snowdon meant that the rain would fall there and not on the battlefield but it made the afternoon darker and that would suit us.

I rode next to the Prince and Sir Thomas was on the other side of him. We were both aware of our role. We were there to protect him. As the Northumbrian brigands had shown he was a target for his father's enemies. King Henry had other sons but Prince Henry was the hope of England and our enemies knew it. I had tried to persuade him to ride in the second rank but he would have none of it. That was his way. Had the Welsh set watchers they would have seen us as we arrayed as we were colourfully dressed. I think I was least decorated of all the riders. Prince Henry not only attracted attention by virtue of his tunic which showed the livery of France and England but also by his standard which Sir Richard Fulk carried behind him. The swan banner was unique and marked the Prince's position better than any crown!

I was watching to the left and saw the arrows rise in the air before I heard the horn. Consequently, I spurred Hawk a heartbeat before the rest who listened for the notes. It meant that I was slightly ahead of the Prince and the earl. It was a position I would not relinquish for Hawk was a powerful warhorse. I heard horns in the Welsh camp and saw knights who had been at the walls shouting for their horses. That was a mistake for it took time to saddle a horse and they should have been ready to fight us on foot. That alone told me that my strategy had worked. We could ignore the battle of the archers for if we won, as I expected we would, the battle of the horses then we could roll the rest up.

I had my spear resting easily on my cantle and I had a shield attached to my left arm so that I did not have to hold the shield. I could have relied on my plate but I had been brought up using a shield and I was more comfortable with one. The Welsh servants and those who had been in the outer camps fled before the thundering hooves of our horses. It did not do to try to stand in front of a horse. It will not deliberately stamp a man but there were so many horses charging them that injury or death were both certainties. The fleeing men impaired the knights and squires as they quickly donned helmets and grabbed pole weapons. I heard their horses neighing and complaining as men tried to saddle them. I had not lost the early lead and was ahead of Prince Henry and the earl. I saw a knight with a green surcoat with a rearing gryphon. He had a pike held in two hands. I would aim for him. The pike was a deadly weapon to use against horsemen as the point could skewer the rider and the razor-sharp blade could hurt a horse. I pulled back my arm and then spurred Hawk. I had been doing this for more than thirty years and knew that timing was everything. The sudden burst of speed threw off the swinging pike of the Welsh knight and as I stood in my stirrups and rammed down my spear towards his open, screaming mouth I saw that, if it hit at all, the pike would strike my left arm and there the shield would bear the brunt of the blow. The pike never reached me for the spearhead entered his mouth and drove down towards his spine. The speed and power of Hawk, aided by my mighty right arm, lifted the knight from his feet and drove him backwards. As I lowered the spear his body slid from my spearhead and hit a second knight who was thrown to the ground. As fate decided it, he fell beneath Hawk's hooves. It would have been a quick death.

And then we were through their first line of knights. We were amongst little parcels of men who ran bravely to stem the tide of metal and horseflesh which swept over them. I speared, in the shoulder, a grey-bearded knight who was just too slow to bring up his shield. He had a coif over his shoulders and the tapered spear tore through the mail and found the gap between his armour. Prince Henry had an extra round plate called a besagew there to prevent such a blow. This older knight did not and he fell. Now that we had broken through, I was able to glance around and saw that Prince Henry had not only survived he still had his bloody spear. Sir Thomas too had been victorious. It was then that the Welsh knights who were left broke. Their horses had been saddled and they mounted but, seeing that we outnumbered them, they turned to head for the bridge and the river.

Raising my spear, I shouted, "Wheel left!"

Had they all been my men then the order would have been obeyed instantly but I was commanding young knights who had the blood in their heads and some pursued the knights rather than doing as I commanded and attacking the men at arms and archers. It did not cost us the battle but men escaped and they would fight us again.

It became much easier as we speared men who were not wearing plate and whose training and weapons were inferior to ours. I led almost two-thirds of the knights and mounted men at arms who had first charged and it proved enough. We passed the bodies of those who had fallen to our arrows and saw that Owen the Welshman and the bowmen of England had managed to hit more than forty Welsh archers. That was a more severe blow to Glendower's cause than all of the knights we had slain and captured. I called a halt to the pursuit as soon as it became clear that their resistance had ended.

By the time we returned to the Welsh camp and the castle the archers had surrounded the survivors and prisoners were being gathered. Some would be ransomed while others, perhaps too poor to be worth a ransom would be kept as hostages in Caernarfon. The Prince was pleased with most of the knights but he berated the ones who had not obeyed my command. Some were young knights brought by Sir Thomas and one of them, Sir Gilbert de Boise, pointed a finger at me and said, "He is just a baron! I obey my earl and my prince."

The Prince was going to speak but I was in the face of the young and arrogant knight in two steps. I physically picked him up in two hands by his mail and I held him close to me, "Speak to me with respect, boy, or I will teach you lessons with my sword!" I threw him to the ground.

26

He began to draw his sword but Owen and four of my archers had returned with us and their arrows were nocked and aimed at the knight. Owen said, "Reach for your sword, my lord, and you will die!"

There was an air of tension which could be cut with a knife. The Prince smiled and said, "Sir Thomas, if I were you, I would have your young knights learn from this. When Sir William speaks it is as though it is my orders and he may be only a baron but he has the confidence of kings and princes behind him."

Sir Thomas nodded and said to Owen, "I ask you to move your bows aside for my cousin is young and foolish. I will deal with him. Sir William, I apologise. Today was a great victory and was yours. The Prince is right to be unhappy with some of the knights. I hope that they can learn before we go to war again!" It was a crucial moment for Sir Thomas was seen to be behind me and I had no further dissension from any knight.

We spent three days ensuring that the Welsh had indeed departed, and then we headed down the coast towards Harlech which we believed still held out against Glendower. We managed to reach no further than Criccieth before we learned that the castle was in Welsh hands. Whilst not as formidable as Harlech, it would still take too long to subdue and winter would soon be upon us. Reluctantly we headed north but this time, when we had passed Caernarfon, we stopped on the shore which lay opposite Beaumaris. The straits looked narrow enough to swim and yet they might as well have been an ocean for we had no ships and could not transport the men. As we stood looking at the castle and those besieging it Prince Henry said, "I have read Tacitus who was a Roman writer and he said that a general called Agricola invaded Anglesey by having his men swim their horses across the straits."

I shook my head, "Then they were either braver or luckier than any warrior I know; probably both. Let us wait until we have ships, in the spring, lord. Use your money wisely."

He nodded, "But I will not leave my people without hope." He mounted his horse and took his banner from Sir Richard Fulk. He rode down the rough ground to the shingle beach and, riding up and down, he waved the standard and shouted, "I am Henry of Monmouth and I swear that I will relieve the sieges of Beaumaris and Harlech!" He repeated it four or five times. Some men might have said that it was an empty gesture for only we heard his words but Prince Henry believed that the land and the sea heard. His riding back and forth, waving his banner would be a sign of his intentions. While some of Sir Thomas' knights shook their heads my men and Prince Henry's knights nodded their approval. We were not beaten but we would need time to gather the men and the weapons we would need.

When we reached Rhuddlan the castle was on the point of surrender to the Shropshire levy which we had left surrounding it for they had had not laid in food for a protracted siege. When the Prince demanded that the Welsh defenders surrender then they obeyed. It was one thing to hold out against the levy but not the mounted knights we took to their gates. We took hostages from the nobles but freed the rest after disarming them.

We parted with Sir Thomas at Shrewsbury and it was there we heard that the King had subdued the north and the punishment he had inflicted was financial although his confirmation of the appointment of Sir Ralph Neville as Sherriff of Westmoreland promised that Henry Percy would be watched. I rode with the Prince to Windsor where he would meet with his father. Its defences had been strengthened and it would be a place to train and to plan his strategy. While riding south I expressed my doubts about the Earl of Northumberland for I did not trust Henry Percy.

"Will, you do not like him and that I can understand for he tried to have you killed."

"It is nothing to do with that. We killed his son and his brother. He is a northern warrior and this has become a blood feud. Better he had been executed and his lands confiscated. It will need to be done sometime. The men of Northumberland are pragmatic. They will ally with anyone, including the Scots, to get that which they want!"

Prince Henry nodded. I saw him looking at the knights who accompanied him and I knew what he was thinking. When he became king then these would be the men he would have to trust. His father was an isolated and lonely man, much as his cousin, Richard, had been. My opinion was confirmed when he asked, in a quiet voice so that only I could hear, "Will, your men are the most loyal of any that I have seen. How did you achieve that?"

I smiled and said, "You should know that Prince Henry, for you have lived in my home at Weedon. They are part of my family. I grew up, as you know, without brothers, sisters, and even a mother. My father raised me but treated me harshly. It was the brothers in arms, the company, who were my family and I have tried to do the same with the men who follow me."

"Then that is what I shall do. When you leave me at Windsor, I will spend the winter becoming stronger in my body for the wound took more out of me than I would care to admit. I will also seek to surround myself with men that I will make close to me. I would have you enjoy the winter with your family. I know the sacrifices which you have made and also the demands my father had made of you. I will not forget them but as this brief foray into Wales has shown me, I need you at my side until I can command and make wise decisions as well as you do."

I nodded and smiled, "Prince Henry, I know that my life and yours are intertwined. Your father and King Richard are the reason for my elevation. I cannot have one without the other. I will serve both you and England for as long as I am able. When I face my death, I will know that I have done my duty."

By the time I had ensured that he was safe and protected inside Windsor's walls, it was almost the end of November and we endured a wet and dismal ride back to Northampton and Weedon. I had lost no men in this brief campaign but I saw, on their faces, that they were weary beyond words. The campaign which led to Shrewsbury and the raid into Wales had kept us from our homes for a long time. The Prince's words told me that we would be spending as long away when the new grass began to grow. I was rich and had power but they came at a price!

Chapter 3

Christmas that year was wonderful for I had two grandchildren to make smile and Northampton Castle was more than large enough for my family to enjoy a comfortable time; there were some advantages to being a Sherriff. It was a joyous time and, looking back, I can see that I should have made more of the happiness which filled my life but I confess that I was distracted for one of my curses was that I always looked ahead and I saw danger for both the King and his son. I did not show that concern to any of my family and that included my two sons but, at night, I spent restless hours fearing for the future and contemplating the threat of Scots, Welsh, English rebels and the increasing threat from France. My family helped alleviate the fears during the days which were, quite simply, not long enough.

When Christmas had passed my wife was anxious to return to Weedon for she was the one who managed all of our estates and Weedon, whilst not the largest, was the one in which she felt most comfortable. Taking only Harry and Abelard we went for a week to Weedon. We had a good steward, John, and the manor was well run but my wife liked to organise and to make certain that all knew what they had to do. She had many lists. Now that only Mary was at home, she was teaching Mary the skills she would need to run her own household when she married. I knew that Mary would make a wonderful wife and mother. She had begged to be left in Northampton for she enjoyed the company and it meant she had fewer tasks than she would if she was at home with my wife and I. For myself, it was good to ride my lands and speak to the farmers and tenants. Most had served with me at some time either as a warrior or as a camp servant. Every man who pulled a bow or raised a sword in my service knows that the reward would be land on one of my manors. Unlike the knights with hereditary titles, my lands had been rewards from King Richard and King Henry for service to England.

It was as we rode around my land that I noticed how much Harry had grown. He had seen more than seventeen summers and was just a few years younger than the Earl of Arundel who commanded Worcester and the Welsh marches. His brother had almost been ready for knighthood at the same age. I now had Abelard to make into a knight and so, as we rode, I asked Harry of his ambitions.

"When you knighted Ralph, you offered me a knighthood and I was honoured for I would be a knight, father, but not yet, if that is what you are asking. Working with Abelard in the last campaign has shown me my shortcomings. When I ride behind you, I see a warrior who is complete and I am far from complete."

"Yet, my son, you have more skill and experience than many who have been knighted already."

He smiled, "You mean like those foolish knights who charged off at Caernarfon? It was they who made me realise that I wanted to be better than they are. Give me the summer campaign in Wales and then ask me again." He lowered his voice even though Abelard was acting as a sort of scout and riding forty paces ahead of us; it was part of his training. "Sir Roger was a good knight but he did not do all that he could to make Abelard a knight. He cannot read and he has other shortcomings!"

"His father was an archer!"

"Which makes him stronger than I was when I began my training and yet if he becomes a knight then he will be rubbing shoulders with those who are nobler. Not all are kind. Would you burden him with such a stigma? I will teach him to read and rub off those rough edges before I am knighted. I like Abelard and I believe he will be a better knight than I for he has his father's build. He is broad of shoulders and already powerful. The training his father gave him with a bow was not wasted."

I nodded for I could see that my son had wisdom beyond his years. "Very well, and then we must find a husband for Mary."

"My sister is younger than I am."

"And you cannot marry until you have your spurs! Mary will see her elder sister and her brother with their children and she will desire to be as they are. Better we find her a husband than she goes to seek one."

"Can she not seek one herself?" In some matters my son was naïve.

"If I was just Will Strongstaff, man at arms, then there would be no issue but she is the daughter of the Sherriff and whomsoever she marries will need to be one who wishes to marry Mary and not my title!"

We stayed longer at Weedon than any of us thought but it was a comfortable experience for this was my true home. My wife had made it so. I had lived there during the odd time of peace but my wife had built it. It had been her vision and she was comfortable. We returned to Northampton at the start of February for I had duties as Sherriff. My son, Thomas, could perform many of them but I had to be seen to at least attempt them. That we had tarried too long became clear when we reached the castle for we were greeted by my son Thomas who had a concerned expression upon his face, "It is Mary, father, she has become unwell."

As my youngest daughter, Mary had always held a special place in our hearts and she was the favourite of both Harry and Tom. That she should be ill was unthinkable for she had always enjoyed the best of health. I felt relieved that there was a doctor who lived in the castle. It was a royal castle and the upkeep was the King's. Harold Beauclerk was a good doctor but I saw from his expression when we entered the bedchamber that he was troubled.

"My lord, I know not what this ailment is; I cannot find a cause for it in any of the books that we use. Your daughter complained, three days' since, of a fever. I applied the usual compresses and gave her the potions which normally bring down such fevers but none appeared to work. I have searched my books and those of my colleagues but cannot find any other answer."

"Her mother is here now and we both know that a mother's love is the best cure for many ailments but I wish you to continue to seek an answer."

As he left, I went to my daughter's side. My wife had brushed past the doctor to be Mary's mother for a mother knows her own child better than any. I saw her with Mary held tightly in her arms. Mary was weeping, "I am cursed, mother! Why am I cursed thus?"

Eleanor's voice was calming and soothing yet I knew that beneath her calm demeanour she would be as distressed as any, "Hush child, it is but a winter fever. Do you remember, your father had one and we sent for the priest for we thought he would die and yet here he stands before you, hale and hearty, the defender of kings? I will do as I did when he was ill. I will treat you with the medicines we used on my father's farm when we did not have enough money to pay for a doctor." If the doctor was insulted, he was wise enough to remain silent.

My wife's family and most of the village in which she had lived had died of the plague and that was on my daughter's mind for she said, "Is this the plague? Are you all doomed by me?"

My wife shook her head, "It is not the plague for I can see that immediately but you are ill for you are burning in my arms. Husband, come and hold our child while I fetch my own medicines."

I had dropped my cloak at the door and so I sat on the bed and my daughter threw her arms around my neck and squeezed so tightly that I thought I would be choked. I could watch men die on a battlefield and not turn a hair but my daughter's distress and her hug were such that I felt myself tearing up. I had to be strong and I had to believe that, between them, my wife and the doctor could rid Mary of this ailment.

"We are here now and we shall not leave until you are well again." I tried to make my voice as calm and reassuring as I could.

She tried to speak but, instead, was overtaken by a coughing fit. She brought forth green spume and white phlegm and her body was so wracked that I thought she would break. "I fear I am dying! Hold me, father, and tell me that I will be well."

"And you will be, child. When you were a bairn, I remember you as the hardiest of our children. You fought off all the agues which afflicted your brothers and sister. You are strong and, with God's help, you will triumph and overcome this pestilence."

My wife returned and she smiled when she saw how tightly Mary and I held each other. "If love can conquer an ague then Mary will be saved. I will take over, husband, now go to the

33

chapel and pray to God. The doctor and I will do all that we can but we need God's help."

Mary said, as I laid her on the bed, "I have been a good girl, I swear. I have not sinned. Surely God will watch over me!"

As I headed towards the chapel, I thought back to the men who should have lived but had died on battlefields while others who deserved to die prospered. God did not work that way but my wife was right and I spent an hour prostrated on the chapel floor begging God to intervene and to save my child. I prayed as I had never prayed before nor since.

My wife's medicine and her love made my daughter more restful but she did not improve. She either could not or would not eat and she lived on broth but each day she became worse. The doctor sent to London to ask a colleague for advice but even he failed to find a cure. It was when Harry became ill that we began to fear for us all. He had spent an hour each day with his sister and after seven days be began with the symptoms his sister had shown. Fearing for my grandson I sent Thomas and his family to Weedon. Abelard insisted upon remaining with Harry and that showed great courage. My wife and I now feared for our son and I wondered if I had been cursed by some enemy. When I went to the chapel to pray, I had to force the anger from my head. My family were suffering and God had not helped.

This time I held my sword before me as a cross and I knelt as I prayed aloud, "God, I beg of you to save my children. I am old and serve my king, my country and my church. If one is to die then let it be me but let my son Harry and his sister Mary live. They have their whole lives ahead of them and mine is almost spent. I beg of you to hear my prayer."

It was four days' later when I received the answer to my prayers, or half of them, at least. On the day that Harry showed signs of recovery his sister slipped away. She had spent three days without waking and my wife had not moved from her side. She cradled her dying body until the doctor gave her the news that Mary had gone. The priest had given her the last rites two days' before she died but she was not awake and we did not have the satisfaction of saying goodbye. We thought that she would recover. I took some consolation that she was with God but from that day my faith in God diminished a little. He had not saved an innocent and precious child and yet others, who deserved death, lived and it made no sense to me.

We did not bury her in Northampton for that was not her home, but in the churchyard of Weedon where the villagers all turned out for the golden child they had all adored as she had grown up. The words Father Michael said over the grave were not meaningless platitudes for he had known her and he spoke with emotion thick in his voice. Mary's death had a profound effect on us all, but especially Harry. He blamed himself for her death for he had had the disease and survived and she had not. Like me, he wished that their places had been exchanged.

It was left to my wife to give Harry some perspective, "Mary was the most loving of all my children. She cared for all equally and would have done anything for anyone. Before she slipped into sleep we spoke and she told me of her dreams for the future. She saw herself marrying some noble knight as her sister had done and she hoped he would be as you are, Harry, for you were her favourite brother as you were closer in age. I know your father tried to make a bargain with God and I believe, in my heart, that your sister did too. Live but live for your sister. Be the knight she hoped you would be and find a wife whom you can treat the way you would have hoped that Mary would have been treated. I shall mourn my daughter and not a day shall go by that I do not place flowers upon her grave but I shall do as I know she would have hoped and live for my children, grandchildren and husband. It is all that we can do."

It was as fine an eulogy as one could have wished. I found the strength to speak without tears coursing down my cheeks, "And I will have a mason carve an effigy of her for her grave shall be marked by stone. She is the first of my bairns to die and the world will know of the family of Will Strongstaff. Unlike my father, we shall not lie in a nameless grave in some foreign field!"

Whilst the death made everyone sad my wife's words spurred Harry and he began to work even harder than he had done before to become the best of knights. He was at the pel from first light and poor Abelard had to join him. In the evening we had to call them in for their food long after darkness had fallen. Even when he was indoors, he was still striving to be the best that he could be and we would play game after game of chess for he knew the importance of strategy. I was a competent player at best and soon he was defeating me each time we played. He began to play against Abelard and soon Sir Roger's old squire became good enough to defeat me more than I won.

It was when the new grass was growing and thoughts were turning to campaigning once more when I was summoned to Windsor to meet with the King and his son. I took my squires and just eight of my men: four archers and four men at arms. We took two servants. I took my men because although the country was quiet, it was not at peace. The north still seethed and the west was in the hands of Glendower and Mortimer. To the east lay a France with ambitions to take over an England which still seemed on the brink of full-blown rebellion.

The first thing I noticed was that the King's affliction which I had noticed after Shrewsbury had worsened and was now clearly obvious to all. His face was almost flaking away as he spoke. I wondered if it was leprosy and then dismissed the idea immediately for his doctors would have diagnosed it as such and he would be away from his son and family. Humphrey, John and Thomas, his other three sons, were there. That it bothered him was clear and he was most definitely distracted by it. I also noticed the clear relief when I arrived and that was from all of the King's sons and King Henry himself. I wondered the reason.

The King's smile was guarded and I knew the reason now; his cracked face looked like a fine pot which was close to splintering. It led him to smile less and that made those that did not know him wary of him. It affected their judgement and opinion of him. Later, when men said that it was God's curse I wondered if it was just that people thought him changed inside as well as out. For myself, I saw a King who now embraced the throne and was fighting to retain it. King Richard, when placed in the same position, had almost thrown it away.

"Strongstaff, it is good to see you! We have need of both your mind and your strong right arm." His voice was strong enough and that gave me hope.

"I am ever your servant."

Prince Henry came and put his arm around me. It was not a royal gesture for the family seemed to fear physical contact with those who were not of royal blood. "And I am sorry for your loss,

Will. Mary was a delightful child and know that I paid for prayers for her soul to be said at the convents and monasteries under my control."

I remembered then that there was but a year between Prince Hal, as she had called him, and my daughter. They had been close when he had lived with me. "That was kind of you. I believe that she is with God now."

Prince Henry was the only one who would have thought of such a gesture. He was not only a good warrior he was a good man and the two do not always go hand in hand.

The King made the sign of the cross; it was something I noticed him doing increasingly often since his ailment had begun, and he said, "We need words and conference with you. I would have all of my sons present for this concerns the kingdom."

Harry and Abelard, as my squires, would wait upon us as would the Prince's squires. We went to the Great Hall which looked remarkably empty for there was just a handful of us. I saw that the Archbishop of Canterbury, Sir Thomas' uncle, was also there. He was not only the most powerful churchman in the land he was also the most powerful man outside of the royal family. That this was an important meeting became clear when I saw him. He nodded at me as I entered. We had not always been friends for he and his nephew had been forced into exile by King Richard and I was still seen, by some, as Richard's man. As prayers were said, before we ate, I noticed that King Henry was more pious showing that his affliction bothered him.

When our squires had fetched our first course and the wine they were dismissed and Prince Henry said, "I will shout for you when we require the next course. Stay without and make sure that none listens to our conference and debate."

I knew that my squires would obey for I would tell them all when we were alone. It was not that I was indiscreet but I trusted Harry and Abelard more than any in the room, save, perhaps, Prince Henry. It was the Archbishop who began. "Know you all that there are enemies in this land. Some are warriors, Glendower, Northumberland, Mortimer, but know, also, that there are others, in the church, who seek to bring down King Henry. The Archbishop of York, Richard Scrope, is one such. There is a belief that Richard, who was king, is still alive and that fosters rebellion." He looked at me as though I was the one who had begun the rumour.

I sighed and spread my hands as though I was tired of having to explain, "King Richard died and I was there when he passed."

The Archbishop nodded, "And that is why you are here for of all the men around this table, nay, in this land, you are the one man was known to be loyal to Richard and, as such, you are in a unique position. Men will believe you!"

"I have told everyone the same words I have just said here."

He smiled, "And that proves your loyalty to King Henry, no, Sir William, you misunderstand me. I have heard rumours that they have one who looks and speaks like the former King. At the moment he is kept hidden in Scotland but if he is produced to discredit King Henry then you become the one man in the Kingdom who can scotch the lie!" He was a clever man and judged his words before he uttered them.

"And I will do so."

The Archbishop continued, "However, there are also those in the south of the land who ferment rebellion and they are equally dangerous. London, as we all know, is a fickle place where the people will change their allegiance with the changing weather. We cannot trust the heart of England and worse, there are people who encourage the French. There is rumour of a noblewoman who seeks to fetch over the French to invade our land."

I nodded, but, in truth, none of this was a surprise. I knew of Scrope's treachery and that there were English noblewomen who did not like King Henry was obvious for many had lost husbands and land.

The King spoke, "We have forgiven Northumberland and he has returned north to his lands but I do not trust him. I wish you to ride to his lands and fetch back his grandchildren to Pontefract Castle where they will be held as hostages for his good behaviour."

I looked over at Prince Henry. I had thought I was to be at his side and, from his pained look, he had thought so too. "But what of the Prince's campaign in Wales? Am I not needed there?"

"The Earl of Arundel is there and besides, we need you for the reasons which the Archbishop gave. Neville is a trustworthy lord but the Percy family see him as a rival and a threat to their power.

You, on the other hand, are seen as a noble knight who serves England and you are a protector of kings. The Percys, we believe, will accept you and my demands."

"But the Earl hated me before Shrewsbury and tried to have me assassinated. I killed his son!"

"And that is another reason why you go, Sir William, for there is a code amongst these wild northerners. You killed Hotspur in single combat and that makes you a champion. That alone will ensure that they hear you out. You will tell Northumberland that his grandchildren will be treated well and he will believe you."

I looked the King in the eyes, "And they will be?"

The Archbishop became angry, "How dare you impugn the King's honour!"

I shifted my gaze to the Archbishop, "I served King Richard and I know that sometimes promises are made which are never intended to be kept. This is not your word which is to be given, Archbishop, it is mine and before I give my word, I have to know that I will not be forsworn."

King Henry smiled, "And that is another reason for this choice for you are not afraid to beard a King." He held his cross, "I swear by all that is holy and at the risk of my soul that no harm will come to the grandchildren of the earl!"

"Then I am content. And when they are conveyed to Pontefract, what then?"

Prince Henry said, "Then you join me at Worcester where, hopefully, we will defeat Glendower and take back my land!"

I was unhappy with my role and it was not that I feared for my life but for that of Prince Henry. Warfare in Wales was the hardest I had ever known and made fighting in Spain and Portugal seem easy by comparison. His wounding by the arrow had been a warning, a sign that while I feared no knight I worried about the archers.

The next morning, he took me with him while we rode through the Great Park. "I know that you are unhappy about this task my father has set for you but it is his way. As you know we have here, at Windsor, Edmund and Roger Mortimer as hostages. He fears that the crown will slip and he will lose the throne."

"May I be blunt, Prince Henry?"

"I would be offended if you were not."

"You and the Earl of Arundel are both young and as we have seen both Mortimer and Glendower are wily old campaigners. As much as I would be with my family, I know that my place is by your side to guide you. You are a great warrior and a good general but I have the experience of many years behind me."

"Then I promise that I will be cautious until you return from the north. It should not take you above a month, Will."

"Aye, if the Earl agrees but if he proves awkward then what can I do?"

Prince Henry smiled, "This is where my experience comes in, Will. If he refuses then, quite simply, you return to Pontefract and tell my father. He will take an army and reduce Percy's home. It is not the solution we wish for the King wishes to keep as many men available to repel a French invasion."

"I know there are rumours but is it likely?"

"They tried earlier this month at Dartmouth. Two thousand Frenchmen tried to invade but they were defeated at Blackpool Sands by the local militia and knights. It was not a well-organised invasion but it shows that they are keen to bring the war to us. My father has sanctioned Sir William Wilford to attack shipping in the Channel as a reprisal and John Hawley and his privateers will continue to harass the French. The war with France will escalate and we could do without this Welsh rebellion." He saw that I was still unconvinced, "Fear not, Will, I know I am not yet ready but someone has to face the Welsh and it is my land. If I cannot defend Wales then I do not deserve to be a future King of England."

I left in the afternoon. It was neither rudeness nor a fit of pique but I needed to get to Northumberland and return to join Prince Henry as quickly as I could. Prince Henry needed me and his words had told me so. The King and his son, Prince John of Bedford, would await my return at Pontefract. The King had decided to give Prince John the north to manage. Although his son was little more than a youth, Ralph Neville would be available to guide and to offer support to him. Humphrey was being sent to Ireland for the same purpose. King Henry would rule the land through his sons.

As we rode north Harry showed that the death of his sister had made him become more thoughtful and more astute. As a squire who served at the table and being slightly older than the two princes, he had been able to talk to the other squires and hear what others thought of the three brothers who would support Prince Henry when he became king.

"I have seen that the King has great faith in his sons but two of them are little more than boys. It has made me realise that I could be a knight for I have fought more times than they have but I will wait until Abelard is a year older."

Abelard said, "I am ready now, Harry!"

Harry laughed, "You are keen enough and there are many tasks that you can do but your reading and your writing need improvement. If they improve then…"

"I will make it so." The determination in his voice made me believe that he would deliver on his promise.

The roads were hard to travel due to the number of people who used them and the weather. The result was that we did not make it home in one day and we had to spend the night in an inn just fifteen miles from our home. By leaving early we were home by midmorning. I would be able to leave for the north once I had seen all of my men and chosen the ones who would ride north with me.

Mary's death had affected my wife more than I might have expected for I had always thought that Eleanor was stronger than I was. She was a strong character and her personality filled every room in our home. Mary had been the last of our children living in the house and Mary's death appeared to make my wife become maudlin and melancholic. When we returned to my home, even though we had been away but days, I saw changes. The clothes she wore were plainer, almost nun-like. When she spoke, she was quieter and more reflective. It was, however, the servants and their worried expressions which concerned me the most. As she took my cloak, Agnes, who commanded the house servants, said in my ear, "My lady spends most of the day in prayers, lord, and the rest in the churchyard tending to Lady Mary's grave."

"Just so?"

"Aye, lord, and she is not the same lady that she was. It began before you left but you and Master Harry were so concerned with your visit to the King that you did not notice," I gave her a sharp look and then realised that she was right. "The other servants and

41

I fear that she is heading towards an abyss and unless she is rescued then we will lose her forever. It is good that you are at home." I heard the plea in her voice but it was in vain. As ever my family would take second place to the demands of the King.

I shook my head, "I leave on the morrow on the King's business."

Agnes' head drooped, "Then the lady is lost."

"No, she is not!" I knew that the problem had a solution and I had to find it. Had this been on the field of battle then the solution would have presented itself soon enough but the world of women was unknown to me. I had grown up without the benefit of a woman's soft touch and was more used to the harsh reality of a world of warriors. I sought Harry who returned from the stables. "Harry, your mother is in low spirits and her thoughts dwell upon Mary. Go to her and make her laugh, amuse her, do anything that you can."

He looked concerned but he nodded and said, "I will try though the house feels empty without Mary's laughter. Where will you be?"

"The King's command has come at the wrong time but I must prepare to obey it. However, I also have a wife I need to save and I will try to do both at the same time."

The village of Weedon and my manor were now almost entirely filled with those who served me and their families. They were people that I knew well. The original village had been small and the deaths of older people who had no children or whose children had drifted away to London meant they had been replaced by those of my men who wished to have families. The largest house, outside of my own, belonged to Harold Four Fingers and his wife, Magda. They lived close to the manor house for Harold commanded the men I left to guard my home. Magda had been rescued from Lithuania and her son, Pyotr, or Peter as he now called himself, was the squire of the first knight I had trained, Sir Henry of Stratford. Magda had endured far worse than my wife and she had survived. I would kill two birds with one stone and while Harold summoned my two captains, Edgar and Alan, I would seek advice from Magda.

Harold was tending his small garden as I approached. He was one of my longest-serving warriors and his days of going to war were long passed. He would be able to defend my land and would do so as fiercely as any warrior but his grey hair and the rounding of his belly told me that he was not hungry for battle any longer.

He looked up as I approached, "Lord, this is a most unexpected visit."

"Aye, Harold, and I am sorry to take you away from your garden but I have something needs tending to."

He laughed, "Once I hewed the heads of my enemies and now it is tares and weeds who fear my wrath and I battle constantly with slugs! They will wait. What is it that you wish, my lord?"

"The King has tasked me with a journey north. Fetch my captains so that the three of us may choose the men that I will take with me. I will await your pleasure here for I have need of words with your wife."

My village and home were small added to which Harold and Magda lived less than two hundred paces from my home. He nodded, "Lady Eleanor?"

"Aye."

"Magda is within. I will not be long."

I gave him a meaningful look, "Do not rush."

I knocked on the door for although I was lord of the manor, I respected the privacy of all who lived on my land. Their homes were theirs. Magda had floury hands as she had been making bread and my appearance flustered her, "My lord, I am sorry I..."

Although she had lived for many years in England her voice still had the Baltic accent. I smiled, "It is I who should apologise for disturbing you but you should know that my visit is important. I will follow you to your kitchen, I will not stop your work for making bread is vital for a family."

I could see that she was torn for the kitchen was not the place to speak with the lord of the manor but she was a practical woman and nodding, she led me through the low-ceilinged house to the kitchen. Unlike my wife, Magda had no servants and we were alone. She looked at the dough which she had begun to work and I said, "I will sit and talk while you work. The dough needs kneading."

She smiled, "It is a living thing, lord, and does not like to be neglected." She began to stretch and pummel the dough and I remained silent.

I watched her powerful and gnarled hands as she turned the roughened dough into a smooth and pliant ball. "I need to speak with you about Lady Eleanor."

She paused briefly and, looking at me, nodded, "Aye, she is a troubled soul." She had learned her English from Harold and it showed in her words and phrases. She lifted her hand to give the bread a mighty smack and then rolled it into a ball. "Sometimes, lord, the dough needs to be treated roughly." She then began to softly smooth the shiny dough into a round, "and sometimes gentleness is needed. Your wife is right to mourn your daughter for she was like a ray of sunshine on a spring morning but there is a time to put aside the past and look to the future." She returned the dough to the wicker basket and covered it with the piece of dampened linen she had left to the side. As I spoke, she went to the jug of water to cleanse her hands of flour.

"You are right, Mistress Magda and, given time, I would be able to coax her back from the edge of despair, but King Henry has set me a task and I will be away for some short time and, even when I return, it will be but a brief visit for I go to war again."

She poured a beaker of beer and handed it to me. I knew that some of the yeast from the beer she had made would be in the bread and already the smell of proving dough in the firelit, cosy kitchen was making me hungry.

"And your wife is alone with her women. Agnes and the others are good folk but they are servants. Thanks to you my husband is a freeman whom you pay and I am a free woman. I am no lady but I am a mother. Would you have me speak with her?"

"We both know that this is not the work of an afternoon. I should have seen her fall and prevented it earlier but I too felt the knife to my heart when Mary was taken."

"Looking back is always easier than looking forward." She rose to put another log on the fire which burned beneath the simmering pot of potage. "My days are filled with little of import these days and I know that had you not come to Lithuania then my son and I would be slaves. You can leave on the King's errand and I will do all that I can for your wife was more than kind when first I came to this land."

Just then I heard the sound of hooves as my captains returned. I nodded and said, "And I shall be in your debt if you can save my wife."

Chapter 4

Unlike my visit to Windsor, my ride north needed a larger number of men for we would be travelling through the land which did not wish to be ruled by King Henry. More than that it was a wilder country with many places where we could be ambushed. The attempt on the Prince's life was still relatively fresh in my mind. My two Captains each led fifteen men. We had spare horses with us and all of us were armed and prepared for war for we would ride armoured and with helmets. I had left Weedon torn between my duty to the King and my duty to my wife but Magda had arrived before I had left with a basket of cakes and biscuits she had made. When she had entered my hall, it had been with laughter in her voice and that was infectious. Agnes and the other servants took their cue from Magda and as I kissed my wife goodbye, I saw the hint of a smile in her eye. Magda had not worked a miracle but she had held my wife from the edge of the brink and would now begin to pull her back. It was what Harold had done quite literally, all those years ago, with her son. In Magda's eyes, a debt was being repaid.

My captains rode next to me along with Harry. The Great North Road was a wide road and it was only when we met travellers heading south that we had to move into pairs. "Father, if Archbishop Scrope is a sympathiser of the northern rebels is it wise to visit York?"

"If the Archbishop plays a treacherous game then we must give him fair warning of the consequences. King Henry sent me for a reason; I am known to be loyal to the crown and I have the King's ear. If I speak then it is as though it comes from the King himself." Harry nodded. "And I slew Hotspur. He was the knight they thought to be unbeatable and sending me will remind them that they lost and that I was the instrument of their fall."

Captain Edgar said, "Aye, lord, but it also puts you in danger for the road twixt York and Warkworth is a dangerous one."

I waved an arm in a full circle, "And I have the best warriors in the land to protect me. I do not doubt that there will be an attempt upon my life but it will not be close to York. Until we reach the Tees they will not attack. That will be partly to alleviate suspicion from the Archbishop of York and also because the land there does not favour ambush. Bishop Skirlaw of Durham is a friend of King Henry; indeed, he was a friend of King Richard and we will be safe in the Palatinate. Newcastle showed its colours when it barred its gates to the Earl of Northumberland. That means if there is an attack then it will be north of Newcastle and south of Warkworth. It is why we have Stephen of Morpeth with us for that is his land and he will know where an attack is likely to come."

Harry shook his head and laughed, "And when did you work this out, father?"

"While the King was telling me my task and while speaking to the Prince. Planning is never wasted, Harry."

I was aware that I was training Harry as I had trained Thomas. Thomas was now acting as my lieutenant in Northampton and I knew that my family was safe as was the road to London.

Travelling with so many armed and mailed men meant that we were noticed. There were northern sympathisers who lived on the road north. Even in royal castles such as Lincoln, there were still spies and one such spy, at least, must have ridden north to York and warned the Archbishop there of our imminent arrival for we were greeted at the gates by a smiling guard from the Archbishop's retinue.

"Sherriff Strongstaff, the Archbishop is pleased that you have come to visit and he has had quarters prepared for you at the palace."

The Archbishop was obviously up to date with events happening further south for he had used the correct title. "And we will just stay one night for my business in the north is most important and commissioned by the King himself."

We were taken through York's ancient and narrow streets to the Archbishop's Palace which was close to the Minster. The Archbishop was slightly older than I was but he had had a life which had been easier than mine and it showed in his paunch and chins. He ate and drank well. He smiled disarmingly as I was introduced and I was on my guard immediately for he was too effusive in his welcome. He had once been a supporter of Henry Bolingbroke and had been one of the churchmen responsible for deposing King Richard but he had now allied himself with the King's enemies. I was not fooled by the smile but I, too, could play the game.

"And it is good to see you, Archbishop. You have a strong city here which can withstand the threat from the north."

He frowned and tried to see the message in my words, "Threat from the north?"

I was being duplicitous and using my words to deceive him, I smiled, "It is well known that the Scots harbour ambitions to take this city and they have been thwarted many times."

He looked relieved, "Indeed, save us from the privations of the Scots is an old adage. Come, I have rooms prepared for you. How long will you stay?"

"As I told your man, overnight only for I must speak with the Earl of Northumberland urgently as the reason for my visit is the King's business."

"What a pity for I had hoped to entertain you here for a few days. You have led a most interesting life and as one who was a crusader in the Baltic, I was anticipating diverting conversation."

I smiled, "My tale will seem dull for, in truth, we did little."

As we ate, he probed me, ostensibly about the Baltic Crusade but the reality was he was trying to gather information. Perhaps he saw me as someone who with the white hairs on my head and beard was getting old and might be careless. I found it easy to deflect his questions with answers which did not seem to follow. I saw that he was confused. I even had time, as we ate and spoke, to think of Peter the Priest, my old brother in arms who ran an alms house by the river. Time would not allow a visit and I found that sad. Old friends were like a good wine, the older they were the more valuable they became.

I had warned my son and Abelard to guard their tongues and they heeded my words. As they served us, I saw that the other servers questioned them at length. I know it was hard for them to avoid divulging information but my son Harry showed his new found maturity by closely watching Abelard and protecting the young squire. My men at arms and archers were housed in the warrior hall but they too were alert and as we headed for Middleham, the next day, they confirmed what I had predicted. Riders had left the city not long after our arrival. Word would have reached Warkworth and there would, I had no doubt, be a warm welcome for us somewhere north of the Tyne. I knew that we would have given any who were following us a dilemma when we left the main road to head for Middleham and the farm of Mistress Mary, Red Ralph's widow, as it meant leaving the road to the north. Four archers trailed us to ensure that we were not followed. We did not have enough time to spend a night at the farm but I needed the services of Sir Ralph and to ask him questions.

When we reached the horse farm Ralph was practising with what I took to be his squire and his brothers as well as other men. They stopped as we approached and waited for us to reach them, "My lord, this is an unexpected pleasure. You should have said that you were coming here and we would have made arrangements."

I shook my head as Mistress Mary emerged from the hall my old friend, Red Ralph, had built, "We cannot stay as we are heading for Warkworth but I would ask you to accompany us for I fear Percy treachery."

"And I will come with you," he turned to his men, "Robin, Richard, you shall come with us. Prepare our war gear for we leave within the hour." He looked at me, "You will, my lord, enjoy some ale and Yorkshire ham with us for my mother will wish to speak to you and Harry!"

I dismounted and handed my reins to Abelard, "Of course."

Mistress Mary had returned indoors when she saw me dismount and by the time we reached the hall and the dining chamber, there was ale, ham and fresh bread awaiting us. She was about to curtsy when I picked her up in my arms and hugged her, "None of that! Here I am Will and you are Mary, the wife of the man who helped to make me what I am."

She nodded and I saw a tear in her eye, "I thank you for letting my son come home to me."

"And now, I fear I must take him away but just for a few days. We ride to Warkworth where I will deliver a message from the King."

"I pray you sit. I know that he still serves you and the crown and for that I am grateful. It is good that he is now close to me and I see him every day; I can endure his service to the King when he is called away." She poured some ale and then, as I began to drink, she carved some ham for us. "And how is your family? The grandchildren will be growing."

"Aye, they are but not all is well for God chose to take Mary to his bosom."

She dropped the knife she was using to butter the bread and made the sign of the cross. "I am so sorry, Will, for she was a golden child and the Lady Eleanor?"

"Has taken it badly, I fear. This journey north has come at the wrong time."

"I know that I was lucky for I married Ralph when his soldiering days were over. The King is lucky to have such a loyal warrior to support him. You will return here on your way south?"

"We will but I cannot tell you when that will be."

"Then we will have beds awaiting you and I will try to write some words of comfort for your wife. I lost a child once but it was in childbirth. I know it is not the same but perhaps they will comfort her."

Ralph appeared at the door, "We are ready, lord."

"Then, Mistress Mary, we will take our leave."

The men had been fed and it allowed us to make good time to the Tees and the bridge at Piercebridge. While we rode north, I told Ralph all for he was like family and I trusted him. "I think that you are right, Sir William. It will be north of Morpeth where the danger will lie. The Scots still raid and the land to the north of Morpeth is still wild. I have ridden with the Lord of the Northern Marches, Sir Ralph Neville, for we scoured the lands north of Lancaster of rebels. He also visited with the Bishop of Durham who watches south of the Tyne. The land north of Newcastle is unknown to me and, I think, filled with those who wish the King and his son harm." He looked at me, "But, more especially, they will wish to hurt you too. I have heard rumours of men swearing oaths to kill the man who slew Hotspur. He was the hope of the north!"

I smiled, "Many men have wished me dead and yet I live still."

We stayed at Newcastle with the Sherriff who was King Henry's man. He confirmed what we already knew. The Percy family still had ambitions to rule the northern half of England and that his stronghold and heartlands went from Morpeth to the Scottish borders. Only the Bishop of Durham's castle, Berwick, barred the border. So long as Glendower and Mortimer were at large the dream of a tripartite division of England between the Percy family, Glendower and Mortimer remained a real threat.

When we left the castle we rode prepared for battle, for although we had just twenty and eight miles to travel, they would be the most dangerous on the whole road. We had servants with the horses and four of my archers guarded them. The rest rode as scouts. Stephen of Morpeth had already told us that the road north had a number of places where we might be ambushed. One was where the road crossed the River Blyth and the other, the more likely place, was Sheepwash over the River Wansbeck for that was a ford and the woods around there made an ambush likely.

We used the same strategy at both sites. My archers left us four miles before each of the crossings and, as they wore no armour, they were able to swim across where there was no ford and approach the crossing from the north. When we crossed the bridge at Bedlington, we had shields pulled up and wore our helmets. Our archers greeted us on the other side. Captain Alan said, "It is clear, lord, and there is no sign that we could see of warriors waiting for us."

"Then, if Stephen of Morpeth and Sir Ralph are correct then the ambush, if there is to be one, will be at the Sheepwash."

He nodded, "We will be there before you."

They galloped off in their two groups. The baggage now just had four servants to watch the horses and spare war gear. I took the opportunity to dismount and tighten Hart's girths. I saw Abelard chewing his lip. I smiled to put him at his ease. "Abelard, you have good mail and a padded gambeson. Your helmet is a good one and the enemy who will ambush us are not archers. They may use bows but Hotspur used Cheshire archers at

Shrewsbury. Archery is not a northern skill. Stay close to Harry and use your shield to protect yourself. All will be well."

I know, Sir William, but I do not want to let you down."

"And you will not. Trust to your fellows and to God and we will prevail."

I mounted and Captain Edgar and David of Welshpool rode before Sir Ralph and I. Stephen of Morpeth rode alone before the Captain and David. Thanks to his prowess Ralph had good armour and wore a helmet like me. Although it was open-faced our coifs protected all but our eyes. The Prince had had a boar's snout sallet at Shrewsbury and it had almost been his undoing. With Ralph riding next to me watching my left side, we headed for the River Wansbeck.

The road turned when we neared the river and headed along its southern bank for there was a steep slope to the right of us. Stephen of Morpeth had warned us of this and so I had some men watching the slope in case we were wrong and the ambush would be the south side of the river. I saw that the ford was close to two small islands and they were both covered in vegetation. Whilst there were few trees south of the river, on the northern bank was a wood. The hairs on the back of my neck prickled and I knew that Stephen of Morpeth was right. There were places closer to Warkworth where we could be ambushed but they would also throw blame squarely at the Percy family, here they could blame it on bandits, brigands or even the Scots. I slid my blade in and out of its scabbard so that when I drew it, it would not stick.

My shield, tunic and the banner held by Abelard marked me for who I was, Strongstaff and I knew that when we were attacked, I would attract the most attention. As we descended to the river, I had to lean back in the saddle for the slope was steep. I kept my shield up as I did so. Stephen of Morpeth had just splashed into the water when the attack began. Four boys rose from the undergrowth and hurled stones at my leading three riders and a flurry of crossbow bolts hurtled towards Ralph and I. Even as I heard the cracks of the crossbows, I pulled my shield up to cover my face. I had a breastplate and mail not to mention a padded aketon beneath. It would take a lucky bolt to hurt me but my face was a different matter. Two bolts smacked into my shield and one penetrated the leather and the wood. Another clanged off my helmet. Hart had continued to pick her way down the slope and as I reached the bottom, I spurred her, not towards the other bank but towards the undergrowth. As I did so I felt a sudden blow to my back. I had fought for enough years to know that it was a stone. The boy slingers were brave but they would pay for that bravery with their lives. I knew that the men behind us would be seeking out the boys and they would be slain. An ambush against men at arms was not for the faint-hearted. If you succeeded then the rewards were great but failure would bring death.

Crossbows take time to reload. Good ones which used a windlass were more powerful but even slower to reload. The crossbowman was still pulling back the cord when my sword hacked into his skull. He died instantly but I had no time for congratulation as a spear was rammed up at my left side. It scraped off my shield and, turning Hart, I stood in my stirrups and brought my sword down to split the poorly made helmet and skull of the spearman. Then I heard the distinctive sound of a longbow release a deadly bodkin tipped arrow. The mailed man at arms who fell at my feet had one of Christopher White Arrow's distinctive missiles sticking from his back. As the rest of my archers let fly so my sergeants tore into the ambushers who were now attacked from before and behind. My men showed no mercy for none would have been shown to us and when I saw Alan of the Woods walking towards me, I knew that the ambush had been thwarted.

Thirty men lay dead and they were all the men of the north. None were knights but twelve were men at arms. The boy slingers had all been killed as had the crossbowmen but at least twenty had escaped which told me that they knew our numbers and had intended to overwhelm us. Had Stephen of Morpeth not warned us then their ambush might have succeeded but our mail, plate and skill had saved us. "Take the weapons and mail from the dead. Leave their bodies here as a reminder of the dangers of attacking warriors such as you! Have the wounded tended to."

Thanks to our foresight none of my men had been killed but I had men who had been wounded. Uriah Longface and Gilbert of Ely had both been struck by crossbow bolts and the two men would not be able to walk well for some time. Four others had slightly less serious wounds. Abelard had also been wounded. He had been hit on the hand by a stone. I admired him for he had not dropped the standard despite the fact that three of his fingers had been broken. It was his left hand and would not impair him although Harry took the standard from him. He had done his duty and my son would now carry the banner.

As we rode the last twelve miles to the castle, we kept a wary eye out for enemies but we saw none. Captain Alan was mortified that they had failed to stop the ambush before it had begun but I shook my head as I answered him, "They were well hidden and it was a cunning ambush. They knew that we would have difficulty controlling our horses at the ford and until they attacked their positions were hidden. It was a risk we took and it has paid off."

We passed through Amble with Warkworth harbour to the sea side of us and saw Warkworth rising before us. It was a well-made castle and I, for one, would not have liked to assault it as it had water on three sides and a bridge covered the moat. Once they raised the bridge then it would take the blood of warriors to take the castle. Of course, as we approached, I realised that they could, if they so chose, close the gates and prevent us from even entering the castle. We were not wearing our helmets and our shields hung from our sides. We had not even donned our coifs for I wanted the Percy clan to see that we were here on a peaceful mission. If they did attack us then that would suit King Henry as it would be perceived as an act of rebellion. As we neared the gatehouse, I knew that they would admit us for the gates remained open and the bridge over the ditch was in place. I turned to my two captains. "Choose just six men to enter the castle with us. I would not be seen to be aggressive."

Captain Edgar nodded, "And besides, if there was to be an act of treachery then we could summon help."

When we reached the gate there was a knight waiting for us. I recognised him as Sir John Pulle who had been with the garrison of Shrewsbury before the battle and had defected to the rebel side. I dismounted and handed my reins to Abelard. He had his own reins in his right hand and he would lead the horses. His left hand had already swollen to twice its normal size. I hoped there was a doctor in the castle who could attend to our wounded.

Sir John did not smile at me. We were enemies and we both knew it. There would come a time when we might have to fight and when we did it would be to the death. "I am here to take you and Sir Ralph to the earl."

"I would have my men accommodated too."

He pointed beyond the gates, "There is ground there for them to use!"

I smiled, "They will do so for they are men but they will remember, as will I, this act of discourtesy; especially from a turncoat who did not have the courage to fight to the end with his master. You are not worth my scorn!" I wondered if I had gone too far for his hand went to his sword and I laughed. "Oh, please, draw your weapon and I will end your treacherous life here and now! You are not fit to be the Hotspur's shadow!"

His eyes narrowed as he moved his hand away from his weapon and he gestured towards the castle, "If you would come with me to the Great Hall."

We walked across the bailey to the steps which twisted around to the door. The castle was of clever construction. A ram could not breach the door as it was above ground level and reached by steps and any assault would have to be by a ladder; such attacks rarely succeeded. The five of us reached the porter's lodge and Sir John led us up a narrow twisting spiral staircase to the Great Hall. That word had reached the Earl became obvious as we entered the hall for he was seated on what can only be described as a throne. Around him were his senior knights. They were all mailed and armed. The purpose of my visit was also present, his grandsons, although it was the son of Hotspur who was the real bargaining counter. The eleven-year-old was dressed in the Percy livery with the blue rampant gryphon prominently displayed upon his chest. I did not doubt that he had been told that I had been the one to kill his father.

I gave a bow for I was addressing the earl. I took out the parchment which the King had given to me. I would only use it in extremis. The Earl said, "I take it you are here from Henry Bolingbroke."

"I am here on the King's behalf."

"How typical that he sends the man who killed my son and heir to me!" He looked around at his knights and they gave him encouraging nods of support. I saw then that he feared me.

"In fair combat!" There was an edge to my voice. The Earl was over sixty but he had a champion who could fight for his honour and I would not be insulted for I represented the King. I had been a King's bodyguard and champion and knew how such matters were.

He nodded, "In fair combat which makes you a man to be feared for my son was the greatest warrior in the land."

"Then I pray that you will listen to the words of King Henry's man and heed their importance. The King has heard rumours that you, Mortimer and Glendower are conspiring to divide the Kingdom of England between the three of you." He said nothing. "I do not ask you to deny it for that is not the purpose of my visit." I pointed my finger at the youngest Henry Percy. "King Henry wants surety for your good behaviour and your grandsons will be held as hostages in Pontefract Castle. You have my word that they will be well treated."

I had expected outrage but the look on the earl's face told me that he knew what I would say before I said it. That told me that there were spies somewhere close to King Henry for I had not spoken of the actual purpose of my visit to any once I had left Windsor. As I had not mentioned my mission in York then it had to be in Windsor, at the King's court. He had yet to find all the traitors.

"Sir William, you are a brave man for you come here to a place filled with your enemies accompanied by one knight and a handful of men but what you ask is wrong."

"My lord, when we crossed the Wansbeck, we were attacked by men waiting in ambush for us. Their bodies lie there still. That is wrong and had I been so minded I could have demanded reparation for the unwarranted attack. I will take your grandsons hence for I have given my word and you know," I looked around the room at the men gathered there, "you all know, that I keep my word! So, my lord, do you agree to allow them to accompany me or shall I leave empty handed and return with an army?"

This was a moment upon which many lives hung. I stared into Henry Percy's eyes and although he held them briefly, it was he who looked down and nodded, "You are right, Sir William, you are a man of your word and, here in the north, we appreciate knights who are courageous and honourable. You may take them but I give them into your care and not Bolingbroke's for he is treacherous. My son and I gave him the crown and then he failed to deliver on his promises."

"Then know that your heirs will be safe in Pontefract so long as you do not join in any rebellion."

The Earl gave us an escort the next day to ensure that we were not attacked again. It was a game he played for he had sent the men to ambush us. He had failed and he would now try something else. The escort meant we stayed in Percy castles to the Tyne. After that, we stayed with the Prince Bishop who gave us an escort to Piercebridge. The boys we had in our care were quiet but Abelard and John, Ralph's squire, rode with them and tried to engage them in conversation. By the time we crossed the Tees, they were smiling a little. Our final halt before we reached the Great North Road was at Middleham where I was able to leave Sir Ralph. I gave him a message for Sir Ralph Neville, I did not commit it to parchment for the message came from the King.

By the time we reached Pontefract the King was already there and awaiting our arrival. I asked for a private audience with him. "Your Majesty, I gave my word that these boys would not be harmed."

He nodded, "And I give my word, too, that they will not. It is in my interest to keep them safe."

"And yet Percy will not keep to the terms of the agreement. He will rebel and we both know that. Will that result in harm to the boys?"

"In truth, Will, I know not but I will do anything to hang on to this throne for I do it for England and not for personal power. If the Earl rebels once more then he is abandoning his grandsons." He smiled, "We will stay here for a few days and I would like you to stay for a day or two as well. I have matters I need to discuss with you. I want a plan to destroy the Welsh rebels!"

I agreed to stay but my heart was not in it. My priorities were my family and then getting to Prince Henry's side. In all the discussions and conversations I had had in Warkworth not once had Prince Henry come in for any criticism. It was his father, the

King, whom men resented and not his son. That made his life even more important! The King and I managed to devise some strategies and plans in the powerful Pontefract Castle and it was on the morning that I was about to leave with him when we received a most extraordinary piece of news. Some English pirates had captured a Scottish ship off the coast at Flamborough and captured the heir to the Scottish throne, the young prince, James! The pirates had given the boy to Sir William of Selby and he was bringing him to Pontefract. In one fell swoop, he had negated any threat from north of the border. With the Percy grandsons as hostages, he could now add Prince James of Scotland The King changed his plans. The Scottish heir would be brought to Pontefract and the King, himself, would take him to the Tower. I left with my men wondering if this presaged a change in the royal fortunes.

Chapter 5

Magda had not managed to work a complete miracle with my wife but there was an improvement. For one thing, she greeted Harry and me with a hearty embrace and a smile and there were no tears. Eleanor had always been interested in affairs of state, mainly because what the great and the good did affected the prices we received for our farm produce, and so I told what had happened. This did bring a hint of the old Eleanor who said, "Then with the threat from the north ended, for this year at least people will spend more on food and less on defence. It is good. I will speak with John and see if we can seed another field with some late wheat." She smiled, "Magda, has made some good suggestions to me. We ought to build a second mill which is closer to Weedon. We now produce more wheat than we can use and we can sell the flour. It fetches a high price."

I patted the back of her hand for it was good that she had a new project, "You know what is best for the manor and I leave that to you. Fear not that we might need more money for warriors; we will not as I have enough from Northampton to pay for them, but you should know that Harry and I must leave for Wales and I would not leave you in low spirits."

"I know and I also know that you watch over my youngest son for you have ever been the good father." She kissed me, "I am feeling a little better now and the world is not so black as it once was."

I handed her the letter from Sir Ralph's mother. "Mistress Mary sent this for you. She thought it might comfort you."

She nodded, "She is kind to think of me for she lost her husband and I still have mine."

Her words made me relieved. This was a different woman to the one who had fallen into such a pit of despair. "First I will ride to Northampton and speak with Thomas. There are things he should know."

Eleanor was a clever woman and I saw her eyes brighten when she read the message beneath my words, "Then you do not take him with you to Wales?"

I shook my head, "We shall not need him. I think this year will be one where we consolidate what we have. Perhaps next year he may be needed but we shall see."

I stayed at home for just three days. I should have stayed longer for some of the men I led were married and had families but I feared for Prince Henry. My son, Thomas, wished to come with me as I had known he would. I refused but I gave my reasons for doing so as I did not wish a rift between my son and myself. "I know that I have not done my duty as Sherriff of Northampton; that is the fault of the King for he gave me an important task and then set me another. We serve the King and we serve England. Northampton and Lincoln are the two most important towns south of York and north of London on this road. There are few men who could hold it but you are one."

He nodded, "And you the other. Yet this does not sit well with me, father."

I pointed to his son, Henry, "When you were his age I was fighting and serving the King. I did not see you grow. There will be time enough for you to take a sword and fight again but, for now, enjoy the time with your family, for I did not."

With Harry and Abelard, I led my twenty-four men to Worcester. I had heard nothing from the west as all my news had been to do with the north. I hoped that Prince Henry was being cautious. This war was being fought at his expense and the knights who followed him expected payment. He had sold his jewels to pay for men to fight for him and until he regained Wales, he would not have an income. King Henry had been clever by giving me Northampton for he had ensured that I would not require payment as being Sherriff brought a healthy income. Added to that, thanks to my wife, I was rich and as far as I was concerned the coins I spent on soldiers was well spent for I was giving money to friends.

The army I saw gathered at Worcester was smaller than I expected and that relieved me as it meant the Prince had not taken it upon himself to begin to recover his land. I dined with the Earl of Arundel and the Prince where I discovered much. The King had kept his son informed of events in the north and the east. Henry knew of Prince James and the hostages we held. I learned that one reason he had not been more aggressive was that the French had arrived off the coast and helped Glendower to capture Harlech and Aberystwyth. That meant the castle at Caernarfon was the last English bastion.

"I have used what men I could to reinforce that castle for I do not wish it to fall. I have little enough coin left to pay for the prosecution of this war." His wound had healed but his face was terribly scarred and as he slumped back in his chair, the despair on his face appeared aggravated by the wound. This was not like the Prince who had lived with me when he had been Prince Hal. Strangely, it was the effect Magda had had upon my wife which gave me the solution. He needed a plan which would give him hope.

"Prince Henry, it seems to me that there are many lords along this border who could be charged with its defence." I used the pots and beakers which lay on the table to explain my strategy. "Here we have Usk Castle in the south. If we head north, we can see that there is Hereford, Ludlow and then Shrewsbury. The north has Caernarfon, Conwy, Rhuddlan, Flint and Chester. You have strengthened the northern castles and used the men of Cheshire to defend them. Why do you and I not ride this part of the border and advise the knights and lords who defend it? Use the loyal Welshmen like Dafydd Gam of Parc Llettis to encourage others to join your banner." I looked at him and emphasised my words, "Your banner and not your father's!"

"I cannot be disloyal to my father."

"And you are not. He was never Prince of Wales! You have that title and even though Glendower has usurped it there are still Welshmen who might join you." I saw him thinking and although the Earl of Arundel looked confused, I knew that the Prince would deduce for himself what I was getting at.

He smiled, "They would be joining a Welsh cause and not be part of an English army!"

"There you have it. I know that this means we will not be reclaiming your land this year but you would be putting in place the building blocks which would enable you to use it next year to make a determined attack."

He looked animated and nodded to the earl, "And you, Sir Thomas, could go to Arundel and gather more men while the baron and I make this land more defensible."

"I confess, Prince Henry, that I have yearned for a visit to my home and now that Strongstaff is here I feel happy that I could go and I would have discharged my obligation to the King."

"And I will stay here on the border until it is strengthened. Mayhap it will be a quiet summer. Who knows?"

We headed for Hereford first which had a good garrison but, as it had been a Mortimer stronghold, Prince Henry had put in command Sir John Oldcastle who was a loyal knight and a good soldier. We spent a month there riding the marches. Ludlow was also a Mortimer stronghold but there its prosperity depended upon trade with England, the mercers and burghers of the town wanted nothing to do with the treacherous Edmund Mortimer. We left it more confident than when we had arrived and headed for Usk Castle. This was in the borderlands and was as close to the Welsh as anywhere else in Gwent and Monmouthshire.

When we reached the castle, my heart sank for it had fallen into disrepair. In addition, the town was half empty having been destroyed by Glendower two years earlier. It explained why the castle had been allowed to become dangerously weakened. Prince Henry was equally unhappy. "I think, Prince Henry, that the task of repairing this castle and making it a bastion in the south, once more, is down to us. I think that we stay here and help the garrison to make it stronger."

He liked a challenge and we set to using the stones which lay close to the castle to make repairs whilst also improving its defences. Autumn was approaching and there had been little action from the Welsh. I was looking forward to a winter with the Prince when Sir Richard Grey of Codnor, the Justice of South Wales, arrived. He had news for the Prince. He was summoned to London for his father was holding a Parliament as he needed money. While the Prince was torn, I convinced him to go.

"Prince Henry, you can leave your men here with me and we can improve the defences. You need the experience of Parliament and your father needs your support. I doubt that the Welsh will try anything this winter but if they do then I have the men to hold them."

He agreed and I was pleased that some of the men who had escorted Sir Richard to Usk stayed on with us. One was Dafydd Gam. We had once rescued him from Glendower's clutches and a more vehement enemy of the Welsh rebel I had yet to meet. After the Prince had left with Sir Richard, I rode with Dafydd while our men laboured on the walls. Already we had improved the defences. The simple act of taking the stones from the ditch had made it harder for an enemy to attack. The river was the border and so we rode along the eastern side. Dafydd was a real character. He was like Owen the Welshman and David of Welshpool, dour but with a wicked sense of humour. I confess that I found myself laughing more when I was in his presence but, as we patrolled the border, his words were serious ones.

"It is good that you improve the defences, Sir William, for Glyndŵr, thanks to the traitor Mortimer, knows that they are weak. If Usk falls then the rebels will flood into England. It must be held!"

"And it will be."

"And yet you have perilously few men! You need a larger force than you bring with you, no offence, lord."

"And none taken. The Prince and the Earl of Arundel will return after the winter with more men. Men cost coins and what is the point of paying men to sit behind a castle's walls in the winter?"

"And yet that is what you will do."

"True but I pay for my own men and I have an income."

"But this is far from your home and even if the rebels won, your lands and manors would be safe. Why do you do this, lord?"

"For my King, my Prince and my country." He nodded for he was a soldier and could understand such loyalty. "But are there other Welshmen such as you? Ones who would fight Glendower?"

"Aye, I have brought eight such with me but there are others. They are not all knights, lord."

"Have you not noticed, Dafydd Gam, that I ride with men at arms and archers. I know the worth of those who are not noble-born."

"Then I will find such men." We had reached the small town of Grosmont. Dafydd waved his arm in a circle, "Here are loyal Welshmen for this is so close to England that they have family and ties to England that even Glyndŵr with his shallow promises of freedom cannot break." He pointed to the castle. "That belongs to the Earl of Warwick but it is abandoned at the moment, lord. If it was manned then the border would be stronger."

"Then I shall write to the Earl and ask him to garrison his castle for it has a good position and would deter the Welsh!"

We spent some time speaking with the men and they confirmed what Dafydd had said. As we rode back to Usk Castle I said, "They are isolated there, Dafydd, and I can see that if the Welsh came then the people of Grosmont would have to suffer great privations before help came."

"And that is the problem all along this border, lord. Between Raglan Castle and Hereford there are many small, prosperous places and the rebels will attack one of them. I am just surprised that they have yet to do so."

"That may well be because they were eliminating our castles south of Caernarfon. I think your assessment is right. When we have finished the improvements, I will institute some patrols. It will help my men to get to know the land in preparation for the Prince's return."

"And my men and I will accompany them."

We had finished the castle's defences by the end of November and I had sent a written message to the Earl of Warwick. I could do no more but I hoped he would heed my warning. All of us wished that we were going home to Weedon but each of us knew that we were the last line of defence against a determined Welsh attack; I had chosen my men well. I had brought both of my horses and I alternated Hawk and Hart as I rode not only along the border but also into rebel-held lands. I divided my men into two groups so that one half always had a day to rest between patrols. Edgar said that I was pushing myself too hard and I ought to rest too. Few captains would dare to question their lord but my men trusted me to respond reasonably.

"Edgar, when the Prince returns with Sir Thomas they will need someone who knows this land well. Dafydd is one such but the King charged me with helping his son and, in truth, I would rather be riding abroad than sitting in the castle and brooding about my family back in Weedon. An occupied mind is a healthy one."

"Aye lord, but your wife grieves and if it was my wife…"

"But it is not and I know Lady Eleanor better than any. She is made of granite within. The sooner Wales is subdued then the sooner I can discharge my duty and return home."

We had a quiet if frozen time over Christmas and into the start of January. When we were able, we rode abroad and when we could not, I fretted behind the walls of Usk Castle. The river never froze and that was a good thing. Our many horses gave us an advantage over the Welsh but a frozen river would allow men on foot passage across the river and into England. It was the end of January and I was leading my patrol along with Dafydd Gam and three of his men when trouble came. We had crossed the bridge into Wales as there had been a snowfall and I wished to see if there was any sign of warriors on the western side of the Usk. Snow caused problems but it also allowed us to see tracks much easier. We had just passed the village of Llanvair when we saw the tracks leading to the river. There were too many of them to be fishermen catching winter food. By my estimate, there were at least ten of them. They had not come from the village and Dafydd, who had spoken to the men in the village, assured me that they were not rebels. "They might not fight for the Prince but they will not fight against him either. They are the sort of men who just want to get on with their own lives which are perilous enough as it is."

We spied the tracks on the eastern side of the river, close to an improvised raft, and I saw that they were headed to the tiny hamlet of Clytha. I took the decision. "We will swim our horses across. By my estimate, the river is but twenty paces across. We will be chilled but some mulled ale at the castle will warm us through."

I saw trepidation on the face of Abelard. Horsemanship was a skill he was acquiring slowly and he had never yet swum a river. It was not hard and none of us wore plate. Indeed, only Dafydd and I wore mail.

"Harry, watch Abelard, eh?"

"Aye, father."

We slipped into the water and I flicked my feet from my stirrups. The cold was a definite shock to the system but once I was wet it did not seem too bad. Hawk was my horse and he enjoyed swimming. The result was that I was the first to scramble ashore and I had the chance to confirm the direction the tracks had taken. Oliver the Bastard was the first to join me, "Wreck the raft. If we cannot find these insurgents then we can make it hard for them to get home!

"Aye, lord."

Once it was wrecked and thrown into the icy waters we headed towards Clytha. We knew that they had reached the hamlet before we saw them for we heard the screams and the shouts. Clytha had just four houses but the folk there had cattle and pigs. I knew then that this was not part of the rebellion but a cattle raid. The pigs would be butchered and the cattle driven back to Wales.

I drew my sword and raised it. The rest emulated me and I put spurs to Hawk. As we galloped over the cleared fields the snow muffled our hooves and, nearing the hamlet I saw light reflecting from swords and weapons. That we had caught them so soon was fortunate for if we had not then I am convinced that the hamlet would have become a graveyard.

A Welsh voice shouted something and Dafydd, riding next to me, said, "We are seen, lord!"

"Spread out! If we can I want a prisoner but take no chances!"

As we neared the houses, I saw one body which had suffered a number of wounds and had bled out. From his clothes, I took him to be a farmer rather than a warrior. I saw that the Welsh, there were twelve of them, had decided that warriors on horseback were too much for them and they fled west towards the river. Hawk was the best horse and he soon caught up with the last of the warriors. Using the flat of my sword I smacked him on the back of his helmeted head. He landed heavily face down. Harry and Abelard, along with Dafydd, were close to me and five of the Welshmen, obviously braver than the others, turned and held their spears and swords towards us. That they had courage was never in doubt and they meant to slow us up to allow the others to escape. I brought my sword down to slice through the spearhead and into the forearm of one Welshman. My sword was sharp and I cut through to the bone. A poleaxe was swung at Abelard who caught it on his shield. His hand was still not fully healed and he tumbled from the saddle into the soft snow. Harry was ruthless and his sword hacked into the shoulder of the Welshman who screamed. Dafydd's sword managed to skewer a Welshman in the eye but the last men ran towards Abelard who was groggily rising to his feet. I whirled Hawk and used his hooves to clatter into the back of one Welshman while Harry leaned from his saddle to lay open the back of the other.

My men were still chasing the other Welshmen and so we reined in. I went to the man whose arm I had laid open but he had bled to death. All five were dead. Harry helped Abelard back into the saddle.

"I am sorry, lord!"

"You had an injury to your left hand. It is my fault for bringing you. Let us ride back to the one who I rendered unconscious."

The man was still prostrate on the ground. Harry took his weapons and helmet from him and as the dented helmet was lifted, I saw that I had split his skull. He began to stir as it was removed and I dismounted, the better to speak with him. "Dafydd, if he cannot speak English then I will need you to translate."

"Aye, lord."

"Abelard, watch the horses."

"Aye, lord."

The man rose to his feet and he put his hand to the back of his head. He stared at the blood on his hand and then seemed to see the three of us with weapons pointing at him. "Where are you from?"

He spat something out and Dafydd backhanded him to the ground. "He said, Wales! You will get nothing from him. Better I slit his throat now!"

"Let us see. Ask him where is Glendower?"

The man laughed and a jabbering jumble of words poured forth. Welsh always sounded like someone was spitting to me. Dafydd said, "He said, not close enough for an Englishman to get him but Captain Rhys Gethin will come soon enough."

I turned to Dafydd, "Who is that?"

"He was the standard-bearer of Glyndŵr but lately he is rumoured to be leading a warband of his own. This man seems to confirm it."

"We will take him back with us." My men had just begun to return and I said, "Captain Alan, go to the hamlet and see if they have any hurts which need tending. Tell them that the raiders are dead or fled and we will take this one back to the castle for further questioning."

"Aye lord,"

"Harry, bind his hands behind him."

I had two of Dafydd's men ride behind the prisoner as we walked south to Usk. The river looped, twisted and turned so that sometimes we were a hundred paces from the edge and sometimes just a few paces. It was as we neared one such place that the Welsh rebel suddenly lurched into one of the horses of the men guarding him. The horse reared and the Welshman ran for the river. He hurled himself in. I do not know if he thought he could break his bonds and he was strong for he managed to reach the middle before I saw him begin to sink, dragged down by sodden clothes, the chilling water and the fact that he could not use his arms. When his head did not rise a fourth time, we knew that he was dead.

Dafydd was angry with his men but I pointed out that we would have learned little else from the rebel. "I doubt that he would have told us where the rebel base is in any case. My guess is that they are close and needed food. This is a warning and has justified my patrols. Some of Glendower's men will have escaped back to tell him that we patrol and it may well be that we are enough to deter raids."

Dafydd nodded, "But not an attack!"

"Aye, not an attack and if an attack comes then it will be with more than a dozen men armed with crude weapons. It will be with an army."

It was the only time we saw any insurgents and as February drew to a close so reinforcements arrived in the area. The first was the Earl of Warwick who brought a garrison for Grosmont Castle. Sir John Talbot brought some well-needed men at arms and archers to swell our garrison and also news that the Earl of Arundel was back in Worcester and that Prince Henry was at Shrewsbury. We were no longer isolated. There was help at hand.

With more men available to us Dafydd left us to return to his own estate which he had neglected over the winter. I confess that

I missed him when he had gone. He was my kind of warrior. The Earl of Arundel was a more common knight. The young nobles did not really understand the reality and brutality of war. I had stood on the bridge in Spain with Sir John Chandos and seen men hacking at each other with nowhere to go. They had heard the stories and ballads of his brave last stand but did not understand the reality. Dafydd had also seen the brutal side of war. More men were sent to the garrison and our task became easier. It was March and I was about to hand over the castle to its new lord who arrived with more than forty men when Dafydd and his men galloped across the bridge.

"Sir William, Captain Gethin is heading for Grosmont. He has more than six thousand men with him and they are heavily armed!"

I knew that the Earl of Warwick had sent some men to Grosmont Castle but he could not have sent enough to fight off such a large force. I sent two of my men, Oliver and John, to ride to Hereford and Shrewsbury to tell Sir John Talbot, Sir John Oldcastle and Prince Henry of the danger. Oliver the Bastard would go to Hereford and I told him what I intended so that we could trap the Welsh between us. I would be the anvil and the men of Hereford, the hammer. I sent one of the men at arms from the garrison to inform the Earl of Arundel of the situation. Leaving just twenty men to watch the walls I led the rest north. The one hundred and ten men I led could not stop the Welsh but I knew that I would be the first to reach the beleaguered town and I would be able to give whoever brought more men to the battle reliable information.

As we rode Dafydd told me that he had been informed of the raid by a loyal Welshman. There were still more of them than Glendower would care to admit. However, the delay in delivering the information meant that the Welsh would already have fallen upon the prosperous town before we could go to their aid. I knew that my riders would not reach Shrewsbury or Worcester before nightfall and that any help might take two days to reach us. My hope lay with the two old knights, Oldcastle and Talbot. They were at Hereford and, with luck, would reach the town by late afternoon.

It was approaching noon when we saw the smoke rising in the distance; they had fired the town. We knew that we would be too late to stop an attack but I had not expected the Welsh to have begun to lay waste to the town so soon. Dafydd shook his head as he saw the smoke, which obviously indicated a large number of houses burning, "This is the way they make war in these parts, lord. They destroy what others have built and hope to dishearten them and make them leave so that their own people can take over the land. It is petty and it is vindictive. This Glyndŵr just wants power and he will do anything he can to get it. He cares not for Wales; he cares for himself and his family and that is why he is so elusive. He surrounds himself with his family and they are the ones who take the risks while he squats safely, like a toad, in his mountain stronghold."

"But thanks to you, Dafydd, and the work we have done, we have the chance to begin to thwart his ambitions."

"With this handful of men?"

"With this handful of men. There is a river they had to cross to reach Grosmont, is there not?"

"Aye Sir William, the Afon Mynwg but it is no Severn. Men can cross it easily!"

"Aye, but if they take cattle, goods and prisoners from Grosmont then they cannot use a ford, they will need a bridge. We find the road which leads from Grosmont to the bridge and we can stop their escape with their ill-gotten gains. We may not have enough men to defeat their army but we can stop them taking from English mouths and by then the two knights to whom I sent for aid should be here!"

"Then the raiders will take the road to Pandy. It is five miles from the bridge there to Grosmont." He pointed to the west. "There is a crossroads coming up and if we stay on this road then we shall pass it."

"Good, Captain Alan, take your archers and ride up this road. I want it blocked to prevent the Welsh from heading back to Wales."

"Aye, lord."

When he took his archers, it left me just fifty men at arms to fight alongside Dafydd and me. It was not a large number and, as we drew closer to the road and saw the billowing smoke in the east, I wondered if I had taken too much on. We saw men driving two bullocks down the road. I knew that Alan would have already blocked the road and these men were going to get a shock. You cannot hide fifty men at arms with banners and spears. The handful of men saw us approaching and they abandoned their bullocks and headed back to Grosmont.

Dafydd asked, "Should we go to capture them, Sir William?"

"No Dafydd, for they serve me. Our intention is to trap the Welsh. To do that I need their attention here so that the men of Hereford can fall upon them."

We stopped where a track led to a burned-out farm. The smoke rising from it told me that the Welsh had already raided and plundered it. There was another farm just a hundred paces up the road and we headed for it. It was not burned out for it was a small stone-built one but there were the bodies of a farmer and two of his sons. They had been butchered and their manhoods sliced off and placed in their mouths.

"Cover their bodies and then tether the horses behind the barn. We will hold them here." I turned to Abelard, "Plant my banner on the roof of this farm. We will let them know that they fight the Strongstaff."

While he did that, I went with Dafydd to the road. There was a hedgerow which was not yet fully in leaf but it would afford some protection for it lined the highway. From behind me, I heard hooves and Captain Alan rode up. "We have cleared the road of the thirty or so men who were taking animals and prisoners back to Wales. The captives I have sent to the burned-out farm for I saw your banner. What would you have of my men and me?"

"I intend to hold them here. I want the archers behind us to thin out their ranks. Have stakes made to prevent them from outflanking us."

"Aye, lord."

"Captain Edgar, have two-thirds of our men spread out on either side of the road behind the stakes the archers are planting. I will need eight of our best men with me. You take charge of the north side of the road. Dafydd, you and your men take the south side. I will use just ten of my men to block the road."

I shed my cloak and took the spear which Harry handed me. There had been cattle in the farm and the farmyard was full of excrement. I waved over Stephen of Morpeth, "Get the men and have them spread the cow dung about twenty paces before us. Let us see how they cope with it."

He grinned, "Aye, lord, for it seems fitting."

By the time it was all done it was the middle of the afternoon and, from the roof of the farm, Much Longbow shouted, "There are men coming from Grosmont, lord. I reckon there are at least five hundred of them!"

I turned to Harry, "So, outnumbered again. Remember Abelard, you stay behind us and use your spear to keep them from before us! God is with us and we fight for Prince Henry!"

My men cheered and although we were outnumbered, we were in good heart! We waited.

Chapter 6

Captain Gethin had sent a large enough force to shift us from the road but they were not led by a knight and they came at us as a mob. We would not be fighting as we did at Shrewsbury. Here we had shields and spears. This was not an open battlefield and I wanted the mob to hit our hedgehog of steel and to die! The Welsh helped us for they came directly for me as there was treasure to be had by either killing or capturing a knight and they hurled themselves at my handful of men standing before the standard on the roof. Alan and his archers thinned their ranks before they even reached us. Bodkin arrows were not needed for the ones who were the closest to us wore no mail. Then men slipped and slid on the animal waste and some were skewered as they lay helplessly before us. The bodies of those we slew caused problems for those trying to get at us. The first eight struck our ash shafted spears and fell at our feet. A couple died quickly thanks to a spearhead in a vital organ but as we pulled back our spears many of the men were eviscerated and lay writhing beneath the feet of their fellows who were equally eager to get at us. It had been some years since I had fought in this kind of battle using a shield and a spear but it was something I had learned from a young age and the familiar action soon allowed me to fight and yet still observe the battle.

With my shield held tightly, I pulled back my right arm, thrust my spear and then, as it struck flesh twisted and retracted. Around me, my men at arms were doing the same while Harry and Abelard and other men at arms poked spears over our shoulders to ram them into faces which had no protection from the sharpened spearheads. Welsh arrows descended but they were aimed further behind us and, more importantly, were hunting arrows and not bodkins. I heard them clatter as they struck helmets and mail but there were no cries from men who had been wounded. I saw more

Welsh arriving and I was able to see them clearly for they rode horses. The nobles and the knights who led this motley crew of raiders were coming to rid themselves of my annoying roadblock which prevented their escape, with booty, back to Wales. We just had to hold out a little longer and I had to pray that my men had reached Hereford.

I heard a Welsh horn and then Welsh voices gave commands. Owen the Welshman shouted, "Lord, they have been ordered to pull back so that their horsemen can charge us."

I shouted, "Captain Alan, horsemen approach and they may be mailed."

"Fear not, Sir William, we are ready." That told me he and his archers had switched to bodkin arrows.

My worry was that they would attempt to outflank us but, as the mob before us departed, dragging wounded friends and family with them, I saw that they only had what looked to be a hundred or so horsemen. That was not enough to outflank us. It was, however, enough to charge us and knock us from the road. I heard Captain Alan shout orders and I heard archers shift position to stand behind us. I glanced over and saw that there were now ten archers there. The Welsh commander had a banner which looked to be that of Glendower: there were four rampant lions, countercharged, two were yellow on red and two were red on yellow. I did not think for a moment that this was Glendower but it was led by someone close to him. As the Welsh commander shouted, his voice indistinct for he was over three hundred paces from us, I saw the men on foot run to the fields. He was going to use those to attack the two sides of the road while his horsemen cleared the blockage.

"They mean to charge us but we hold them and trust that our archers will thin their numbers before they reach us."

I was counting on the fact that there were fourteen bodies before us and some were piled into a human barrier. Before them, closer to the animal waste, were more bodies. Although the knights and nobles were five men wide at the moment, the bodies littering the lane would affect their cohesion. We would need to trust to our shields, our armour and our spears. At last, and with the sun lowering in the sky behind us, the Welsh horn was sounded and the hooves clattered along the road. I heard the

Welsh cheers from beyond the hedgerows but my attention was on the horsemen. The tight line with which they began their charge became disjointed as soon as they reached the first of the bodies. Horses always try to avoid stepping on men and in trying to avoid them they either slowed or veered to the side. Then the arrows flew from behind us. They were bodkin arrows and could penetrate not only mail but, plunging from on high, plate too. It was as the man holding the Welsh standard slipped from the saddle that I heard a distant horn, from the town. I knew that it was not Welsh. It had to be the men from Hereford.

"The horn means we will not be alone for long! Hold the line! Hold the line!"

A horse was hit by an arrow and as it dumped its rider its falling body slewed across the lane. The leading three riders had almost reached us and our archers chose targets further away. As I had expected the three came directly for me and the leading noble who had a surcoat with a red gryphon on a yellow background thrust his spear at me. The man had used a spear from the back of a horse before but not often for he failed to stand in his stirrups. The result was a weak strike which I easily deflected with my shield. My spear found the flank of his horse which was without a caparison and it scored a deep line along the side of the animal which tried to pull away from the weapon. Just then I heard a wail from the east and knew that Sir John Talbot and the men of Hereford had reached the rear of the Welsh. The hammer had struck and we just had to be the anvil and to remain firm.

Pulling back my arm I thrust again and this time the rider, in attempting to control his horse, had raised his arm. I stabbed at his chest and, unbalanced, he fell to the ground. I knew from his surcoat that he was important and so I stepped from the line and had my spear at his throat even as he tried to rise.

"Yield or perish, rebel!"

He nodded and, dropping his weapon, said, "I yield."

Although I was exposed my handful of men had clambered over the Welsh dead and formed a barrier of spears. I saw Stephen of Morpeth with another knight as a prisoner. The rest of my men at arms and archers, seeing that the Welsh were broken, dropped their spears and bows and ran amongst them to drag them from their horses. Some were taken prisoner but others were slain. When I heard the clash of metal on metal, I knew that knights had struck the Welsh.

Dafydd Gam shouted, "They have broken! They are fleeing!"

I looked down at the noble I had captured and gestured for him to rise, "What is your name?"

"I am John Hanmer!"

He said the name as though I ought to know it but I did not. David of Welshpool laughed, "A fine prisoner, lord, for he is Glyndŵr's brother in law."

I saw Stephen of Morpeth gesture for his captive to rise and he asked him his name. The man spoke only Welsh and David of Welshpool said, "Another captive worth keeping, Sir William, he is Owen ap Gruffydd ap Rhisiant, Glyndŵr's secretary."

Not only had we defeated the Welsh we had two men we could keep as prisoners and use to bargain with the Welsh. By the time it was dark there were no more belligerents on the field of battle. It was, indeed, Sir John Talbot who had brought men to aid us and we headed towards the town of Grosmont. The small garrison sent by the Earl of Warwick had held the castle but they had been too few in number to prevent the loss of houses. More than one hundred houses had been burned and the commander of the castle, Sir Humphrey Granville, was embarrassed that they had been so impotent. "I will send to the Earl for more men. Had the two of you not arrived with your men then things would have gone ill."

Sir John and I agreed but there was little that could be added for it was not Sir Humphrey's fault. Sir John said, "I sent to Worcester and the Prince should be here soon enough."

"Then I will stay although my men should return to Usk. I left few enough men to watch the walls and although we slew many men there are still more at large."

It was noon the next day when Prince Henry arrived. I had not seen him since the autumn and I saw that he had grown over the winter. It was not just physical growth, he had matured. Sir John, Sir Humphrey and I each told him of the events. He nodded to Dafydd Gam, "We are in your debt Sir Dafydd. Thanks to your warning you have saved us from greater harm."

"I serve myself too, my lord, for until Glyndŵr is gone, I am in danger too!"

The Prince looked at me, "Sir William, I need a word." He led me to one side. "How many of our men did we lose?"

"We lost less than fifteen men and that includes men from the castle garrison, Prince Henry, but the town lost more than a hundred houses and two hundred men from the town perished. Some families were burned in their homes. Grosmont has suffered a grievous loss."

"And the Welsh?"

"We captured five knights including the secretary of the rebel leader and the brother in law of Owain Glendower and more than eight hundred bodies were recovered."

"Then it is a victory." I nodded. "You should know that the reason I did not return was due to Parliament. My father and I have spent the winter trying to extract money from a parsimonious and self-serving Parliament who refuse to fund us and this just war." He shook his head, "I saw not a single face from the battle of Shrewsbury! These were not the knights who defended us against the rebels. These were the ones who profited from the war."

"It is ever thus, Prince Henry, there are warriors and there are those who have neither nobility nor courage and they will be the ones who skulk in Parliament."

"Aye, you are right and I am right glad that I have surrounded myself with men like you. When I am King I will ensure that it is my men who are the council of the King." He lowered his voice. "You should know that my father is not well."

I nodded, "The skin complaint?"

He looked surprised, "Aye, but how did you know?"

I laughed, "I watched over your father from the time he was younger than you. Like King Richard before him, I know him well. He can recover, can he not?"

"Perhaps, but he tires more than he used to. It means more of the burden of the Kingdom will fall upon my shoulders. I know that you have spent longer here than you expected. Return to Usk for a short time and I will send Sir Richard Grey of Codnor to relieve you for he is a doughty knight. I will take these prisoners back to London and speak with my father. When you are relieved then return to Northampton where I will join you so that we can plan our strategy."

"But, Prince Henry, the border!"

"We have hurt them and this will buy us time." He smiled, "Do you not wish to return home?"

"With every part of my body, aye, but we are not done here yet."

"No, but I see a chink of light and that gives me hope. Sir Richard will be with you by early April."

I returned to the castle but I was not convinced. I had lost none of my men and they were in good spirits for all had profited from the battle. There would be a ransom for the two men we had captured and all would benefit from that. Abelard was the one changed the most by the battle for he had killed a mailed man. His thrust over my shoulder had been well delivered and entered the eye and brain of the Welshman. It changed Abelard. He took his first real steps to becoming a replacement for Harry.

Sir Richard Grey did not reach us until the end of April. The knight was apologetic for the delay but the weather had been atrocious and some of his men had had commitments on their farms. However, he brought a sizeable force, so much so that we struggled for accommodation and stabling. I spent two days showing him the land around the castle and I sent for Dafydd Gam. Dafydd had returned to his manor in Llantillo but I knew that he would wish to meet my replacement.

He arrived but not in the measured way I expected. I was with Sir Richard at the gatehouse surveying the River Usk when I spied riders racing to the castle. I had put in place systems and procedures for surprise attacks and the horn summoned men to the walls.

"Leave the gates open for a while." I saw that a dozen riders who galloped towards us were being pursued. Of course, this could be a trick, indeed I had used such a trick myself but, as they neared, I saw that it was Dafydd Gam. "Archers, shower those pursuing once Dafydd and his men are within the walls!"

I saw that those who were pursuing were a good two hundred paces behind and we would have time to raise the bridge and close the gates before they reached us. As the last man galloped through, I heard the creak of the windlass as the bridge was raised. The archers released a whoosh of arrows and the horsemen stopped. I saw that it was a sizeable army. In fact, there looked to me more horsemen than in the one we had defeated at Grosmont. Behind them, I saw men on foot running down the road.

Dafydd raced up the stairs and stood close to Sir Richard and myself. He pointed to the Welsh, "It is Gruffudd ab Owain Glyndŵr, himself! It is the son of Owain Glyndŵr."

Sir Richard frowned for he was new to the border, "I do not understand, why would the son of the leader of the rebels chase a handful of you?"

"They were not chasing me; they were coming, my lord, for this castle. They believe it is still weak and after Grosmont, they need a victory. I discovered this from some loyal Welshman and I was about to come here when your messenger found me. It just so happened that I was on the road at the same time as they were. They have brought many of the knights who followed Owain Glyndŵr when he captured Harlech and Aberystwyth. They are the best that they have."

"And Mortimer?"

Shaking his head Dafydd said, "He and his English rebels are in Harlech!"

I smiled at Sir Richard, "Then I think that they are in for a shock, Sir Richard. Thanks to the men you brought and the men at arms we have within these walls I think that we can hurt these rebels. We let them assault the walls, for they think the ditches are still full of rubbish and do not know that we have repaired old mortar and replaced stones. When the attack fails, we will ride forth and destroy this army of Glendower."

"A good plan. I will have my knights mounted and ready."

"Aye, Abelard, go and prepare our horses. Harry, fetch my helmet and weapons and then join Abelard. Dafydd, can you and your men ride forth or are your horses spent?"

"My squire and I will ride for I would not miss this opportunity to defeat the rebels."

I saw that the Welsh leader had halted his men and that showed that he was not stupid. Six of them lay pierced by arrows from my archers. They were the eager squires who had neither plate nor mail. This son of Glendower would wait until his foot soldiers arrived and let them attack. The Welsh hated the English for a whole variety of reasons. They fought not for money but for their freedom and for Glendower. They would bleed to get at our walls.

By the time I had been dressed for war Sir Richard had the knights he had brought gathered in the outer bailey. The walls were manned by archers and twenty men at arms, mainly mine. To the Welsh, it would look as though we had few men. When we had first arrived, it had been the land to the north which had been the part which needed the most repairs. The son of Glendower obviously thought it was still the weakest part for he moved his army around the castle, outside the range of our archers. That suited me for when his attack failed, we could send our knights from the castle through the main gate. My men mirrored the movements of the Welsh and we positioned ourselves on the north wall. I saw that they had not brought many ladders. I only counted six. They thought to climb the walls much as they might climb rocks to get to their sheep. I also noticed that the knights dismounted and their horses were tethered. The ordinary Welshmen would breach the walls and then the better armed and mailed men would exploit the breach.

I sent a couple of men to open the gate and lower the drawbridge for the foolish Welsh had not left it watched; it was a mistake which would cost them dear. With the whole of the Welsh army to the north, we would have plenty of time to secure them if I was wrong. I saw a monk, he looked to be an Abbot, blessing the Welsh who all knelt. It was a sure sign that they were about to attack. My archers each nocked an arrow. These were war arrows which would cause terrible wounds to men who wore neither mail nor plate. I could see that most of the Welsh who faced us had a helmet at best. There were at least a thousand or more waiting to attack us.

One of Dafydd's men was near to me and he said, "Lord, the one leading them is Captain Gethin and, next to Gruffudd ab Owain Glyndŵr is his brother Tudur. He is the one looks the most like his father."

I saw the two he meant and they were close to the banner I had seen at Grosmont. This was an attempt to break the English hold on this part of Wales. If they succeeded then Wales would, apart from Caernarfon and Conwy, be in Welsh hands!

A horn sounded and the Welshmen raced like greyhounds across the open, rising ground. Captain Alan commanded the archers and he was patient. The ditch had been improved so that it had two steep sides. Men could break ankles jumping in and once in the straight sides were almost impossible to escape. They were in for a shock. Captain Alan waited until the Welsh were just one hundred and fifty paces from us knowing that although many would reach the ditches, they would be so close to the walls that they could be easily hit. Men lifted shields but our archers were accurate enough to hit wherever they chose. Had we had more archers then none of the Welsh would have reached the ditch. As they reached the ditch, I heard the sound of screams as men fell to break their ankles on the bottom. The only way out would be once the ditch was filled with dead and dying men and they could climb and clamber over corpses.

I turned and shouted down to the men waiting in the bailey, "Sir Richard, prepare to leave the castle. We will wait until their first wave falls back!" He waved his acknowledgement and I turned my attention to the failing attack. Some of our archers were hitting Welsh warriors as they crossed the ground to the ditch but most were now aiming at the men trying to clamber out of the ditch. Two of the ladders had managed to reach the walls and each time someone tried to climb out an archer hit the man. One ladder broke when two men fell across its middle. I saw the Welsh leaders conferring and preparing a second wave. This time they were stiffening the ranks with men at arms wearing mail and plate. I said to Captain Alan, "I leave you to command!"

"This is not war, lord, it is slaughter!"

He was right but this was necessary if we were to secure Wales for the Prince. I mounted Hawk and, raising the spear given to me by Abelard, I said, "Sir Richard, take the west side and I will take the east. Dafydd, you know this land, ride with Sir Richard! Ride for their standards!"

As a plan it was basic but I hoped it would be effective. After we had crossed the bridge I turned to the east. The Welsh would see us once we cleared the walls but, by then, it would be too late. Their knights, nobles and men at arms would have to get to their horses. We would be riding at full speed and only a fool faced charging horsemen on a stationary horse! As we cleared the castle, I saw that the second wave was advancing rapidly and the odd survivors from the first attack were making their way back. When we were seen we sowed confusion amongst the Welsh. Some of those retiring began to run while those advancing halted and presented spears and shields. We were not attacking the ordinary warriors, I wanted the leaders and the nobles.

I saw the nobles mount but it took time and we were approaching rapidly. I had slowed down a little to allow my men to form a line alongside me. That was one advantage of riding with men who knew me; I did not need to issue orders. This time, too, Harry and Abelard were close to me with spears and shields. It would be Abelard's first charge on a horse. All I hoped was that he would stay in the saddle. Anything else would be a bonus.

The Welsh were horsed but their natural escape route, to the south and the west, was blocked by us and the river. They had but one way to go, towards the northeast. What they did not know was there was a large pond there and they would have to divide themselves to get around it. There would be confusion and, in such chaos, lay disaster. Sir Richard would take those on one side while I would take those on the other. We were gaining on them for they begun their ride not from a canter but from a halt and we had speed. I saw the banners and knew that the two sons of Glendower would be on my side. Before I could reach them, I had to negotiate groups of fleeing Welshmen. My spear came up and back, punching into men who, at best, managed to turn to face me.

I heard Harry shout, "They are turning to face us!"

I pulled my spear from the side of the bleeding Welshman and saw that Gruffudd son of Owain Glendower had realised the futility of flight and was making a stand. They wheeled their horses and came towards us. They would be going no faster but at least their front would be to their enemies. The two brothers and their lieutenants and standard-bearers came directly for me. I had no standard with me but my surcoat stood out, uniquely, on any battlefield. I realised then the danger in which I had placed my squires. They would both be facing warriors. I spurred Hawk and his legs opened to take me away from my squires. If I could draw their spears then it gave Captain Edgar and my men at arms the chance to protect my son and squire.

Both of the Welsh knights who faced me wore open helmets and I saw the one they said was the twin of his father. It was he, Tudur, who came at me. The Welsh knights were trying to keep boot to boot but Tudur Glendower was keen to get to me. He had a spear but I did not think he had used one too often for it wavered as he galloped towards me. I kept my spear resting on my cantle. As we closed, I lifted it and pulled it back. His lunge at me was poor and I took the weak blow on my shield. I punched hard at his side with my own weapon and when I hit his shield, he lurched towards his brother driving him further from me but, alarmingly, closer to Harry who was on my left. Another Welsh knight barged his horse into mine and his sword clattered off my helmet. Abelard came to my rescue. His spear rammed into the arm of the Welshman and he had to drop his shield. Abelard had been trained for a few years as an archer and his quick hands punched again and this time, he drew blood. The Welsh knight wheeled his horse around and tried to flee. Abelard had the bit between his teeth and he urged his horse to pursue the knight. I turned too for Tudur Glendower was not yet beaten. He drew his sword and showed his strength for he backhanded my spear and it flew from my hand. I had been careless and in watching Abelard I had failed to see the danger my enemy represented.

He saw his chance and came at me. Even as I drew my sword, I lifted my shield to block the blow from his sword. Behind me, I heard Captain Edgar shout, "Protect the Strongstaff!"

It was as he shouted that I realised my son would be fighting Tudur's brother! It made me determined to end this quickly, Already Sir Richard was driving other Welshmen towards the pond and I saw mailed men and horses falling into its murky waters. I spurred Hawk and his head reared around to bite at the Welshman's mount. He did not have a courser and it tried to get away from us. It gave me the chance to pull my sword and to swing it hard at his shield. I knew my first blow had hurt him and caused some damage to his shield; the spearhead had torn into the wood and gouged a line along it. The next strike with my sword also hurt him but this time he shouted and I wondered if I had broken a bone in his hand or arm. I lifted my sword again as he swung a weak slash at my shield. I barely felt it but he expected another strike at his shield. Instead, I twisted the point to ram it towards his armour. He had a breastplate but my tip found the gap and the end ripped through links in his mail and came out bloody.

He was afraid; I saw it in his eyes. My name was known as protector and champion of kings. Perhaps he thought me old, many men did, but the first blows we had exchanged had shown him that was not true. He tried one more swing at me, this time aiming at my head. I flicked up my shield and sent his blade harmlessly above my helmet while I hacked down at his leg. Like me, he was armoured for horseback and although he had greaves, he had no armour on his thighs and my sword hacked through the mail and into his leg. That was enough for him and he turned his horse. Sadly, for him, it was not a warhorse and it was slow to turn. I was still worried about Harry and rather than asking him to yield I brought my sword across him, striking him across the side of the head. He fell from his horse which fled the field. I did not stop to see how he fared but I turned my horse. His brother's squire rode at me. He was not a young warrior; he was in his twenties and was a huge brute of a man. Behind him I saw Harry and Gruffudd Glendower sparring; to get to them I had to deal with a squire armed with a war axe.

He urged his horse towards me and began to swing his axe. Any connection with me would be dangerous and potentially fatal. The axe head could shatter mail and break bones. I had to use his own strength against him. I held my shield out before me and invited a swing to shatter my shield and break my arm. I saw his eyes widen in anticipation as he swung the long weapon. I pulled back the shield and the axe-head swung into fresh air. I stood in my stirrups and hacked down at the haft of the axe. I hit it and, more importantly, knocked it from his hands. I lunged, more in hope than expectation, at his body and he reeled. He was a big man and, with an unbalanced horse, he pulled the horse on top of him. He screamed as the horse landed upon him and then spewed forth blood. He was dead!

I whirled around and saw that my son had unhorsed the leader of the Welsh and he had his sword at his throat. "Surrender or die like your brother."

I saw the Welshman look around for a way to escape as I dismounted and walked over to him. I placed the tip of my sword close to the corner of his eye, "Gruffudd ab Owain, I care not if you live or die but if you attempt to leave without surrendering then I will kill you myself."

Handing his sword hilt first to my son, he stood, "I will yield but you will not hold me for long. My countrymen will free me."

The sun was setting but there was still enough light to survey the scene of carnage. Bodies were piled around the pond and riderless horses wandered around. I waved my sword towards the castle. The ground was covered in the bodies of the men slain by my archers; Captain Alan had led them from the castle to finish off the Welsh archers and their foot soldiers. "And where will these men come from? Has your father another army hidden away somewhere? We destroyed one at Grosmont and another here. These are knights and nobles I see here and they cannot defeat us. What hope do those who work the fields have? You can have the mountain passes! Let your men eat grass." I turned, "Owen the Welshman, take four men and guard this one. Oliver the Bastard, take his brother's head and plant it on a spear. For the rest, throw them in the pond. We do not need the water and Pwll Melyn will remind Welshmen for all time of the folly of rebellion."

As we searched the battlefield, we saw that the Captain, Gethin, who had raided Grosmont and caused them so much harm had perished too. Barely eight knights escaped the slaughter. We had little ransom but we had won and that was all that was important.

Leaving Sir Richard to secure his new castle I led my men and our prisoner to Worcester. Dafydd Gam came with me. To my surprise, Prince Henry was there along with his father and the Earl of Arundel. Their faces told me that there was trouble.

Chapter 7

Before they gave me their news, for I knew that they would wish to do so in private, I said, "Your Majesty, Prince Henry, I have here Gruffudd ab Owain Glendower, captured by my son, and can advise you that his brother Tudur ab Owain Glendower is slain."

Dafydd tutted and said, "It is Glyndŵr."

I smiled, "However you pronounce it, he is our prisoner!"

I saw that the King's face was becoming worse and when he smiled, I saw the pain it caused, "You are the best of knights, William Strongstaff! I come here with dire news and you bring me a prisoner. Come, we have much to tell you. Arundel, have the prisoner taken under strong escort to the tower to join the other prisoners! You go with them to make sure that he does not escape."

I took Harry with me for I had a request to make. We were taken to a small chamber in the castle and I saw that the Archbishop of Canterbury was waiting. He smiled, "The bearer of good news again, eh Sir William?"

King Henry waved an irritable hand. I suspected his illness was affecting him. "The north has risen in rebellion. Sir Ralph Neville has been given orders to meet them. The rebellion is led by Scrope!" He glared at the Archbishop. "The Archbishop of York!"

"I did not appoint him!"

"Your Majesty!" I heard the anger in the King's voice at the apparent lack of respect.

"Who else was involved, Your Majesty?" Sensitivities would get us nowhere.

"Thomas Mowbray, the Earl of Norfolk and Henry, Earl of Northumberland! I have forgiven that snake enough and now I will take all of his lands!"

Prince Henry said, "First, father, he has to be defeated. It is why we are here, Sir William. How stands the Marches? You have won two battles. Can we take the army from here to go to the aid of Sir Ralph?"

I felt every eye boring into me and I knew that they wanted me to say, aye, but I could not. I would tell the truth and if they did not like it then so be it. I had fallen foul of King Richard by doing so but I could not change my nature. "No, Prince Henry, we cannot. We could take some men and send them but the castles we have we must hold. I thought Grosmont would result in victory but that was less than two months ago and they have come again. We have yet to see Mortimer outside of castle walls and Owain Glendower remains elusive and hidden. My advice would be to send some men north but not all."

When Prince Henry smiled, I knew I had done the right thing especially when the King said, "Your words concur with my son's but I cannot let this rebellion go unpunished."

I had trained Henry Bolingbroke and, to me, he was still a youth, "Your Majesty, you trusted the border to me and I did not fail you. You have trusted the north to the Sherriff of Westmoreland and I know him to be a doughty warrior. Trust the loyal knights in the north."

"I have ever trusted your judgement and I will do so again. Nonetheless, I will leave when Arundel's men return from London and I will take what men I can from here."

Prince Henry said, "And I will thank you, Sir William. What boon do you wish?"

I pointed to Harry, "That my son Henry of Weedon be knighted, Prince Henry, for he was the one who defeated the rebel."

"And gladly will I do so!"

And so my son ceased to be Harry and became Sir Henry of Flore, taking over Sir Roger's old manor. Some of my men had been wounded in the battle and so I sent them with my son to Weedon. Even though he wished to stay I knew that Harry, Sir Henry, needed to speak with his mother and to use the coin from Flore to hire men and buy horses. If the north had rebelled then he would be needed, sooner rather than later.

Harry shook his head and said, "I would rather stay with you, father, for we have two rebellions to fight and I do not wish to be just watching, I would serve my King and my country."

"And you will but you are now a knight, a lord of the manor and you have responsibilities. You have to provide the King with men and horses from your manor. You need a squire and you need to be dressed and equipped as a knight. When that is done then you shall return but not before. Remember, Harry, that I am your lord now as well as your father. It is my command that you must heed."

He saw that I was right. Turning to Abelard he said, "And now he is your responsibility. I have no doubt that you will discharge your duty well but it is a great weight that you now bear."

"I know, Sir Henry, but you have shown me that it can be done and it will be done!" They did not leave immediately and it took a couple of days to ensure that the wounded had been tended to and were able to ride.

They had been gone but one day when Sir Thomas Fitzalan returned from London. From the state of his horse, he had ridden the animal almost to death. He was breathless but his eyes were bright with excitement, "King Henry, the rebellion is over! Sir Ralph tricked the Archbishop of York and the army of rebels is disbanded. He has the Archbishop Scrope and both he and the Earl of Norfolk are held in Pontefract Castle. The Earl of Northumberland, along with Lord Bardolf have fled to Scotland. God be praised!"

The relief was clear in the King's voice. The worry and fear I had heard while we waited for Sir Thomas, was now replaced by hope and optimism. "Then I will hie me to Pontefract and show these rebels the price for rebellion. My son, I charge you with the protection of these Marches on the Welsh border. Let us prosecute this war too so that England shall be at peace once more. Fitzalan, you shall come with me and sit in judgement upon these rebels."

After the King had gone to prepare for his journey and while an exhausted Sir Thomas Fitzalan rested in preparation for another punishing ride, Prince Henry and I enjoyed a beaker of celebratory wine. "This is a joyous day, is it not, Will?"

"If we had Percy with the other two then I would empty this jug of wine but Percy is in Scotland and while the King of Scotland can do nothing directly for King Henry holds his son, there is nothing to prevent him from supporting the Earl of Northumberland and I can tell you, Prince Henry, that there are Scots who would follow any leader to do mischief in England. Do you remember Shrewsbury and Douglas?"

Prince Henry was reflective. "You are right, of course, and yet you sour this moment for me."

"That is your lot in life, Prince Henry. I served King Richard as well as your father and I saw hope dashed many times over. No matter how secure you feel you are then you must know that there will be new threats which emerge from rocks you do not even see yet."

"And that is why King Richard and my father kept you close."

I shook my head and my voice was filled with bitterness, "Little good it did King Richard for he still died alone and friendless. I do not call these rebels friends of King Richard for they were conveniently absent when he needed them."

"I, too, liked King Richard for he was kind to me and it was he dubbed me but we cannot live in the past. We live in the here and now." I nodded. "What do we do about the Welsh?"

I smiled for I saw that Prince Henry's joy had evaporated with both my words and his own thoughts, "There I can offer hope, Prince Henry. We have hurt the Welsh. The hostages will not end the rebellion but in two battles we have rid ourselves of some leaders. There are now just two enemies we must deal with, Glendower and Mortimer. We know not where Glendower is hiding but we know where to find Mortimer: in Harlech. Harlech is well made. Even though it had a small garrison of thirty-six men and according to reports of the prisoners we exchanged they had but three shields, eight helmets, six lances, ten pairs of gloves, and four guns, it still held out for a long time. If you are going to take it then you will need cannons to batter down the walls and they will take time to make and to transport to Wales."

He nodded, "And they are both expensive to make and require skilled men to operate them." He beamed, "Then I have a task. I will send to find men who know about such weapons. It may surprise you to know, Sir William, that I had already thought about this. When I was in London and had to endure the tedium of the Parliament I spoke at night in the alehouses by the river with hired swords." He smiled, "Others may shun such company but I learned from you that these men, whilst not noble-born, are men from whom a future king can learn. The best gunners are Dutchmen and I shall send to that land for some gunners but as I have no cannons as yet, that will have to be for the future."

I smiled at the increasingly mature Prince of Wales, "In the meantime, we can use our horsemen to push further into Welsh lands. You now have bastions at Usk, Grosmont, Raglan, Hereford and Shrewsbury. We have lost few horsemen thus far and we use them to push into Welsh lands. The chevauchée we used was a most effective weapon. Let us raid the borderlands and make life uncomfortable for the rebels."

"That sounds like a long process, Sir William, and I am keenly aware of the sacrifices you have made for me."

"If I may speak openly, Prince Henry?"

"Always."

"Then when the autumn comes, I will return home for neither you nor I will be needed here over the winter. Your garrisons can contain the Welsh and that gives you the opportunity to have your cannons built so that we can begin to reclaim Wales. Harlech and Aberystwyth are now Welsh. The end of the rebellion will come when they are taken. When you have the cannons then we might have to endure a winter in Wales. Until then my men and I will enjoy winters in Weedon and Northampton."

"Ever the practical man. I will ride to my castles and instruct the commanders."

"And my men and I will be your escorts for while the Welsh have not proved a danger in an open battle, they are adept at ambush!"

We had but one week of such rides for more dire and unwelcome news reached us. The French had landed in the west of Wales. The numbers were unknown but we knew that there would be knights and crossbows amongst them. In open battle, they were a threat to us and so we sent word to King Henry and gathered as many knights as we could at Worcester. We held a council of war and all were agreed that the French would strike for England and that meant heading towards Worcester. Prince

Henry showed his maturity for there was a balance of old and new at the council. Men like myself, Sir John Talbot, Sir John Oldcastle were the older heads while Sir Thomas Rokeby and Sir Richard Grey were the younger ones.

The Prince summed it up when we had discussed and debated for some hours. "It seems we must abandon the land to the west of the Severn and keep our castles there as annoyances to the French and the Welsh. We will gather every knight that we can here so that we can contest the crossing of the Severn. Return to your castles and fetch back our knights. This will be our first real test as Prince of Wales and I pray to God that I will not fail. Fighting a battle against Welsh peasants who are ill led is one thing but a French army is quite another."

While his nobles returned to their castles, we devised a plan to discover the whereabouts of the French. I told the Prince that I would take some of my men and we would ride to Haverfordwest, which was where the French had landed. He forbade me to do so and was supported by my captains. Instead, we sent Owen the Welshman and David of Welshpool. They had played the part of traitors for us before and they would ride to the coast to bring back accurate numbers of the French and the Welsh. Both Prince Henry and I knew that numbers given by those who had fled would be grossly exaggerated.

It was while they were away that we learned of the vengeance of King Henry. Archbishop Scrope and Sir Thomas Mowbray had been summarily executed. It was not their execution which caused outrage but the fact that the Archbishop had not been tried by a jury of his peers. The King had used the Earl of Arundel and Sir Thomas Beaufort to sit in judgement and they had sentenced both men to death. The Archbishop had asked the axeman to use five strokes to emulate the five wounds suffered by Christ. The manner of his death and his request ignited more anger, especially in the north, and led to the belief that the King was cursed. It was true that his skin complaint worsened and he had fits where he was incapacitated but I had seen signs of this for a year or more and I did not believe in the curse. Others, especially the common people, did. We did not know it then but power was slipping away from King Henry who was seen in public less and less. Visions of King Richard filled my thoughts and haunted my dreams.

My two Welshmen returned to us just a week before the French and the Welsh arrived at the River Severn. The French had captured our last stronghold in south-west Wales, Carmarthen, and were advancing through central Wales with a Welsh army. The fact that none of the notable nobles from France had accompanied the army gave me hope and Owen had recognised Glendower. The rebel would be close enough for us to take. However, the army was somewhat larger than we had anticipated. It was not the Welsh contingent which was made up of idealists who had fled English universities and men who thought they could get back at the English for perceived past wrongs which intimidated us, it was the French knights and men at arms who numbered more than 2,500. We had less than one thousand.

Prince Henry sent for more knights from Bristol to swell our numbers and we waited along the west bank of the Severn. It meant that we denied them the bridge over that river and if they headed north towards the next one, we could mirror their progress and block their crossing. Owen and David confirmed that they were indeed heading for Worcester and their ranks were becoming swollen by those affected by English raids, the raids I had begun. A chevauchée always had risks.

I had sent for those men at arms who had recovered from their wounds but I also sent word to Harry and Tom, along with Wilfred, John, Richard and Henry, my other knights, that they were to stay in the east. I did not need to risk them. When the army finally reached us, I recognised Glendower and his standard and we saw that the French were led by John, Lord of Aumont. His livery was distinctive: arms argent and a chevron between seven martlets. His nickname gave an indication of the sort of knight he was. He was called. 'the Brawler'! They made their camp to the east of Woodbury Hill.

Once again, we held a council of war. This time Prince Henry was less bellicose for he had seen the size of their army. We were outnumbered in terms of heavy cavalry and their archers outnumbered ours. If we added the ordinary Welshmen then it was hard to see how we could win especially with the hill as a central point in their defence.

"I think we form our battle lines and send them packing!"

I looked at Sir Richard Grey. He was a brave knight but apart from a brief spell as Admiral of the fleet he had been, largely, a politician and administrator. The Prince looked at me and I nodded, "Sir Richard if we were to advance across the open ground before the hill then the Welsh archers and the French crossbowmen would fill it with dead knights and horses. If we were to advance with dismounted men then we might reach their lines with fewer losses but we would be outnumbered in a close battle even a peasant with a bodkin dagger can kill a knight."

"Then we cannot win, Sir William?"

I smiled, "I did not say that. Sometimes a victory can come about when you do not fight. The French and they are the real threat, are, like us, a mounted army. What is the biggest problem facing horsemen?"

Sir John Talbot snorted, "The same as always, grazing and fodder, not to mention water."

"Exactly. We hold the river and they must take their horses elsewhere for water. Eventually, they will use all the local grazing and whilst we have the lush valley grass, they do not. They will either have to attack us or to disperse."

Sir Richard was like a dog with a bone, "And if they attack us?"

"Then they have to endure the same as we if we were to attack. Our archers would make the ground between us a place of the dead and if they used the Welsh to attack," I nodded to the two Sir Johns, "as these gentlemen will attest, it becomes sword practice to kill them. I do not think they will attack. Glendower has had two defeats and he cannot risk a third."

For three days both armies arrayed for battle a mile apart and each night retired to their camps. Ours was the more comfortable for we had Worcester and halls where we could eat and even sleep. On the fourth day, a herald came for a parley.

The Prince took me and Sir John Talbot with him. I saw that Glendower was accompanied by the Brawler and another knight whose livery was arms gules and two bars ermine. I think he was Robert of Beaumesnil. The fact that Glendower had not brought a translator meant that we would speak English and that, in itself was a victory. We reined in and faced each other. Behind us lay our armies and they were all ready to fight. Was this the preliminary to a battle or an attempt to negotiate land?

Although Glendower spoke first, I could see that the French leader, John of Aumont, was ready to begin an argument. His fingers played with the hilt of his sword and his eyes darted between the three of us. I could see that he had earned his name well for he was looking for a fight when the rules of chivalry meant that there would be none!

"Henry of Monmouth, I am here to demand that you return my son and the other prisoners you captured on Welsh soil! And I would have an apology for the way my son, Tudur was treated after death!" His eyes flicked to me; he knew that I was responsible.

He had insulted the Prince by not using his title but Henry was too sensible to make much of that. Instead, he countered the Welsh claim. "As both battles, which you lost, took place on this side of the border I am at a loss to see how you can make such a claim!"

"Those lands are historically Welsh and we demand their return!"

It sounded petty and petulant but it showed me that we had rattled Glendower by our victories and I hoped that Prince Henry would not relinquish the advantage he held. He smiled and shook his head, "That will not happen. They will remain as prisoners in the Tower."

Glendower was nonplussed. I think he expected us to ask for a ransom. "Then we shall pay a suitable ransom for them. What will it take for you to free them?"

Prince Henry's smile became broader, "That is simple. Return the traitor Mortimer to us and the castles that you have taken. Then we can begin to have meaningful peace talks."

Glendower reddened, "Boy! You speak to me thus! I rule Wales and all you hold are a few castles in the north and that is all!"

"Then we have no more to say except that I find it sad that you had to hire mercenaries to fight your battle for you! Are there no Welshmen left that you resort to hiring creatures such as this?"

It was a deliberate insult and as the Prince had expected the Brawler rose to the bait. "My honour is impugned and I demand satisfaction!"

The Prince stared at the huge knight, "Are you a Prince that you can challenge me, Frenchman, or do you not know the rules of such things?"

He was nonplussed and he blustered, "Then I will fight one of your choosing!"

"Like Sir William here? He is the champion of my father and of me. Would you cross swords with him?"

My eyes had never left the Frenchman and when he turned, he saw steel in them. He was a brawler and like all such men, he was a bully and that made him a coward. He might be willing to take on a callow prince but not someone with my reputation. He was younger than I was and, who knows, he might have defeated me, although I doubted it. I made my voice as low and threatening as I could, "I will happily fight you now, Lord Aumont. It has been some time since I slew a Frenchman but the last time I did, his blood flowed as quickly as any other man."

He snarled, "I do not fight those who are not nobly born. We are wasting time, my lord, let us fight them! We outnumber them and they are led by a boy!"

The Prince earned his spurs that day, "Then we will return to our lines and prepare for battle. There will be little enough ransom this day for the Welsh are as poor as church mice and the French will run for their ships as soon as a blow is struck. If there is nothing more?"

Glendower was defeated and it showed in his eyes. He whisked his horse's head around and led the two French knights back to their own lines. We deliberately stayed watching them and then, as we turned, our army all began to cheer and bang their shields. The victory was compounded.

The French and the Welsh stayed another four days before heading west. We awoke one morning and found them gone. The Prince sent Dafydd to follow them and when he returned, at the end of the month, it was with the news that they were back at Haverfordwest. When the Prince heard the news, he wrote a letter to his father, now returned to London and becoming the recluse he would be for the rest of his days as King. The Prince told his father what he had done and suggested that he send the English fleet to intercept the French. We later learned that the King declined as Parliament had, once more, failed to find the finances for the ships.

By the time autumn came the rebellion had fallen into a stalemate. The Prince could not afford to continue to maintain his army and the Welsh had to sow winter crops for they had failed to do so in summer. It would be a lean winter for Wales. I got to go home after almost a year away and I was happy for the stalemate for a stalemate meant that while we had not won, we had not lost!

Chapter 8

It seemed such a long time since I had been in Weedon that when I finally reached my home it was like visiting a new country. As I rode along my lanes, I found myself looking at trees which were so tall that they might have been planted by another and not me. I saw faces smiling and waving at me and they looked like much older people than when I had left. And when the door of my hall opened and I saw a white-haired woman waiting to greet me, I almost did not recognise my wife. In a year she had grown old. Guilt wracked me for having deserted her when she needed me. I would put my knightly pursuits behind me for a while.

I turned to Abelard, "Put the horses in the stable and then the time is yours. I thank you for your efforts but you need not serve me now that we are at home. We ride abroad in the morning but until then I shall not need your services."

"Thank you, lord, I think I will sleep tonight in the warrior hall and then visit with my mother for the rest of the time. I have missed her but tonight she will welcome my father back. They need time together and besides my father will have seen enough of me!"

I forgot, sometimes, how young Abelard was. As he led the horses away, I saw my wife turn and say something to the servants. Then she opened her arms and beckoned me. The welcome my wife gave me was as warm as it had always been. The embrace was held longer than I could recall.

"Husband, I have missed you! Tell me that you will stay here awhile."

"I will, wife. The campaign is over and the Kingdom of England is safe, for a while. And, how are you?" It was not a platitude for I really meant my words and I could not tell if she was still in the pit of despair.

She linked my arm and led me into the cosy room the two of us used when we were alone. It was the chamber with just two chairs, a table and a fire which made the whole room seem comforting. I saw that she had been knitting. She normally did that when there were babies. I would let her tell me the news in her own time. Two of the house servants hurried out of the room having placed a jug of ale and some savoury pastries for me. I smiled my thanks at them and knew that my wife would not answer me until they had left. They closed the door and I poured myself a beaker of the ale.

She looked up at me as she sat in her chair, "Do you mean have I found my smile once more after Mary was taken from us? Aye, for Alice has had a baby, Beatrice, and she was born in January. God took one from us but sent another in her place. It is for her I knit and, I confess, I can see Mary in her. Is that not strange? Magda said that is how the sisters work. I fear that Magda has something of the witch in her but it does make sense to me."

I suppose I could have been upset that no one had told me but then I had not written home once while I had been away. It was good that there were more grandchildren. I wondered if Thomas and Mary had begun to enlarge their family. It would be good to speak to my sons.

"And where is Harry?"

She beamed and, putting down the knitting took my right hand in hers and kissed it, "I forgot to thank you for having him knighted and then sending him home where he is safe. He is well and busy making Flore as prosperous as Weedon. He has been there but a short time and yet he has become more popular than even Sir Roger."

"That is good. I will ride, when time allows, to see my sons." It would not be a long ride. Flore was just over a mile away and Northampton but nine. As my wife click-clacked away with her wooden needles, I stared into the fire. When I had been with the Blue Company the only warmth that I had known growing up was the burning campfire for my father had had little to do with me. The fire around which the men of the company had sat became comforting to me. There was, in my eyes, nothing finer than a log fire into which I would stare. I saw things in the fire which others did not and my mind often wandered. Thus it did as I watched the flames burning the elms that had been copsed three years since. In three years, our country and my life had changed beyond all recognition. I had gone from gentleman to baron to Sherriff. My sons had been squires and were now knights.

I heard a laugh and came back to the room and away from my thoughts. I saw my wife shaking her head, "Will Strongstaff, but you are a deep one. I have been talking to you for some little while and you were just staring into the fire."

I laughed, "Aye, you are right and I was just thinking of the position we hold and how we made the journey. We both had nothing and by sheer dint of hard work, and a little help from the Good Lord, we are now respected folk and others look up to us."

"And there are many noble-born who cannot say that." She shook her head. "Prince Henry is a good boy but I put that down to you. That Robert de Vere, he was evil and there you have it. Both were noble-born and yet they turn out as different as can be. Still, you have done your best, as have I, and Prince Henry is the man he is because of you and, I like to think, a little of me." She stood, "And food will not prepare itself. Tonight will be plain fare for I have had no time to plan and to tell the cook what to prepare. It will just be potage, bread, ham and cheese."

"And there is nothing wrong in that!" I meant the words I said. Our potage was one of my favourite meals. Begun on Sunday with the leftovers from the best meal of the week it was kept warm and each day something new would be added with the daily water to replace what had been eaten the previous day. It was the same in the homes of every common born family but we were lucky. Rabbits, hares, squirrels and game birds would all be added and even by Friday it would still be more than just edible, it would be something to which I looked forward. I had arrived home on a Monday and so it would be mutton based and that was good.

That night I slept better than I had since last I had been home. The bed in the castle at Usk had been a good one as had the bed in Worcester Castle but they were not mine and I woke refreshed. After a hearty breakfast, I went to the stable and mounted my horse which Abelard had prepared. "Abelard, I do not need you. Go to your mother. I will send for you when I need you next."

I rode Hilda, my stout palfrey. Too old for war she was a comfortable horse to ride and I would be able to rest Hawk and Hart. It was just a mile or so to Flore but it took me a long time to reach it due to the conversations with those who worked my land and walked my roads. I liked to think that I was well thought of but a lord never really knew for they all owed you service and you were their master. Freedom was an illusion even for me. When the Prince and the King demanded then I came running. Harry was stripped to the waist and working with some men. They were using a treadmill crane to lift some stones into place. He was building a tower to defend his manor.

He jumped down and ran to me, "I heard you were back and had you not called I would have visited this night."

"Then come anyway for your mother is organising a feast and I do not eat as much as I once did. I shall need your healthy appetite to help me to demolish the mountain she will prepare!"

"And I will be there. I have yet to find a cook." He waved a hand at the men and youths around him, "Instead I hired warriors first." I looked at them and saw that they were all strong but they were far younger than my men. That was to be expected. Mine had been with me for a long time. "I have yet to find a squire but I will find one. I thought it more important to secure my home and train my men. I only need a squire when I go to war and, as you are home, then I do not think that will be any time soon!"

I nodded and told him all that had happened since he had returned. "So, you missed nothing except for the humiliation of a French lord. I will not stop your work. We can speak this night. I ride to Northampton to speak with your brother and see if I am needed as Sherriff."

The road between Flore and Northampton was quiet for it was a country road and this was approaching the middle of autumn. I had my sword hanging from my belt and I felt safe. I was Sheriff of the county and if I was in danger then it was a poor state of affairs. Once I reached the main road then the traffic became heavier and I was anonymous for these were not my people. My cloak hid my livery and the people I met were heading north or south and trying to travel quickly. They probably took me for a merchant. I quite enjoyed the anonymity. Once I reached the gates of the town, of course, all of that changed. Two of the sentries escorted me to the castle, clearing the way for me. Both had served me until they settled down with families and my son took them on as part of the garrison.

Thomas was now twenty-two. He no longer looked young although he had not yet grown the paunch which many in his position might have done. Even Henry of Stratford had a bigger waist than when he had been younger. We embraced for I had not seen him for a long time. It had been Shrewsbury when last I had spent any time with him.

"Father, it is good to see you. Are you home for good?" I heard the plea in his voice. He was now a husband and he would have visited my wife often. The loss of his sister would have made him aware of his own mortality. As warriors, we were used to the prospect of death on a battlefield but there was something more frightening about the randomness of death from some ailment which had neither name nor cause. It had taken Mary and spared Harry. Why?

"For the winter and spring at the least, Thomas, and I hear that you are an uncle and I have a granddaughter."

He nodded, "And she is a delight. I have seen her but a few times but she is more beautiful each time I see her; my sister and brother in law are lucky. We hope for a girl next time for we plan to have more children. Come, Mary will be pleased to see you." I did not mean to react but Tom's wife and my daughter shared a name and the use of it struck me like an arrow. "I am sorry, father, I..."

"It is I who should apologise. It took me by surprise is all. Now take me to my daughter in law and your son!"

Mary was a delight and always had been. As soon as Thomas had said he wished to marry her it was as though it was meant to be and I could not have chosen a better wife for him. She completed him and together they were better than they were as man and woman. As for Henry, my grandson, he was growing and he hurled himself at me as soon as I entered the room. Thomas was right, he had grown and he took after my side of the family for he was stockily built.

"Grandda!"

He could speak and I found myself laughing and crying at the same time as I swung him around. "Who is this mighty warrior you have kept hidden from me, my son? He looks like he could stand in a shield wall."

I put him down and he said, "Me is Henry!"

Mary said, "I am Henry! Have you forgotten? You are the son of a lord and you must speak properly."

He nodded and stood straighter, "I am Henry like my uncle!"

He sounded like he had been practising. Tom said, "We heard that you were on your way home and when we told Henry he pestered us asking when you would come here."

I knelt. "Well Henry, I am here now and I shall try to see you as often as I can!"

He looked crestfallen and Tom said, "I told you, Henry, your grandfather will be busy for he is Sherriff."

Shaking my head, "I promise that I will visit here and play with you as often as I can and I will take you riding." I looked at Tom, "He can ride, can he not?"

"After a fashion but with you to help him he will get better."

I spent a delightful few hours with Henry. My son took me to show me Henry's pony. The boy could sit on it but he was so young that he could do little more. I was able to give him tips as I walked the pony around the inner ward. I was loving every moment of our time together but, inevitably, the steward found me and I was forced to spend an hour in a chamber reading and signing papers. I knew that I had neglected my duties and while it was not my fault, I would have to try to make up for the time I had lost.

I left after lunch and headed back to Kislingbury to see my daughter and her family. Sir Richard had a fine manor but there was no castle and no guards. It was a fine hall with a moat but that was its only defence. Servants must have seen me coming for I was greeted at the door.

"Congratulations Richard. Thank you for my granddaughter!"

"She is lovely and her big brother adores her. He is very protective of her. We have often spoken of you since you have been away but I confess that he may be shy for he does not know you."

"And that is my fault. I will be grateful if he does not run away screaming!"

In the event, it all went well. Part of that was the fact that my daughter, Eleanor, when she saw me enter, handed the baby to a nurse and rushed, weeping, into my arms, "Father, you are home and you are safe. I have prayed each night for you."

"And I am safe. Your daughter seems to be everyone's favourite but where is my eldest grandson? Where is Master William?"

Shyly he came from behind his mother's chair where he had been hiding. He had retreated there when I had entered. I had seen him but aware of Richard's words I had allowed Eleanor to greet me.

He stood straight and said, "I am William, granddad!"

I bent down and gently picked him up. I did not risk hugging him in case he burst into tears. I smiled, "And have you not grown? You will grow to be a warrior like your father."

His eyes lit up and he threw his arms around my neck. He squeezed so hard that I thought I would choke and yet I would not stop it for I felt a peace inside me I had not felt for a long time. It was the purity of a child's love."

He pulled away and said, "Will you play with me?"

Before I could answer Eleanor said, "Now, Will, your grandfather needs to see Beatrice."

William nodded, "Bea is my sister and I love her." The way he spoke made me think that he had practised for I had seen other children his age and he could speak better than they. I put that down to his mother who was so well-spoken.

Eleanor stood and handed me the baby. She had blond hair but I knew that many babies began with blond hair and then it changed. I was fearful I would crush her and I was glad that I had not donned mail and just wore my houppelande. It was well made and soft. I looked at Beatrice who opened her eyes. They were the bluest eyes I had ever seen. I could not help smiling and when she smiled back, I thought my heart would break. She was so delicate I thought she would break but that smile stole my heart forever. I think it was because I had lost Mary and that I had not said all I should have said to her while she was alive. I would not make the same mistake with my first granddaughter.

I stroked her cheek with my forefinger and she smiled even more and giggled. I spoke quietly for my words were intended just for her, "I am your grandfather, Beatrice, and I will do all in my power to see you grow up safely. Whatever you and your brother need, you shall have and know that I will always be there for you and William as well as your cousin Henry. Now I shall hand you back for I do not wish to push my luck." I handed her to Eleanor who looked fit to burst. "She is beautiful, like her mother." Then I turned to William, "Now then, what shall we play for I have seen that you already have the skills of a scout? Shall we play hide and seek?"

I spent the rest of this short day with my daughter and her family and when I left to ride home, I was reluctant to do so.

The ride back was lonely for it was dusk and it was cold and damp. It was exacerbated by the fact that Will had cried when I had left and that had upset me. He had not wanted me to go and I had not wished to leave. Richard had laughed and told me that he would soon get over it. That was cold comfort to me for I felt I was the cause of the tears.

As the last of the harvest was gathered in and the days grew shorter, colder and wetter, I got into the habit of not having to wear mail and being able to ride alone as I travelled to Northampton and to Flore. I did not always ride alone; sometimes Abelard came with me and sometimes Harry. I managed to see my three grandchildren four or five times a week. Often, I would take a detour to see my daughter and my other grandchildren on the same day that I saw Henry. I could not get enough of them and my days were filled with them. When I was not playing with my three grandchildren, I had to be the Sherriff and any spare time I had was given to my son, Harry, and his new defences. I went to bed each night exhausted but I minded not for this was my work for my family and not my work for the House of Lancaster.

We moved to Northampton for the twelve days of Christmas. I invited all of my family to be there with me for I wanted us to be together. Although it meant leaving Weedon my wife was happy to have her family all around her. This was the first Christmas we had spent together since Mary had been taken from us and she was remembered by us all but not in a maudlin way. We spoke, as we dined or sat before the huge fire in the hall, of what she would have made of the three grandchildren who would have been her niece and nephews and it was as though she had not died but was in another room. I can explain it no better than that. There were no tears but there were fond smiles of remembrance for a girl who would have grown into a wonderful woman, mother and wife.

When we all left after the twelve days of Christmas to return to our own manors, I felt sad that we could not all continue to live in the one huge castle but as my wife pointed out on the way home, it was the King's castle and could be taken from us at a whim. Weedon was our home and my wife decided, as we neared it, to begin improvements and make it big enough for our expanding family. It was the final act in healing after Mary's death for the project gave her purpose and she bustled about as she had in the days before Mary had died.

Once the days began to lengthen, I took it upon myself to help Harry find a squire. Old Sir Geoffrey Fitzwaller lived at Althorp. His son and daughter in law had both died. His son had fallen at Shrewsbury and his wife died, it was said, of a broken heart at his loss. Old Geoffrey was not a well man but he did his best to look after his grandson, Edward. Edward was eleven years old and a charming boy. I visited the old man regularly for I had known his son and I had seen him fall defending the King's standard. One day the old man beckoned me to his side, "William, I am dying. The doctors try to hide it but a man knows when his body is failing. I am prepared to meet my maker and be reunited with my family but I have a grandson who needs care."

"And I will have him as my ward, my lord."

He shook his head, "No, for I would have him become a knight and to do that he needs to be a squire. Your son, Sir Henry, needs a squire. This way you could watch over him and he could fulfil my dream."

"But does he want this, Sir Geoffrey?"

"He does but you should ask him and if he says nay then he shall be your ward. I leave him my estate and money in any case."

The old man was right and Edward was delighted to be given the chance to become a knight as his father had been. When Sir Geoffrey died, at the end of February, we closed up the house and I took him to Flore. One life had ended but another had begun. Such was our world. Harry took to the boy immediately and I saw, once more, the fingers of fate pointing and directing whence we should go.

I knew that my time at Weedon was coming to a close for Prince Henry would be keen to get back to Wales and end the rebellion. I knew this from the letters he sent to me. They were brief, almost terse, but that was Prince Henry's way and I liked it. There were no flowery phrases nor lengthy salutations. He came to the point quickly. From his missives, I learned that most of the French had left Wales in November. That was dictated by the climate and the country; their horses needed vast amounts of fodder and there was little to be had in west Wales. His father's condition had worsened and he rarely left Windsor. That was confirmed by news from travellers on the road and the gossip in Northampton market. I also learned, from the market, that there was much disquiet in the land about the arbitrary execution of the Archbishop of York. It fuelled the ill-feeling in the north and I knew that the rebellion there was not over.

A week after Sir Geoffrey had died, we also had an unexpected visitor. It was Sir Ralph, my former squire. He brought a gift of two horses and news that he had married. His bride was the niece of Sir Ralph Neville, Anne Willoughby. His joy in the marriage was obvious and his visit meant we all decamped to Northampton for Thomas and Harry were great friends with Sir Ralph. In a quiet reflective moment, Sir Ralph warned me about the danger in the north. "The King should know that the Lord of the Northern Marches, Sir Ralph Neville, has an almost impossible task, Sir William. The King confiscated the Percy land. There are many people who are still loyal to the Percy family and do not like the fact that King Henry has brought the rule of England to Northumberland. North of the Tyne is now a dangerous land and the Sherriff of Newcastle barely controls the land around his walls. The land controlled by the Earl of Westmoreland, close to Middleham and Richmond is loyal but York is filled with malcontents who are drawn to the city like flies to a dunghill. The Earl has strengthened Raby Castle and his castle at Sherriff Hutton is as strong as Windsor. Loyal folk will have a refuge but if the rebellion comes it is hard to see how we could stem the tide for the Scots would support a rebellion. They resent the fact that the heir to their crown is in England as a prisoner."

I knew from Prince Henry's letters that King Henry had rewarded Sir Thomas Rokeby who had been with us in Wales with the title of High Sheriff of Northumberland. He still lived by the Tees but he was another ally and I told Sir Ralph of him. "He is a good man and although young, he is loyal to the King."

"That may be, my lord, but his lands are far from Northumberland. It is said that Lord Bardolf's family, who have lands in Nottinghamshire and Leicestershire are also unhappy that Lord Bardolf is forced to live in exile in Scotland. When I came south, I heard disturbing news in the inns. Rebellion is being spoken there and the ordinary folk say that the King's ailment is a punishment from God for his execution of Archbishop Scrope."

I shook my head, "Superstition, for the King was ill before the Archbishop died. It is like this belief that King Richard still lives!"

"That is as may be, lord, but it is what they believe and no amount of rhetoric from a Sherriff will change that!"

When Ralph returned north, laden with gifts for his mother and new bride I wrote to Prince Henry to inform him of the new threat from the north. That his father did not act immediately could have had dramatic ramifications on the north but that threat was seen the lesser of the two. Wales was still the priority.

As I rode back to Weedon with Harry and my family I discussed with him the problems we faced. "The north is one thing but if Nottinghamshire and Leicestershire rise in rebellion then we are threatened here in Northamptonshire. My castle is the only one which could withstand an enemy. I will have to ride to Nottingham and speak with the High Sherriff there."

"But are they not changed each year, sometimes sooner?"

"Aye, and that makes it even more urgent that I travel there for the new Sherriff may either have no idea of the threat or he may be part of it."

"Then I shall come with you." His voice was firm and this was no longer my young squire and son. This was a lord in his own right who would not let me go into danger.

"Aye. That might be for the best and it would give your new squire the chance to learn more about becoming a knight."

I took a healthy escort for the relatively short ride north to Nottingham Castle. I discovered that the new Sherriff was a man called Sir Nicholas Montgomery. I knew little of him and that, in itself, was a worry. I knew all the knights who were loyal to the King for I had fought alongside them at Shrewsbury. I did not know Sir Nicholas Montgomery and that would influence my judgement when we met.

This was Edward's first excursion as a squire. He was able to ride but he had no idea of the other tasks which would be required of him as a squire. Abelard rode with him and coached him on the sixty-odd miles north. As Sherriff of Northampton, we were accorded hospitality on the way north but we only made one stop. Nottingham Castle was imposing and the bustling town was slightly larger than Northampton. In the time of King John, it had been the centre of that King's power but things had changed since and King Henry, as King Richard before him, had made their home closer to London; the north was abandoned. I wondered at the wisdom of that. My banner was well known as was my association with King Henry and we were treated civilly when we arrived.

I noticed his captain of the guard at the gate. I did not recognise him but I recognised the type. He had been one of those who had served in the Free Companies; he had been, like me, a mercenary. There were few left in France and Spain now and those who had survived came back to continue to ply their trade. This one had the tanned face of one who had served abroad and the white scar which ran down his face showed that he had fought hard. I might have spoken to him and asked whom he had served had not the look he gave me shown such derision. He had recognised me and, for some reason, had cause to either hate or, at the very least, dislike me. Perhaps I had fought against him while serving under King Richard or King Henry. I knew not and I dismissed him from my mind.

A steward whisked us through the inner bailey to the Great Hall where Sir Nicholas Montgomery awaited us. I did not recognise him nor his livery and that told me that he had not been at Shrewsbury and that made me suspicious of him. He was not young but neither was he ancient as I might appear to be. I took him to be in his thirties. He had a well-made houppelande trimmed with Leicester lace. He was a rich lord who could afford such things. Unlike me who just wore a single ring with my seal upon it, the High Sherriff had fingers adorned with rings. I did not like that for it made me suspicious of someone who had to show his wealth and power on his hands!

"My lord," he bowed, "this is an unexpected honour. What brings you to my humble castle?"

I had to play a part until I got to know the man and that meant I had to dissemble. "We are both Sherriff and I thought just to pay a visit. As you know, Northampton is a royal castle and I am the guardian of the King. I protect his road south."

His eyes narrowed and then he smiled. He gestured for us to go to the table close to the fire. It was a chilly day, "Come, we shall have some honeyed, mulled ale to take away the cold and we can speak." He glanced at Harry, "And who is this young knight with you, Baron?"

"Sir Henry of Flore, my son!"

"Ah, the hero who captured the son of the Welsh rebel. It is an honour to meet such a warrior."

We sat and servants brought us ale. The Trent's waters made for fine ale and the beer was good. I smiled at the Sherriff and said, "So, Sir Nicholas, where are your lands?"

"My lands?" I saw a little fear in his eyes and yet my question was harmless and I had only meant it to fill the silence before I questioned him about the state of his county.

"This office is temporary; where is your manor?"

He waved a vague hand, "North of here, my lord and how is the King? We have heard rumours of dire ailments." He smiled, "The common folk ascribe superstitious causes but you will know the truth being such a confidante." The fact that he changed the subject so quickly also made me suspicious.

I began to get the measure of this man, "He is a little unwell but we are lucky that his son, Prince Henry, the hero of Shrewsbury, is close at hand." He nodded and his eyes were hooded so that I could not read them. "Tell me, Sir Nicholas, were you at Shrewsbury?"

This time my sudden question had taken him by surprise and he almost started, "I am sorry that I was not. I had business in France else I would have fought."

I wondered on which side. "Tell me Sir Nicholas, does this land and the lands north of it stand for the King or the northern rebels, the Percy and Bardolf family?"

He said, too quickly, "Why they are solidly behind the King, of course. What makes you ask?"

"We have heard rumours of discontent and conspiracies of those who would use the Welsh war to further their own ends. The King and his son are aware of factions in the land who would oust him and yet do not have the courage to face him in open battle. I, for one, admired Hotspur, for he showed his colours and fought for them."

Sir Nicholas let his guard slip as he said, somewhat bitterly, "And yet you slew him."

"Aye, warrior to warrior. God gave me the strength and I had the right."

"And we thank God for that for you have given us a safe land and the people here are hardworking and are more than happy to heed my commands. This is a peaceful and loyal city. Will you dine with us or will you return south directly?"

It was as clear a message as I could have been given. He wanted me gone and I had been right to come here. He was not an open rebel, yet, but in his year in office, he would do all that he could to undermine the King. A Sherriff had the power to do so. Taxes could be misplaced, supporters of the rebels given non-existent sentences, lands given to the enemies of the King. I would have to tell Prince Henry and his father all that I had discovered.

"We will stay and return in the morning if there are rooms for us."

"Of course. My steward will take you and your son to your room."

Once in our room, I spoke quietly to the three of them. "Abelard and Edward, tonight you will serve at table. Play the innocent; say little and hear all. Feign stupidity if you must but learn all that there is to know about this castle. Sir Henry and I will also listen but I fear that we will learn little."

In the end, we did learn something. We learned that Sir Nicholas was not as popular as he led us to believe. There was a local lord who had been in the castle to ask for help with brigands and bandits. He had come with his wife and his daughter. He had not been accommodated in the castle but I think the Sherriff had to invite him to the feast for Sir Humphrey Calthorpe was related to the Phelip family and they were powerful although the knight came from a lowly manor and had little money.

Sir Humphrey and his wife were seated close to me and his daughter, Elizabeth, was seated next to Harry. It meant I was able to talk to a local landowner and that would give me an insight into the way Sir Nicholas worked. It soon became obvious that he did not think the Sherriff was doing a good job. He spoke quietly, "Sir Nicholas thinks that because I have little influence at court and my manor is small that I can be ignored. I have written to my father's uncle, Sir William Phelip, but he is busy with affairs of state. I have to hire men to guard my lands against those who would hunt my deer and steal my animals. The High Sherriff is supposed to protect landowners but all that he does is look after those of his own family as well as the incomers who have been given lands under dubious circumstances."

"I can have a word with him if you wish. I have no actual authority here but I am still the King's champion and that must count for something."

His eyes lit up, "If you would, then I should be grateful."

"I do not promise but know that I am a friend and my manor is just a two-day ride down the Great North Road."

I was the senior noble at the feast and it was incumbent upon me to be the first to leave. I stood and said, "Thank you, Sir Nicholas, for a fine feast. I will leave early but I would have a conference with you before I go."

"Then I shall make myself available, Sir William."

Once in the room, we pooled our information. Abelard and Edward had garnered the jewel. Sir Nicholas was related to the Bardolf family and his journey to France had been on the rebel's behalf. That alone might be enough to arrest Sir Nicholas. Harry's news was less political and more personal. It seemed that he was smitten with the young Lady Elizabeth. I smiled for this was truly mysterious. He had shown no interest in any of the young ladies his mother and his elder brother had introduced to him at Weedon and Northampton and had I not come north then he would never have met Lady Elizabeth. I did not think, for one moment, that this would lead anywhere but at least he had shown enthusiasm for something that was not to do with his manor.

The next morning Sir Nicholas was waiting for me with the four knights who had been closeted with him the night before. "Sir Nicholas, I spoke last night with Sir Humphrey of Stanton and he complained of bandits."

The High Sherriff frowned, "He is a trouble maker and uses his relatives in Suffolk to threaten me, however, I will send my men to scour the forests again. They have done so before and found no trace of the animals he alleged were stolen!"

"I thank you."

"And will you speak with the King soon?"

I shrugged, "There is little that I have heard to confirm the rumours. I will speak with him but not yet. I have more places to visit. I bid you farewell."

We left for home and I had much to think on. I decided that I would ride to Windsor and speak with the Prince. I was disturbed and worried that a delay might help the enemies of the King and his son. I would also discover when we were to return to Wales.

Chapter 9

The King was abed when I reached Windsor. He had had some sort of fit and his face had worsened so much that he was heavily bandaged. It was the Prince who heard my words. Like me, he was concerned. "I know not this Sir Nicholas but Lord Bardolf is a proven traitor. I will speak with my father when he is a little better."

I could speak openly with the Prince, "You know the people think this illness is a sign from God?"

"I do and we both know that this is nonsense but nothing we say will change their minds. I must take the place of my father as the figurehead."

"And when do we return to Wales?"

"My gunners are hired and they are making the weapons. It may not be this season that we retake Harlech for I would rather wait and ensure success than rush and fail. I have instructed Sir Thomas Fitzalan to harry and harass the Welsh along the border while we prepare an army. Now that Sir Richard and Sir John are there, I feel happier but your news about Nottingham makes me worry that there may be other areas of disloyalty. Perhaps I should go to Nottingham and confront Sir Nicholas."

"I am not certain that is a good idea with your father ill, Prince Henry. Leave it for a month or so and I will try to visit other lords along the road to the north. Lincoln seems to me to be somewhere that the rebels might target. I will need to have some time at home first but I promise that I will visit Lincoln and assess the threat."

"Do not tarry too long for we must deal with these potential rebels harshly! The King has been too lenient."

I knew what he meant. The Earl of Northumberland had rebelled twice already. Had he been punished by death then it would have only been one rebellion and the north would be much safer. That there were spies in Windsor should have come as no surprise to us but the Prince and I had spoken in private and yet I received news, five days after I reached my home, that one of the King's household had vanished and stolen a horse. The Prince of Wales suspected he was a rebel spy and that he feared we were getting too close to them. I knew that I had to leave for the north sooner rather than later.

Despite the need for urgency I was not going to let slip my visits to my son and my daughter for I had grown accustomed to the pleasure of my grandchildren. When I arrived in their respective homes, they swamped me with demands to play with them and I loved it. I did not care that I often looked foolish, cavorting around on all fours with either William or Henry on my back. Their giggles and laughter made up for any embarrassment I might have felt. Harry had persuaded me to ride with Abelard to accompany me and I had agreed although I felt that he had little to enjoy for I was silent both going and returning and when I was in my children's homes I was preoccupied. Abelard had grown and changed especially since we had taken on Edward for my son. He could do for Edward what Harry had done for him and my silence on the road back from my daughter's home did not upset him.

It was that silence, as we rode home on an evening when darkness had fallen earlier, thanks to heavy rain clouds, which gave us warning of the danger ahead. Wrapped in my cloak I was riding Hart and anticipating, with more than a little dread, my impending trip to Lincoln. We were warned, thankfully, by my clever horse who alerted us to the threat. We had left Kislingbury and headed down the tiny lane which wound between high hedgerows when her ears pricked and she snorted; a sure sign that there was trouble ahead. I was silent but I was not distracted. I knew danger was close. I hissed, "Danger!" and drew my sword. I had a sheepskin-lined scabbard and the sword slid out silently. Abelard had come on well of late and he also drew his sword. I knew I had my dagger in my left buskin and another in my belt but I knew not what the danger was. Neither of us wore mail. The silence helped for I could hear movement ahead. It had been years since I had been the young scout searching for food for the company but some habits are so ingrained that you do not even know that you are using those skills. There were men ahead and to the right. That, alone showed that they were not the best for if they were then no matter how good I was I would not have known where they were. A good assassin would come from our left where it was hard to protect ourselves.

I edged Hart so that I gave some protection to Abelard and I whispered, "There are men to the right. I will speak nonsense but when I shout *'now'* then ride like the devil for home. We have just two miles to go and we have good horses. It is dark and you can swash with your sword."

"Aye, lord." His answer was equally quiet.

I raised my voice and made it sound casual, "Well, Abelard, soon we shall be at home and I hope that cook has made her meat pie. I am in the mood for a pie and a... *Now*!" I spurred Hart who leapt forward as though she had been stung by a wasp. I had my sword behind me ready to sweep at any enemy who came close.

The men waiting for us had been taken by surprise. They had been listening to our voices as we approached and gauging the moment when they would attack. They might have had weapons drawn but their horses were not ready to attack. The result was that I saw the first warrior as his horse lumbered reluctantly from between the hawthorn trees. The trees were not the best place to hide for they tore at the rider and horse as he emerged. He was a large man and wore mail but he only wore a coif. I swung at his head and my sword hacked through the coif and into his skull; it was a mortal blow and he tumbled from his horse. I heard shouts and, as the accents were northern, I guessed they were from Nottingham as I heard certain inflexions I had heard when visiting the Sherriff. Even as I fended off a hurriedly struck blow from the dark and our swords rang together, I was deducing who had sent these men to ambush me.

"Abelard, ride to my shield side!"

My squire's horse was young and lively and he quickly placed her next to me. It meant we almost filled the narrow lane and he would be protected by my bulk. They would have to get through me to get to him. I heard horses behind me but I had no idea of numbers. They had done as I would have done and ahead, in the almost jet-black dark, their last sentinel burst from the hedges and rode towards me. All that I saw was a dark shape on a horse. We were to all intents and purposes trapped. The last sentinel would block us and the others catch us and butcher us.

We had ridden this path so often that I knew it intimately and even in the dark was aware of what lay ahead. There was a field ahead belonging to Old Oswald of Fenton. It was an isolated piece of land for the rest of the land he farmed lay to the east of us but there was a gap in the hedge to allow him access and it was coming up soon.

"Abelard, take Oswald's field!"

Abelard had grown up in this land and he had hunted with his father, Alan of the Woods. He did not reply but steered his horse towards the gap. Hart followed. It was a race between us and the last sentinel who hurried down the lane towards us. He could see the gap in the hedge and his voice shouted a warning to those behind, "They leave the road! They leave the road!"

It was one thing to know what we were doing and quite another to be able to stop it happening. It did little to aid those following for they did not know which side we would be leaving the lane. I saw the shadow ahead rise up and knew that the last sentinel had his sword ready to swipe at Abelard. My squire had improved since the time he had watched and followed Harry. He lay flat along his horse's head. A blow struck in the dark at a shadow was hard to aim at the best of times but when you are galloping then it is almost impossible. The sword missed and his horse, still racing down the lane, loomed up before me. I swung my sword as I jerked Hart to the left and my sword struck mail. I heard a grunt which told me that I had hurt him and spurred my horse through the gap.

"Abelard, ride for home. I will follow!" The field was open and we would soon be close to my manor.

"Are you sure, lord?"

"Certain! Be not silent as you ride and alert the manor." I sheathed my sword and spoke to Hart, "Ride hard, my sweet. This is our land and we can outrun them!"

This was ridge and furrow land. Old Oswald had recently ploughed it and it was not a smooth surface. Worse, for those following who were mailed, it had recently rained and the ground sucked at Hart's hooves making her slip and slide a little. That was all part of my plan to escape. The men behind were mailed, with helmets, coifs and hauberks. I wore a houppelande and cloak and without armour so that I was at their mercy if they caught me but they had to catch me first and I had the advantage that I knew the ground over which we rode. Abelard was already heading towards the gap in the hedge which led to the open grazing closer to Weedon. Risking a glance behind I saw that they had spread into a line and I counted seven shadows. They were playing ducks and drakes and trying to cut off any escape I might make. Instead of following Abelard I jerked Hart to the left to ride towards the corner of the field. I was the one they wished to kill and not my squire. After two strides I looked back and saw that they had taken the bait. Five strides later I turned to head back towards the gap Abelard had taken. Four of those following would have to ride the wettest part of Oswald's land. There was a patch of clay in that part of the field where the water never truly drained away. Although I had turned before it, at least three of the men following would have to struggle through the cloying clay which Oswald cursed each time he ploughed.

The gap was ahead of me and, again, I knew it would aid me. I could gallop straight through but they would have to take it one at a time and they would be strung out again. Once on the open grazing of Weedon's pastures then they would have a better chance of catching me. In the dark, ahead, I heard Abelard as he shouted for help. We were within a mile of Weedon and although we kept no sentries my men at arms and archers would hear Abelard. His father's smallholding lay just a mile to the west of us and my manor was even closer. I reined in a little to conserve Hart in case I needed to push her later in the chase. That my pursuers were close became obvious when I heard a Nottinghamshire voice shout, "He is tiring! Quickly, on him!"

They might have been scouting me for some days to see if there was a pattern to my movements but they had not explored the land. The road we had been taking looped around the fields and we were closer to the manor than they thought. I saw shadows ahead and knew, instinctively, that it was my men. For it to be enemies would have meant that my manor had fallen! I slowed even more for I knew that there was a small beck ahead. Hart could jump it but with my men approaching I did not want to jump and risk her hitting one of them. I saw four of the shadows ahead stop and I knew that they were archers. That meant I could clear the water safely and I jumped the beck, slowing to a stop. I saw Uriah Longface and Stephen of Morpeth as they raced towards me and each held a poleaxe in their hands. Neither wore mail and I could not let them face the chasing horsemen alone. I heard the whoosh of my archer's arrows as they loosed at the shadows racing across the field. Whirling Hart around I saw that there were now just six horsemen and a horse wandered away from my waiting men. The first arrows had yielded a result.

Their leader realised, as another four arrows descended and my two men at arms flanked me, that they could not complete their task. I drew my sword as he shouted, "Back! We have failed." Even as he turned an arrow smacked into his back. He kept his saddle. When eight arrows descended then I knew that more archers had come to our aid. This time three men fell from their horses and then the rest disappeared into the darkness.

Abelard rode up, "Are you hurt, lord?"

I shook my head and sheathed my sword, "Thanks to the alarm you shouted, no." I dismounted and handed Hart's reins to Abelard. "Put our horses in the stables." I cupped my hands and shouted, "Form a line of beaters. Let us find their corpses!" I led Stephen and Uriah, along with my archers and the other men at arms who had hurried from my manor, across the field. We found the three who had fallen from their horses quickly. They were all dead. One had been killed by an arrow which had torn into his neck while the other two had been struck by arrows but had their necks broken by their fall.

"Oliver, have some men take these bodies to the manor where we may examine them."

We found the leader by the gap in the hedge. He had been dragged by his horse but he was dead. I took the foot from the stirrup and turned him over. It was the final proof I needed of the involvement of Sir Nicholas. It was the captain of his guard and I recognised the long scar down his face.

"Take this one and his horse back to the hall. I need this head! Have it placed in a barrel of vinegar! Let us see the Sherriff squirm his way out of this."

We walked back to the lane to make certain that all had been accounted for and then returned to my hall where an anxious

Eleanor awaited me. "You could have been killed! You should take an escort when you ride abroad!"

I laughed and kissed her head, "The day the Sherriff of Northampton cannot ride five miles from his home without an escort will be a sad day."

My two captains had joined us and Edgar said, "Her ladyship is right, my lord, and we have been remiss. We sit and practise here when we should be riding your roads to look for strangers. I will implement the change forthwith."

"A little like closing the stable door after the horse has fled but it can do no harm however, you need to put this off until after we have returned to Nottingham. Send to Sir Henry for I need him, his squire and his men. I need quill and ink for I must write a message to the Prince."

My wife shook her head, "You have almost touched the River Styx and yet you would still put your life in danger."

"That is my lot in life. This is the man you married; would you change him?"

She shook her head, "I just hoped that becoming older would slow him down a little." She turned to head into the kitchen, "Food will be ready shortly. You had best wash up."

I turned to Oliver the Bastard. "What did you discover from the bodies of the three slain men?"

"That they all wore mail and were sergeants at arms. They had rid themselves of their surcoats but one had a dagger with the mark of Nottingham about it."

"Then bring that with us. We ride at dawn. I will need a messenger to ride, at first light, to Windsor. The Prince needs to be informed of this treachery."

My letter was both blunt and concise. I informed the Prince of the attack and my course of action. My son arrived as I was finishing my food. I told him what had happened and what I intended to do. "I will need you and your men. In a perfect world, I would have the knights of Northampton but I do not want this snake to escape. We ride with the men we have."

"And if he simply bars the gates to Nottingham and denies you entry, what then?"

"Then we have won for that will be proof for all to see that he is guilty." I had thought all of this out as I had eaten.

I led just fifty men north but they were my men and that made them twice as good as any other men in the land. We rode hard, stopping just once to rest. It was as we rested that we discovered that our archers had been more successful than we had thought. A man at arms had died on the way. His body was at the local churchyard awaiting burial. We went to examine it and I recognised him as one of the men who had been at Nottingham Castle for he had been stood next to the Captain of the Guard.

As we approached Nottingham Castle, early the next day, I saw that the gates were wide open and there were no sentries there. I knew, even without asking, that our prey had fled and taken his men with him.

"Secure the gate, Captain Edgar. Captain Alan secure the walls. Put the head we brought on the spike on the city gate. We need it not to prove the Sherriff's disloyalty. Let us use it to show other traitors the folly of treachery."

The steward was at the entrance to the hall, anxiously wringing his hands, "I am sorry Sir William, I knew nothing about this treachery."

My eyes narrowed, "What treachery?"

"Men returned late last night and Sir Nicholas immediately packed his belongings and took his men. When I asked why he struck me but one of the servants overheard the conversation and learned that an attempt had been made on your life."

I had not thought the steward would be involved and his words confirmed it. "And where has he fled?"

"They took the road north."

"And the rest of the country is vast. Be more specific. Where would you think he went?"

"His family have estates in the north, lord, but I know not specifically where they are. He has a manor at Alfreton but I think that is too close for him." He was aware that his words were not telling me what I needed to know and fear was in his voice. "I am trying to help you, lord."

I heard the panic in his voice and knew that I had terrified him and yet I knew not how. I made my voice softer, "Did he just take men?"

"No, Sir William, he emptied the treasury. There were taxes which had been collected but not yet sent to London. They were taken."

"We will await Prince Henry. He will need chambers preparing."

"The future King comes here?" I nodded. "Then I must away."

There were some members of the garrison left in the castle and I discovered that they had been here before Sir Nicholas had come. It became glaringly obvious that Sir Nicholas had secured the appointment to ensure that the next rebellion would succeed.

The Prince arrived late the next day. I had begun to wonder if he would arrive at all. He came with a large number of young knights. I knew most of them for they had been with us in Wales. As soon as he dismounted and before I had time to greet him, he began, "Where is this traitor? I see a head upon the gate is that Sir Nicholas?"

I shook my head, "Sir Nicholas has fled and the head belongs to his Captain of the Guard. He was the one who led the assassins who tried to kill me."

"And for that, I apologise. I should have done as you said and acted quickly." He waved forward a knight I did not recognise. "This is Sir Robert Fraunceys and he will be the Sherriff until I can find another. I trust Sir Robert and we can leave the castle safely in his hands. It is the reason I am late for he has a manor just south of here, close to Newark." He took off his gloves and propelled me towards the Great Hall. "We cannot allow this viper to escape justice. More, I wish to find out the magnitude of the rebellion. Until it is scotched then we put the assault on Wales to one side. We can see who are the Welsh rebels, here all dissemble."

"I believe that Sir Nicholas has a number of manors north of here but if I were to put money on the outcome, I would bet that he will be in the one closest to Northumberland."

The Prince smiled, "And you have worked out which one?"

I nodded. "Through his mother, who was a Hepdon, he has claims to the small manor of Hetton-on-the-Hill. It lies halfway between the Tees and the Tyne and, more importantly, is not part of the Palatinate. I know nothing more about it and would not have known this if the servants had not had such sharp ears. They were happy to tell me of Sir Nicholas' holdings for he did not treat them well."

"Then we ride there tomorrow. It will give me the opportunity to visit York on the way north and to see how the new Archbishop is coping."

I was more confident about the new Archbishop than I had been with Scrope. There had been two attempts by the Pope to have another Archbishop appointed before Henry Bowet, the Bishop of Bath and Wells was appointed. I knew him as Henry for he had been a clerk under King Richard and I had seen him, often, at Eltham Palace. He was loyal and that was all that we could ask.

Sir Robert had enough men to garrison the castle and so the Prince led our column north. We stopped in Lincoln briefly before pushing on to York. I suspect that if the King had arrived his greeting would have been chillier than the one accorded to Prince Henry but he was as popular as his father was unpopular. Crowds cheered us as we rode through the city.

Henry Bowet had just grown older; he had the same smile and manner as he had always had and was in contrast to the political animal that had been Archbishop Scrope. We stayed but one night and learned that most of those associated with the former Archbishop had fled to Scotland with the Earl of Northumberland. He was confident that he was secure in York. It helped that he was a good friend of the Bishop of Durham. Scrope had resented the Palatinate and its loyalty to the crown.

When we left we hurried north, not towards Piercebridge but to Thornaby and the ferry to Stockton. The castle there was in the hands of a loyal knight although he was on a pilgrimage to Rome. His absence partially explained why Sir Nicholas had chosen the manor of Hetton-on-the-Hill to hide.

Lady Isabelle was a gracious hostess and was pleased to be able to accommodate the Prince. Everything about the visit reassured me that the Tees was as loyal as anywhere. You can learn more from speaking with the servants and burghers of a town than you can ever learn from conversations with their lords and the people were behind the King and they confirmed that the lord and the lady of the manor were too. We also picked up useful information. The manor at Hetton had no castle and the fortified house was not particularly strong. Both Prince Henry and I had feared that there was a castle and that a siege would provide a rallying call for other rebels.

We left early for we had just twenty odd miles to travel. There was but one main road in this area and we headed up it. The nearest castle along our route, apart from Durham itself, was Newcastle and that was held by loyal men. The traitor must have had men watching the road for none passed us heading north and yet, as we neared the manor, we could see the signs of a hurried flight. Every door was open and there were just five terrified servants who dropped to their knees when we galloped up to the hall.

The old steward, Jocelyn, pointed north and west, "Sir Nicholas went but an hour since, Your Highness."

There was little point in berating a steward who could have done little about it in any case. I turned to Harry, "Sir Henry, take my archers and find the traitor. Send us word which road he has taken and do not try to take him yourself. We will rest briefly and follow."

He grinned for he now had his chance, "Aye, f... Sir William!"

When he and my men galloped off Prince Henry said, wryly, "That should have been my command!"

"Aye, Prince Henry but in the time it would have taken you to ask my advice and for me to give it then the rebel would have been even further away. My son knows what he is about. We should water our horses and take some food."

"One day I shall make such decisions as quickly as you but, until then, I am content to follow your advice for it is sage."

As I ate, I ran through all that I knew of the land. There was a castle close to the Wear at Lumley. It was in the Palatinate and would hold against Sir Nicholas for Prince Henry had sent riders ahead to warn the Bishop of the Sherriff's flight. Sir Nicholas and his men, we learned he had more than forty, would have to cross the Wear and that meant it would be downstream from Lumley. He would need to keep heading north and west for while he might be able to ford the Wear the Tyne was a different matter and to get to the heartland of Northumberland, he would have to reach the Roman bridges which lay close to the Wall. If he reached the Wall then we had lost him for the borderlands were Percy land.

We set off with the knowledge, gleaned from the frightened steward, that Sir Nicholas had five knights with him and the rest were men at arms. He had no archers. However, it meant that all of his men were armoured and would fight hard. They knew that their fate had been sealed once their attempt at assassination had failed.

Much Longbow met us on the road. "We have not caught up with them, lord, but they forded the river northeast of Lumley. Sir Henry thinks it would be quicker to cross the river at the castle for you could save time and he will continue to trail them."

My archers all had good horses and without the need to carry mailed men could travel faster. This made sense. "My son has come up with a good plan. I advise that we take it."

The Prince nodded, "Take the message back, Much, that we will do as Sir Henry advises!"

When we reached the castle, the Prince asked for some local men to act as guides. The lord of the manor, Sir Hector, was no longer young but he gave us ten men who knew the land. As we headed along the road which led to Ovingham our new guides told us that the river could be forded there.

"Not an easy ford, Your Highness, but from what you told his lordship these are desperate men. If they took the ford over the Wear then we have a chance to catch them." Old Walter looked up at the sky, "But we may not reach them until after dark and to speak truly your horses look all in."

The Prince said, "Ovingham sounds like a risk, Sir William, for Prudhoe Castle lies close by."

"And it will be dusk when they cross. By the time the castle is alerted they may be across but from what Walter said we may catch them before they reach the castle. My horse still has some miles left in him and my squire has Hart. She may not be a warhorse but she is a good one."

"We have cast the die, Sir William, we push on!"

It was getting dark when we passed the hamlet of Tanfield and we had had to leave ten men behind whose horses could go no further but we caught up with my son whose horse also looked exhausted. He pointed triumphantly north and west. "They are less than half a mile ahead. They think they have lost us for they have slowed."

"That may be because they wish to cross the Tyne under cover of darkness. You have done well. You can rest here if you wish. The Prince and I have more than enough men to deal with Sir Nicholas."

"My mount is one of Mistress Mary's best and they are hardy animals. He will finish the task and then he can rest."

The Prince nodded approvingly, "Your son has the same heart as his father. Let us push on. If we start them, like game, and they run then it will alert Prudhoe's garrison."

He was right and we put spurs to our mounts. Although it was poorer light, we could still see them ahead, and they, in turn, could see us. That Sir Nicholas knew the land became obvious when the column suddenly left the road and, riding over open fields of winter barley and oats, headed north.

Old Walter said, "He is heading for Spen Burn, Your Highness. There are trees and trails there. We could lose him and he could escape."

The Prince was angry for he did not want to let this traitor escape. "I will be damned if he will. Sir William, take your men and continue north and west. Then ride north to cut him off. If he rides through the trees then they will slow him down. I will follow the beast!"

It was not the decision I would have made but, at least, he was thinking and reacting quickly. I shouted, "Men of Weedon, follow me!" I knew that my son and his men would join us too. We were splitting our forces and the Prince had the greater number of knights but I had archers. As we rode, I shouted my orders, "When you close with them, Captain Alan, then dismount and hurt them until we can close with them. Then it will be knife work for it will be dark."

Archers were the deadliest of killers. Not only could they use a bow and kill at distance, once they were in a mêlée, they knew the weak points in armour and any knight they found had better surrender or he was a dead man walking. I saw a village ahead and guessed that the beck ran through it. There would be no cover there and we hastened towards it. The night was so close that we could almost touch it but there was still enough light to make out the stream and the thin undergrowth.

I heard Alan shout, "Dismount and string your bows!" We did not slow although I felt Hawk weakening a little.

The first of the men led by Sir Nicholas emerged from the undergrowth and the trees. The beck had been shallow and they had made good time but we had made better. I drew my sword and turned Hawk to cut off Sir Nicholas from his escape through the village. I heard shouts from further down the waterway as Prince Henry and his knights caught up with the slower ones at the rear of the column.

Sir Nicholas was no coward and he roared a challenge as he galloped towards me, "Royalist lickspittle! You will die, old man!"

I had been insulted many times and I ignored it. I had no shield but neither did Sir Nicholas. I know not if he had discarded it as unnecessary weight or forgotten to bring it but it meant that we were evenly matched. Except that we were not for I had forgotten more about fighting than the traitor would ever know. He made his first mistake when he came to me rather than waiting for me to descend into the water. It meant he was leaning forward and his horse was struggling to climb the slippery, grassy bank. I owed this rebel nothing and I swung my sword at head height as he came towards me. With no shield, he flailed his sword above his head but it merely slowed down my sword which struck his sword and then his helmet. His horse's hooves found purchase on the bank but I saw, even though his face was shadowed, that I had stunned him. His ears would be ringing and he would find it hard to concentrate.

Twirling my sword, I struck a backhand blow at him and this time he managed to block it with his sword but I had the initiative for he was reacting to my strikes. I was in command of the battle. I used Hawk. My horse was tired but he did not need to move. He just had to fight and fight he did. As I jerked his head towards Sir Nicholas' charger, Hawk snapped his teeth and Sir Nicholas' horse pulled away and exposed the knight's side. I lunged with my sword. He wore plate but there was always a gap between the breastplate and backplate and my tip found the mail beneath and slid into a mail ring. He had good mail but my sword was better and it first enlarged and then tore the link before sinking through

126

the gambeson and into flesh. It was not a mortal wound but he was hurt and his scream was almost feral.

He whirled his horse away from my mount and my blade and as he did so I reached down and pulled my dagger from my buskin. He would not run away for he could not do so. My son and my archers lay between him and the Tyne while behind him came Prince Henry and his knights. His only escape was through me. He spurred his horse and launched himself at me. Maybe he thought I was old and my reactions would be slow but I knew how he would strike before he unleashed his sword for he pulled it behind him. He was going to use a long sweep and knock me from my horse. I had my dagger in my hand and, dropping my reins, I blocked his strike and swept my own sword towards his unprotected left side. There was nothing to slow down my blade and it crashed into his plate armour. The knight had good metal and my blade did not penetrate to the mail beneath but it did not need to. I was still a strong man, despite my age, and the blow broke ribs. He was bleeding from one wound and now he had to endure broken ribs. Kicking Hawk in the side made my horse lunge forward and the other horse shied away. Standing in my saddle I brought my sword from on high. His ribs hurt as he pulled back his arm to swing and counter the blow. His parry did not materialise and my sword hit and split his helmet. Even before it began to slice open the coif and tear through the arming cap his skull was fracturing. I saw his eyes begin to roll into his head as he dropped his sword and my blade carried on into his skull and ended his life. He fell from the saddle.

I was dimly aware, as his body slipped into the beck, that no-one else was fighting. Even while I had been fighting, we had won for the others had either been slain or, seeing that they were surrounded had surrendered. All of the knights who followed Sir Nicholas died but his men at arms sought mercy and the Prince granted it. We had ended one threat from rebels but the rebellion still smouldered.

Chapter 10

We learned little from the prisoners because they were not noble-born and had been little more than swords for hire. Prince Henry showed a steelier side to him when he had one summarily executed who would not answer our questions. The others answered but it became clear that they knew nothing. They were sent south to languish in Windsor Castle. They would be an example to other rebels who were not noble-born. We stayed in Newcastle for some months. King Henry was still unwell and so the Prince rode abroad to let all know that it was the King's family who ruled this land. We travelled as far west as Westmoreland and as far north as Berwick. When we headed south, we left a north that was cowed but not yet defeated. It could not be defeated until Henry Percy was dead. So long as he lived then the rebellion was alive and we now knew that we had to defeat the North before we could tackle the Welsh. We could not fight a war on two fronts.

It was a leisurely ride back and the Prince and I discussed our plans for the following year. Prince Henry would ask his father to demand that the Duke of Albany, who ruled Scotland in the absence of the boy King, should hand over Percy. It seemed a good and workable plan but I knew that if the Duke refused then we would have to invade Scotland and we did not have an army which was large enough. We needed for Percy to venture south.

We stayed a day in York and it was there that my son showed that he had grown. The Prince and his knights were talking with the Archbishop and Harry asked, "Father, I know we have a new Sherriff in Nottingham and I doubt not that he will do a good job but I now doubt that Sir Nicholas would have done anything about the bandits who were bothering Sir Humphrey of Stanton."

I confess that I had forgotten about the knight but when I called him to mind then I understood why Harry had remembered them. He had been much taken by the knight's daughter, Elizabeth.

"You may well be right. I will speak with the Sherriff when we reach Nottingham."

Harry shook his head, "At the pace we are going that could take another fortnight! We said we would aid the knight and I do not think we have."

I felt uncomfortable for he was correct. I had abdicated responsibility when I had told the Sherriff of the problem. In the past, I would have acted myself and I would have dealt with the problem. I knew there was more to this than a carping complaint from my son, "What would you do?"

"I would take my men and ride ahead to Stanton. You can speak with the Sherriff but I can show the lord that we keep our word."

"You can manage this yourself?"

"If I cannot deal with brigands and bandits then you should not have had me knighted." It was a blunt statement and showed me that Harry was now a man.

Nodding I said, "I will speak with the Prince and he will, no doubt, sanction it but take Captain Alan and my archers too. The forests there are not suited to men at arms and Alan of the Woods is well named."

I sought out Prince Henry during a lull in the conversation and he was happy to accede to Harry's request, "Although I have no doubt that Sir Robert, the new Sherriff, will exert his authority soon enough!"

"Yes, Prince Henry, but we both know that he must scour Nottingham first of all those who secretly support Sir Nicholas and the rebels. Besides, my son has another reason for this quest. I think he hopes to win the hand of a maid."

The Prince smiled, "And that will please you and Lady Eleanor." He sipped his wine, "This is good, Sir William. Your family is the very antithesis of the Percy family. England needs loyal knights such as you and your sons and they need sons of their own."

"And what of you, Prince Henry? Do not you need a wife to ensure that there will be future kings of your blood? King Richard lost his crown because he had no heirs."

"Ah, Sir William, you forget two things: firstly, the King is still alive. He is ill but alive and secondly, I have brothers. They are being trained for kingship even as we sit here. Besides," he touched his scarred face, "this will not win me a fair princess, will it?"

"Prince Henry, the right woman will look beyond the disfigurement and see the nobility within."

"Sadly, Sir William, unlike you and Harry, I will have little choice in the matter. This will be arranged either by my father or my advisers. King Richard was lucky in that he found the love of his life in Anne of Bohemia. I may not be that lucky."

My son left before us the next day. A royal progress was, perforce, slow as Prince Henry had to meet the leading nobles in each town and castle through which we passed. Riding north we had an excuse to race but now we did not. Prince Henry was consolidating his father's grip on the north however, he was not using the mailed gauntlet but the velvet glove and his engaging wit. Where there were frowns when we arrived, they were replaced by smiles when we left.

When we reached Nottingham, we learned that my son had first spoken to the Sherriff who was happy for the help. As he said to the Prince and I as we dined with him, "Not all of Sir Nicholas' supporters left with him. There are lords of the manor who skulked back to their homes and I am still finding out who is loyal and then there are those who were not noble who fled to the forests. There may be less banditry and brigandage but it still exists and your son, Sir William, will discover that winkling them out will take a long time."

The Prince said, "And you, Sir Robert, will pay Sir Henry and his father for the men he uses." I saw the frown on the Sherriff's face as did the Prince. "Do not worry, Sir Robert. You will not lose out. I intend to confiscate Sir Nicholas' estates. The money he took from Nottingham will be returned and the taxes he stole will be replaced. You will pay them the same rate as though we were at war; 100 marks per month."

The Sherriff nodded, "Aye, lord."

I knew that my son would have done this without payment but it was good that he was being paid for my men deserved reward for their work.

We received good news when we reached London where King Henry waited to greet us. The Welsh had not been able to take any more castles and, indeed, had lost much of the land they had captured in the Welsh Marches. The captives we had taken had hurt them more than we had realised for they were the better of the Welsh leaders. King Henry was delighted with the quashing of a rebellion before it had even begun. Although he had recovered a little, his skin complaint still made him look leprous even though it was not that disease. The King and his son both shared facial disfigurements but for entirely different reasons.

The three of us, the King, the Prince and myself, dined alone on the night before I returned home. "We have still to ensure that we can pay our army, my son. Parliament withholds the funds that you need."

"I have begun to put in place plans which will change that, father. I have confiscated Sir Nicholas' estates and when the Sherriff of Nottingham has completed his scouring of the shire then there will be others. It may not be next year when we retake Harlech but by the time we are ready then I will have men and cannons which will ensure that it falls!"

The King nodded, "And I have sent to my son in Ireland to ask him to attack Anglesey and relieve the siege of Beaumaris."

The Prince turned to me, "Sir William, I know from our journey south that you have connections in the north. Sir Ralph of Middleham Tyas was once your squire and now he is close to the Lord of the Northern Marches?"

"That is true, Prince Henry."

"Then I would have you keep in close contact and give the Lord of the Northern Marches as much aid as you can."

It was interesting that the roles of King and Prince had almost been reversed. Already Prince Henry was giving commands and his father did not gainsay them.

When I returned home, I went, first, to Northampton. I needed to speak with my son Thomas as I was keenly aware that I had kept him safe for the sake of his family but that protection might have to end soon. However, the warning had to wait for I was greeted when I arrived by my son and a pregnant Lady Mary. "You are to have another child! This is great news!"

I kissed Lady Mary who said, "It is just to please you, my lord, for playing with Henry makes you so young that we thought to give you twice the pleasure and extend your life even further."

I grasped my son's arm, "Does your mother know?"

He laughed, "I will beard any knight in the land but I would never dare to keep such news from my mother. She is delighted and her tears ably demonstrated that fact!"

"Then I shall stay the night and return home on the morrow."

He became serious, "With an escort of your men at arms!"

"Of course."

I played with Henry until supper and then, after we had eaten and Lady Mary had retired, I sat with Sir Thomas and told him all that had occurred and my predictions for the future. "The King has charged me with keeping watch on the north. That is not such a hardship as the journey to Middleham is less than the journey to North Wales but I will need knights that I can rely upon. That means I shall need not just Harry, but yourself and Alice's husband, Sir Richard, as well as Sir Wilfred and Sir John."

"And you know that all of us have been itching to follow you! We could have been at your side many times before now."

"Since Shrewsbury, I have not needed you but I know that I shall need you in the battles to come. When the north rebels once more it will be the last throw of the dice for Percy. It will be a fierce battle and they will do all that they can to recover their lost lands and to have vengeance upon the man who slew their son, Hotspur the hope of the North."

"You!" I nodded, "And yet they accept that it was in fair combat."

"I agree but their son, the champion of Northumberland, died and I live. When I am dead, they will be happy. The Prince and the King are even further from the north than are we so that it will be the men of the north who fight the northern rebels. Can you not see the dilemma and the size of the problem? More than half of the north wish King Henry gone. Many believe, erroneously, that King Richard lives. This will not be an easy fight."

He looked me in the eyes, "Do not fear for me, father, I am of your blood and earning my spurs at Shrewsbury tied me irrevocably to Prince Henry and his father." I hid my smile with my hand. It was ever thus. Henry Bolingbroke was not likeable.

He never had been and when men fought it would be for his son and not for the King. Prince Henry was a King in waiting and I wondered just how long he would wait.

I left the next morning and headed for my home. The year had passed quickly and yet I had not been to Wales. From what Prince Henry had said I would not be going any time soon. The Prince had confided in me that he hoped the Welsh would simply tire of the rebellion. Their nobility had been slaughtered and the already poor country was becoming poorer. The peasants could not fight and grow crops. They could not rear animals and families. If the rebellion continued in this fashion then all that would be left was a land filled with carrion and corpses. I think that was the real reason that the Prince had called a halt to his attempt to recover his land. He needed a land which was worth ruling. He wanted to be Prince of a Wales which had prosperous people.

My wife was delighted to see me but I saw the worry on her face when she realised that my archers and Harry were missing. "Fear not, wife, he is scouring a wood in Nottinghamshire of brigands."

She adopted a grimace, "And why does my son have to do that which is the responsibility of the Sherriff of Nottingham?"

I sighed, "There is a fair maiden involved and a promise our son made. All will be well."

"A maiden?" She was mollified immediately. "A lady?"

"Of course, and one with whom our son is taken."

"Then why did you not tell me immediately instead of making me fret and worry?" She kissed my cheek, "And, how are you? I hope you suffered no wounds."

As ever, the family came first and then me. It was ever the way and I did not mind. I knew my place and I was grateful for it.

Our son arrived as the last of the crops were being gathered in. I had not been worried for if anything had happened to him then a rider would have brought us news. He came, first to Weedon and I saw that although some of the men he led had minor wounds there were no empty saddles. After his mother had given him a tearful welcome, she scurried off to get her youngest some food prepared. I sat and spoke with him. His news disturbed me.

"The '*brigands*' father, were hired men paid for by the Sherriff himself. It is why we tarried so long in the north for the problem

133

was more widespread than we thought. The new Sherriff brought men to aid us when I informed him. We managed to capture some and questioned them." He smiled, "My men at arms are quite adept at extracting information. The ones we captured we let go but they are marked by the loss of fingers and a brand on each of their foreheads."

"What was Sir Nicholas' purpose?"

"From what we deduced it was to ferment unrest in the north. Sir Robert learned that Sir Nicholas blamed everything on King Henry. The King's ailment did not help and people believe that the King is the cause of the malaise in the land. We have rid the land of the brigands and bandits but the problem still remains. There is unrest which borders upon rebellion."

This was the worst of worlds and I knew that I would have to write to the Prince to inform him. However, any action would have to wait until Spring and that meant we had a winter to prepare and to await the birth of the next Strongstaff!

As my son quaffed the beaker of wine I said, with a smile playing upon my lips, "And the Lady Elizabeth had nought to do with your tardy return?"

He flushed and then nodded, "I confess, father, that I am smitten and the lady, I think, returns my affection."

"Then do something about it. Life is too fleeting and we both know knights, like Sir Roger, who died before they had either wife or children."

"But will her father accept me? He has connections to the Earl of Suffolk."

"And you are the son of King Henry's champion and you are the friend of the next King of England. Besides, until you ask, you will never know!" He nodded, "However, first, speak to your mother. She feels that she is not part of your world and she still pines for Mary."

"I know and I will but I find it hard, sometimes, to speak to her."

"And that is my fault for I took you to war when you would have been close to her. Make the effort, my son, and try."

"I will!"

His words were well chosen and his mother was delighted. She even offered advice on what to say to Lady Elizabeth's parents.

He left for Stanton a short while later. My wife sent gifts for her parents and she made certain that he was dressed as a young noble should be. Our poor mason also discovered that all the work he had done was to be restarted for my wife wanted even more rooms now. She wished all of the family to be accommodated in what had once been a humble hall. I smiled and was grateful that I could get on with the work of Sherriff of Northampton, a task I had neglected for some time.

When he returned it was with the news that Sir Humphrey had accepted my son's proposal of marriage but they felt that she was still too young to be wed and the date which had been set was September. My wife and son would have to wait a winter, spring and summer before there would be a wedding. I needed that time for I could not afford to relax my vigilance.

One advantage of being Sherriff was that I could employ more men at arms than I could as Baron Strongstaff and I began to hire more men in Northampton. My son had lived there long enough to be able to weed out those who would not stand in a shield wall and he and I selected the men we would leave to garrison both Weedon and Northampton when we were called to the north. I also wrote a long letter to Sir Ralph Neville to explain what I had planned and I sent it with four of my men who would also buy four more horses from Mistress Mary. Her manor at Middleham Tyas was key to my plans. I also wrote one to the Bishop of Durham. His support was vital if we were to hang on to the north.

I had realised the dangers of riding alone in a land still riven with conflict and assassins. The Welsh and the Percy family would both like me dead for I was linked not only to their defeats but also to King Henry and his son. When I travelled from Weedon to Northampton I did so with eight men and Abelard. I also took to spending longer at Northampton so that, as the short days of winter arrived, I was not travelling in the dark. I was not afraid of my enemies but it was a foolish man who gave them an advantage.

My men and the reply from the Lord of the Northern Marches had arrived by Christmas so that I was able to enjoy the celebrations with my family. My second granddaughter, Margaret, was born on Christmas Eve. It seemed appropriate somehow and Mary and Margaret were both healthy. It made that

Christmas, quite possibly, the best we had ever enjoyed. I had bought some barrels of wine from Bordeaux and I had some special ale brewed for the garrison and my men. In celebration of the birth of my granddaughter, I gave each of my men at arms and archers five pounds. I still remembered how such acts endeared men to their lord from my time in the Blue Company. Captain Tom had always been generous when he could. I was more than generous because I knew just how good were the men I led.

When, after Christmas, we were back in Weedon I spoke at length to Eleanor about my plans. I think she now understood them and was able to listen without becoming upset. "I may be away for most of the summer; it may not be this year when the north rebels again but I think it is likely. It means that I may not be present at the wedding. If events conspire then Thomas and Richard will also be with me on the campaign. Harry will understand."

She put her hand over my mouth, "And I understand. You pay the price for the life we lead and I think I see that now. There are too many men who put themselves before the country and I thank God that you are not one of them. The King and his illness put the country in danger." She made the sign of the cross when she mentioned the illness for my wife also believed, I am sure, that it was a curse from God. "You and Prince Henry will have to keep the land safe but I would you were at my side in the church at Stanton."

"And if God is willing then I shall be."

Prince Henry visited with me at the end of January and he brought news which both encouraged and disturbed me in equal measure. His father's condition had worsened and Prince Henry feared that he might never be able to appear in public again. "It is not leprosy; the doctors have told me that but it looks as though it is and people are afeared when they see him. In addition, he now endures fits and we cannot allow him to be in public when such a fit occurs."

"You will take the crown?" I could be blunt with the Prince for he knew my motives were not tainted by personal greed.

"No, for that is not my way. At least not yet. The doctors are trying some new remedies and so we will see if they work. All of this means that I will need to stay close to London and my father for I will have to work with the King's Council and Parliament. I intend to make the Council more supportive. I will not be able to help you and I wanted to tell you that to your face."

"I had not planned on involving you unless I had to."

I told him my plans and he beamed, "Your mind is ever working. I like the plan and I also bring good news. Anglesey has been taken by knights from Ireland. Beaumaris is relieved and there are just the castles of Harlech and Aberystwyth which are thorns in our side. My gunners have the cannons made and when the north is secure then we can take Wales but it may not be this year for that will depend upon the northern rebellion. This year we protect what we have and it will be next year that we retake that which is ours." He smiled at me, "And I shall not be alone. My brothers, John and Humphrey are preparing to bring men to aid us when we fight Wales. They will do so at their own expense."

"And your Uncle, the Duke of York?"

He frowned for Edward, Duke of York, had been a supporter to King Richard and was now held as a prisoner in Pevensey. The news had rocked the court for it was thought that the Duke was loyal to the King but there were now doubts. "I do not believe he is treacherous. His younger brother, Richard, is a different matter but my uncle is safe in the castle at Pevensey and that safety works both ways for I fear there are those who would use him to their own ends. If you can manage the north, along with Sir Ralph Neville then I believe there will be hope for us!" He lowered his voice, "The Bishop of Norwich is a clever cleric and he has a network of spies in France. My father asked him to begin to gather intelligence once the French invaded Wales. He has learned of their civil war and he is preparing information which will be advantageous to us when we decide to reclaim our birthright. He has heard a rumour that the Earl of Northumberland is gathering an army. I cannot believe that he would attack in winter but spring is a different matter. It might be prudent to leave for the north earlier rather than later."

"Aye, Prince Henry, you may be right."

Before he left, he gave me a chest of gold to help to pay for the army in the north. I would not need it for my men but I knew that the Lord of the Northern Marches was not as rich as the lords further south.

I took my sons and son in law with me. There were more than enough men left to guard their homes and the north was not Wales. It was closer and they could, if the northerners did not rebel, be back home within seven nights.

Chapter 11

It was a hurried goodbye but that was no bad thing for I needed no tears before I left my home. Sir Wilfred and Sir John had both arrived promptly and with Sir Richard and my sons living so close we were able to leave as soon as we were mustered. We were able to allow Harry to visit with his bride to be on our way north. As we rode the rumours of a northern rising were told to us in both Nottingham and, more alarmingly, in York. I spoke with the new Sherriff of York, Sir Thomas Rokeby.

"My Lord Sherriff, I think we should prepare to call out the levy for these rumours grow stronger the further north we come."

"I too have heard the rumours but I find it hard to give them credit. The ground is still frozen and winter is still upon us."

"Aye, and that alone makes me think it might be true. Percy is a northerner and he knows his people cannot till fields yet. Further south men are finding the land warm enough to plough but, in the north, it is still winter. This strikes me as the perfect time to strike. I will be at Middleham Tyas with my men. If you hear any news, either good or ill, then send for me and I will serve under you. I will have riders ready to summon Sir Ralph Neville and the men of Westmoreland."

Even as we left the city the summons was being sent out for the loyal knights and men of Yorkshire to gather. It was a gamble for they only owed the Sherriff forty days service and if the Percys did not arrive in that time then they would be disbanded. When we reached Middleham Tyas I was disturbed to see that the lord of the Northern Marches was not at home. After settling our men into the farmhouse, I went with Sir Ralph and my sons to Middleham castle. There were just ten knights in residence and they had with them just one hundred and forty men at arms and archers. Sir James, who commanded the castle in the absence of the earl, told me that the Earl was still in Westmoreland, at

Carlisle, for he did not think that the Northumbrians would move until Spring. It was disappointing for he must have heard the same rumours that we did. Why had he not reacted?

I demanded that Sir James send a message to him informing him of the urgency and necessity of his return. I then sent Harry and four men to Durham. I needed the eyes of the Palatinate to watch for the rebels in the north. I was now even more convinced that they would choose this cold and miserable time to head south. Henry Percy, with his last throw of the dice, hoped to catch us napping!

Harry was the reason that we had prior warning of the rebel army which had crossed the Tyne and was now heading across the Tees. The Bishop of Durham had received word of an army moving south and even as he was confirming it my son arrived at Durham. Harry was quick thinking and he headed back south to tell us. He encountered them south of Yarum and he managed to avoid the Northumbrian army which was augmented by Scottish raiders and, as such, busy ransacking churches and stealing cattle. Sending one of his men to York he hurried to Middleham Tyas. When he gave us the size of the army he had seen I knew that we would struggle to hold them without the aid of the men of Westmoreland. That we were unprepared was an understatement. With a handful of knights and barely two hundred and fifty men we could not stop a Northumbrian army. I raised the local levy and that brought us another one hundred men. We headed east for the enemy would be making for York. York had always been the capital of the north and if Percy held that city then he could hold Yorkshire to ransom and use it as a new power base. I had too few men to send out large numbers of scouts and we headed towards the Great North Road like a man walking along a cliff in a fog. I did send two of Sir Ralph's men to make contact with Sir Thomas Rokeby. The Sherriff had a sizeable force and they were my hope.

It was coming on to dark when we reached Knaresborough and there we had word of the rebels. Their army had been spotted by Sir Thomas Rokeby and his men. The rebels now knew they could not take York by surprise as the levy had been mustered. Sir Thomas had sent men to order all the towns and villages to bar their gates to the rebel army which was marching south. It was time for me to make quick decisions and so I changed my horse and rode one brought by Sir Ralph. Leaving Sir James in command of the army and with orders to rest for at least five hours, I rode with Captain Alan and my archers through a darkening evening towards Wetherby. I had to find the rebels. Sir Thomas would be doing the same but he was highly visible for he had a large army. My men and I were so small that we were invisible and Henry Percy and Lord Bardolf did not know that we were close.

The rebels had already passed through Wetherby when in the dark of night, we passed through. People were just returning to their homes having been attacked when Percy and his marauders passed through. The town had been pillaged and ransacked. Food and animals had been taken and I wondered why they had not stayed in the town and then, as we headed towards Bramham, where the survivors said that the rebels had gone, I realised why. They had destroyed too much of the town. They needed somewhere that they could defend and we found that place. Bramham Moor was a tiny hamlet but it lay on top of a rounded moor. Their campfires alerted us to their presence and we dismounted to walk through the dark to their camp. They had chosen a piece of high ground close to the small settlement of Bramham. This time they had not reduced the hamlet and that explained its choice. Percy would sleep with a roof over his head while he waited for the men of Yorkshire.

We made our way back to our horses and I sent two archers to ride around the army with orders to fetch Sir Thomas Rokeby. We retired to the hamlet of Clifford where there were just six houses. We were close enough to the enemy to be able to keep watch if they moved and yet we could move north if we were threatened.

"Matthew the Millerson, ride back to my knights and have Sir James bring our men here at daybreak."

When he had gone, I sat with Captain Alan in an empty house in the village for when the rebels had passed those who could had fled for family who lived further away from the wild scots and Northumbrians. I did not want the flames from a fire to alert the rebels but it was so cold that we needed the warmth. Only three of the houses were occupied and so my men and I were able to take shelter from the cold February air. We cooked some dried ham in water. It would make a broth to warm us and chewing the leathery meat would make it feel as though we had eaten.

Abelard asked, "Do you have a plan, lord?"

His father tutted, "Do not be impertinent, boy!"

"Let him be, Alan, he does right to question me for one day he will be a knight and he will have to make decisions such as I make." I turned to him, "The simple answer is no. If Percy runs, we follow but if he stands and fights then we have to join battle. It depends upon the terrain and on Sir Thomas. I know not how close he is. Let us say, Abelard, that I am glad that most of the men we bring are mine for I know how they will fight and for the rest then we are in the hands of God."

Alan nodded, "You see, son, that battles are not won by kings and princes, but men like us. Kings can have plans and strategies but if we do not carry them out then they will fail. For myself, I am confident for the enemy army is led by Lord Percy. He has escaped justice so many times that I am convinced that God will give us the victory for we deserve it and we are led by Sir William. We could be faced by ten times the number who face us but right will win!"

I rose before dawn and sent half of the archers to watch the enemy. A weary Harry Fletcher rode in and said, "Lord, the Sherriff is heading for Bramham. He will be here after noon!"

"Then we have them. Captain Alan, when the men arrive, take all of the archers and head for the rebel camp. Keep yourselves hidden for my plan is to wait until their attention is fixed upon Sir Thomas Rokeby. I will bring our mounted men at arms to fall upon their rear and you will distract them with your arrows."

He grinned, "Aye, lord!"

My men began to arrive and Captain Alan organised the archers. I gathered the knights around me. I knew my sons, son in law, Sir Wilfred, Sir John and Sir Ralph but not Sir James and the men of Middleham. "Today we have a chance to make the north secure for the King and his son. More, it will be safe for you and your families. With James of Scotland a hostage our only northern enemy is Percy!" I was pleased to see their eyes brighten as I spoke. They knew of the odds but my words had put steel in their hearts. "I intend to wait until Sir Thomas focusses the attention of the rebels on their attack from the east and then attack from behind, using our archers to weaken them."

One of the Middleham knights, Sir Jocelyn of Otley said, "Lord, is that not dishonourable?"

I laughed, "Sir Jocelyn, if you think there is any honour in war then you are deluded. Dishonour is allowing a coward like Percy, who let his son fight his battle for him, win. Follow my banner and do not even think of ransom. This day we fight for England and not for coins!" I saw that they all now understood my words. "We move east but we walk our horses and we do not progress beyond my archers' horses. We will need to be patient this day but when we do begin, we will mount and move as though the Devil himself was behind us. If their position is strong then we will attack on foot."

Sir Wilfred smiled at me as we walked our horses towards the battlefield. He was now the oldest of my knights. He had recently married but his wife was an older woman, a widow and he would have no children. "I am glad that you summoned me, lord, for since Shrewsbury my sword has become a ploughshare and that is not my way. It is good to be fighting for England again."

"And I am glad that you are here. I ask you to watch Harry when we fight for he is young."

"Fear not, Sir William, I have no bairns of my own. Your kin are my kin!" I was satisfied.

I led Hawk and my men towards Bramham Moor. It rose above us but the hedgerows and many small woods hid it from us and, I hoped, us from the enemy. It was Walter of Sheffield who halted us. "My lord, Captain Alan said to tell you that the ground betwixt us and the enemy, who are waiting, is uneven and rocky. He advises that your horses would not be able to keep a continuous line and you would have no speed."

I saw Sir James give me a strange look for I was listening patiently to the advice of an archer. I would listen to my men for they knew how we fought. I turned. "We leave our horses here."

I would not tell knights and men at arms which weapons to take. They were fighting on foot and each man would know their own weapon of choice. I took a spare roundel dagger and held it in my shield hand, along with my shield and I would take my sword. I removed my cloak and left it on my horse for I would not need to be encumbered by that. The chilly day would soon become warm when I began to hew heads. I estimated that it was about noon when we moved once more. As we were not on our horses, we were able to reach our archers unseen by the rebels who were in their prepared position and awaiting the men of Yorkshire. Handing my shield and helmet to Abelard I joined Captain Alan who sheltered behind a large oak surrounded by saplings and scrubby shrubs.

Pointing through the trees he said, "We cannot see them yet but they are beyond the slope we see. They have formed battle lines and face the men of York. I had one of my archers ride to Sir Thomas to tell him of the enemy disposition."

"Has he returned?"

"Not yet, my lord, but, in truth, I would not expect him. If he was seen hurrying west then it would alert the rebels to our position. He would take a circuitous route to avoid detection. We have not been able to count them, lord, and so I do not know the numbers we face. I thought that surprise would be lost if they knew they were being watched closely from the west. You will have to trust me, Sir William, they are there and they know not that we are here."

"You have done well. We wait."

I suspected that the fact that the rebels waited was evidence of their lack of numbers. This was not the army they had brought to Shrewsbury but that was not a surprise. Both sides had lost many men that day, but the rebels and their Scottish allies had lost their best warriors. In addition, Henry Percy was not the gifted warrior his son had been. He was waiting on the top of this piece of high ground to try to win a defensive battle and then march into a York stripped of its garrison. The hidden rebels like Sir Nicholas would them emerge like disturbed insects from the holes in which they hid. No matter what happened at this battle those hidden rebels would remain and the King and his son would still be in danger. Peace was still some way off.

When we heard the horns above us then we knew that Sir Thomas was approaching the rebels. They were preparing to fight the Yorkshire levy. That was our signal too. I donned my helmet and took my shield and dagger. Unsheathing my sword, I raised it and led the men at arms and my handful of knights from the shelter of the shrubs. Captain Alan and his archers, with strung bows, scurried up the hill like greyhounds. I waved my sword to make us into a long line like beaters at a hunt. As we began the walk, I saw why Alan of the Woods had advised us not to use horses. There were holes which had been the homes to rocks at some time. The rocks had gone leaving a trap which would have broken an animal's leg. Walking on foot we could avoid them.

Even with a helmet, coif and arming cap, I heard the whoosh of arrows from the east. The battle had begun. Captain Alan and his archers would form a line and nock arrows but they would wait for our arrival unless they were seen by the rebels. I was feeling my age as I struggled up the slope. It was not steep but I had not fought on foot since Shrewsbury and that had been some years since. I was no longer the young man fighting as King Richard's champion. Glancing around I saw Sir Wilfred struggling to keep up with Harry. The clash of arms told me that battle had been joined and I wondered if we had left our climb too late. Then my line of archers came into view and beyond them, I could see the battle. The enemy horses were to the south of us and were tethered and unattended. Lord Percy and Lord Bardolf were using all of their men to fight. I saw Percy's standard but this would be a bloody battle for, even as our archers drew back on their bows, I saw many wild Scotsmen amongst the rebels. They would fight and die hard!

Raising my sword, I shouted, "Loose!" The arrows soared and fell amongst the many rebels who were yet to be engaged. They dropped and struck some around Henry Percy's standard. As our archers nocked another arrow and drew back, I shouted, "For King Henry and the Prince of Wales!" We marched forward. Our archers were not a continuous line and we passed between them. The first arrows had come as a surprise and each had found a mark. The second flight was almost as effective as men turned to face the new threat. The third flight would be Captain Alan's last for by then we would be engaged and they would drop their bows and become the deadly killers I knew they were.

The rebels now turned to face this new threat. We were few in numbers but we had surprise on our side and I knew that Percy and Bardolf would be dismayed that their flight was now barred. We were between them and their horses. For one of the first times that I could remember I was not the first to strike the rebel line. My two sons had that honour. Thomas had not fought since Shrewsbury but he had trained each and every day. When the wild Scot raced at him wielding the deadly poleaxe my son did not falter and he rushed towards the Scot so swiftly that the poleaxe was only swung halfway before my son's shield smashed into it and his sword hacked across the thigh of the Scot. His leg half severed, the borderer fell to a bloody death. I barely had time to register that Harry was fighting a knight before I was engaged and it was Lord Bardolf himself who faced me. His blue shield was distinctive. He held a war axe in his hand and a shield. Seeing me he lowered his visor and came towards me. The rebels were now engaged all around but for me, the battle was the small circle which separated Lord Bardolf from me.

He had the advantage and I knew it. A war axe was a heavy weapon and the head alone could break steel plate and the bones beneath. In contrast, my sword was almost a lightweight weapon. I had my rondel dagger in my left hand and that weapon might be the one to win this fight for me. I had one advantage over him and that was the weight of his weapon. Once he began to swing then he would be committed to the swing. He could not feint and he could not change direction. I had to allow him a free swing at me, He was so eager to get at the knight who had killed Harry Hotspur that he put all of his efforts into the first swing which was aimed at my shield. If he could break my shield and my arm, then I would be at his mercy. I had anticipated the blow and held my shield, not tight to my body but away from me. It was a risk but it paid off. As he swung, I withdrew the shield and stepped back on to my left leg. His axe still connected but it just scored a line down and across my shield. My step back allowed me to swing my own weapon at him but I did not aim at his shield, which he expected, instead, I swung at his plate protected leg. I turned my sword so that I hit with the flat of the blade as I did not wish to take the edge from my sword. I heard his cry from within his helmeted face. I had hurt his leg.

All around me my men at arms were protecting me from others who wished to come to the aid of Lord Bardolf. I saw Wilfred obeying my orders and fighting to keep the enemy from Harry. In this way, we were clearing our part of the battlefield.

As Lord Bardolf pulled back his arm for another swing I stepped forward on my left leg and punched with my shield at the rebel. My shield was strapped to my arm so that I could hold my dagger. The shield hit his right shoulder and my dagger hit his besagew. The round plate was intended to protect the armpit and my dagger severed the fastening holding it. The besagew swung loosely from his shoulder. We were now so close that swings were impossible and so Lord Bardolf tried to use his weight to push me over. I had the advantage for my legs were placed well apart and he had an injured one. As he lunged at me, he slipped and I used the pommel of my sword to batter his helmet as he slid to the ground. He was stunned and so I placed my sword where his besagew would have protected him and plunged my blade down into his flesh. When the axe slipped from his hand, I looked for another opponent. Lord Bardolf was out of the battle.

Glancing around I saw that my sons, Sir Richard and Sir Ralph still lived and were hacking and hewing their way towards Henry Percy who had tried to retreat towards his horses. I noticed that Sir Wilfred was limping. He had been hurt. Around the Earl of Northumberland was a ring of household knights and his standard-bearer still held the blue rampant lion aloft. I shouted, "Take the earl! Take the head of the snake and the beast will die!"

I adjusted my shield and began to move towards the ring of steel around the last rebel, the earl. A young knight lunged at me with a poleaxe. He had quick hands and was strong; I barely had time to deflect the spiked head with my shield. Had he managed to strike me he could have used the hook to pull me over and once on the ground I would have been slain. I hacked at his weapon and it cracked. The better poleaxes had steel reinforcements and plates along the haft. This did not. I know not if he knew his weapon was damaged but he lunged at me a second time and when the head hit my shield the haft broke and fell into two pieces. His look of shock lasted a heartbeat for I swung my sword at the side of his head. He tumbled to the ground and putting my weight on my sword I drove it through his open mouth. His eyes had glazed over and I doubt that he knew much about it. Thomas and Harry, along with Captain Edgar had slain some of the younger knights around the Earl and I heard Sir Ralph, the son of Red Ralph, hired sword, roar out a challenge, "Face me, old man, for I am a loyal knight and a lord of the north who wishes the Percy family gone!"

It was a challenge which could not be ignored and meant that no other would interfere. I caught glimpses of the combat as I fought to get at the standard. When that fell then the battle would be over regardless of what happened to the earl. Most of the pole weapons, spears and pikes had been broken and now it was swords and axes which determined the battle. It meant we were all closer and long swings were harder to employ. This reminded me of the fight at the bridge when Sir John Chandos had perished. I knew that in this type of fight victory or defeat hung by a thread.

I punched my sword into the open face of a knight and, as he reeled, I rammed my rondel dagger up under his right armpit for he had no besagew there. The tip caught on the plate over his shoulder and I had to twist it to remove it. He screamed in pain and bright blood spurted as I tore a vital artery, Sir Ralph was trading blows with the Earl and wearing him down. The Earl was ten years older than I was. More importantly, he had not fought for some years. Ralph had been at Shrewsbury and fought many times since. It would be a matter of time.

The standard still fluttered and I shouted to Thomas, "The standard!"

The two of us began to move towards the flag. There were fewer men in our way now. Sir Thomas Rokeby and his levies would be hacking and slashing their way through the Scottish mercenaries and border brigands but it was we who faced the knights of Northumberland. It was sword on sword and my son and I worked in unison to swing, slash and block almost as one. The knights we encountered fought alone and that meant they exposed their sides. One knight with a bastard sword swung it at my head but I blocked it with my shield. My arm was numbed by the force of the blow but a two-handed sword meant you either struck your enemy or you exposed yourself. He was exposed and I swung my sword at the top of the skirt which protected his groin. I had practised the blow many times and it demanded accuracy. I managed to find the gap between the breastplate and skirt and the blade's edge had yet to be blunted. It sawed through the mail and the gambeson. Coming away bloody I knew that he was hurt. He lifted his sword above his head to finish me off but I punched, almost blindly with my shield and dagger. The blade tore through his cheek and he did not complete the blow but stepped backwards towards the standard. As he did, I pulled my sword to swing at him.

I saw that Sir Ralph was winning and the Earl had lost his shield and was using his sword two-handed to fend off the blows rained on him by Ralph of Middleham Tyas. Blood was pouring from the Earl and he would not last long.

I, too, was tiring and although my two sons and my son in law were now fighting the standard-bearer and the last two of the Northumberland knights, my enemy was still a threat. He swung his bastard sword at my head and I did the unexpected. I dropped to one knee and rammed my sword up under his plate skirt. There was neither plate nor mail to hinder my sword and I drove it up deep within his body. As he fell, I stood and saw the standard fall and then Sir Ralph swing his sword and smash into the side of the earl's head. I looked around and saw that the battle was over. Sir Thomas Rokeby and his levy were pursuing the remnants of the rebels.

I shouted, "If you wish to surrender then do so now!"

There were still four or five men with swords including at least one Bishop. They dropped their weapons. Sir James had lost four of his knights but my men and sons were alive. I walked over to Sir Ralph, "You have done well and the earl's armour and horses are yours. I shall tell the King and there will be more honour for you."

"I am happy, Sir William, to have served my King and my country."

I sheathed my sword and handed my helmet and shield to Abelard who had obeyed my orders and stayed close behind me to guard my back. I walked back to Lord Bardolf and took off his helmet. He was dead and I had killed him. Sir Thomas Rokeby rode up to me and I saw that his surcoat was so bloody he could have been a worker in an abattoir.

"A great victory, Sir William, and I see that your men have slain the beast!"

"Aye!"

He turned to the men with him. "Have Lord Bardolf and the Earl stripped of armour. I want them hanged drawn and quartered." It was a brutal but necessary sentence. The body parts would be sent to the four corners of the kingdom whilst the heads were prominently displayed. The Sherriff had lost men. I could see their corpses amongst the rebels and he was not in a forgiving mood. He looked at the prisoners and recognised two churchmen amongst them. The Abbot of Hailes wore armour while the Bishop of Bangor did not. The Sherriff said, "Bishop, you may lay down your sword and return to your church where you can beg forgiveness of God for your rebellion." He turned to the rest, "As for you, kneel and ask God for forgiveness now!" His men held them while he strode along the line, swinging a twohanded sword and taking their heads. "Now put these heads upon spears so that all the world may know the fate of traitors."

I turned to speak to my sons and I saw that Harry was not there with Thomas. I saw him close to the place he had helped me fight for the standard. He was kneeling and I feared that he was hurt. As I reached him, I saw that he knelt over the body of Sir Wilfred. My old friend had died. Harry looked up at me and shook his head, "He was wounded, father, but he never left me. When two Northumbrian knights came at my shield side, he placed himself between me and their blades. He slew them both and then succumbed to his wounds." I could see that he was distraught. "I never got to thank him! He died saving my life and I said nothing!"

I put my arm around my son, "His soul is but a little way above our heads, Harry, and he knows. My father did the same for me. He died and I did not get the chance to thank him but I believe he knew I was grateful. Sir Wilfred was obeying my last orders. I asked him to watch over you and he did. He died a warrior and he died happy. See the smile upon his face."

Harry shook his head, "I did not want him to die for me!"

"And had you asked him he would have said that better an old man dies than a young knight who will have children of his own one day! You and Tom are the future! Come let us bury my old friend here, at Bramham Moor and we will remember him each time we talk of this battle, the battle that finally ended the threat of the Percy family!"

It was a brutal world in which we lived but that battle at Bramham Moor ended the northern threat. King Henry and his

son were safe and it meant that Prince Henry and I could turn our
attention to Harlech and the Welsh rebellion!

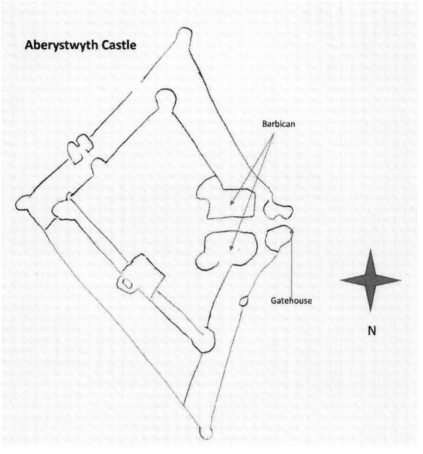

Chapter 12

We left the battlefield two days later. Sir Wilfred had a wooden cross but Harry swore that it would be a stone one. The dead were stripped and the mail, plate, weapons and horses equitably distributed. Sir Ralph and his men were rich because of the battle. The Earl had gold upon his person as did his retainers. To the victor go the spoils. My men at arms and archers all benefitted as did my knights and I. We took horses, mail, plate and weapons, along with the heads of the two leaders with us. We left one head, Lord Bardolf's, at Lincoln for that was the start of the north. Leaving my sons to return home I took the head of the Earl of Northumberland to London. Prince Henry came with me and it was he placed it on a spike upon London Bridge. It was a sign to all in the south that the rebellion was over.

"You and the Sherriff have done well and now, when the fields are planted, we can go to Aberystwyth and Harlech and end this other ulcer's cancerous growth!" My face must have fallen even though I tried to hide it for he said, "But a little more, Sir William, and then, with a secure kingdom, I can learn how to rule this land."

"Rule this land? Is the King…?"

He shook his head, "He lives but his illness means that he cannot go forth in public and I will have to establish my own control for there are parties who might not wish to rebel but have their own ideas of governance. They will learn that I am not a man to cross!"

I heard the steel in his voice. He reminded me of his father when he had been Henry Bolingbroke and seeking the crown. Was Prince Henry making a move to take the throne? If so then I would have to stop him as much as I did not wish to. I had sworn an oath to the King and only he, or God could release me from it.

As I headed home, I was lost in my thoughts. I knew that Prince Henry would make a better King than his father but the King had to choose to abdicate the throne. King Richard had allowed Henry Bolingbroke to take the crown and if he had not then I would have fought him. I knew that the Council who advised the King were the real power in the land and they were the ones who could apply pressure. If the King's ailment prevented him from appearing in public then the Council would, effectively, rule the Kingdom. It was a dilemma and I knew not how we could get around it. I also had Wales on my mind. Prince Henry now had his cannons and his gunners. He had plans to sail them to Aberystwyth from Bristol and save a journey through Wales which would be beset by dangers. To that end, he had asked me to join the Earl of Arundel at Shrewsbury and to bring the men who would assault the walls across Wales. That, in itself, was a nightmare. Welsh rebels would hide behind every rock.

By the time I reached Weedon, I had my plans in my head and I shelved them there for I wanted at least two days without thinking of battles or politics. I wanted two days with my family, all of them. What I wanted and what I got were two entirely different matters. I had forgotten that our son, Henry, was due to be wed in September. At the table that first evening my wife was in a good mood and the food was well cooked and to my taste. I enjoyed wine from Bordeaux with the food and felt replete until she brought up the subject of the wedding.

"Now that the north is safe, and I thank God for the safe return of my men, then we can concentrate upon the wedding in September. We have much to plan."

I held up my hand for I knew that if I did not mention the Welsh war sooner, rather than later, then my wife would be even angrier and more upset with me. "I may not be at the wedding, my love, for the Prince wants me to be at his side when he attacks Aberystwyth."

Her face darkened like a sky before a thunderstorm and I braced myself to weather it. "Are there no other knights who can aid the Prince? Is it you alone who fights for Henry Bolingbroke and his son?"

"Thomas and Harry need not serve. It is only myself who may attend the wedding." I realised when the thunder clapped and my wife spoke that I had said the wrong thing.

"How thoughtful! You will allow the groom to attend his own wedding! Such generosity! Will Strongstaff you are…"

I never learned what I was for she burst into tears and ran from the room. I had learned, over the years, to let her calm down in her own time. I finished the jug of wine and stared into the fire. I reflected that we might be in a position, by September, to end the siege of Aberystwyth and that meant I might be able to return for the wedding. I would not promise that yet but it was something to have in case I needed it. I also began to work out which men I would take with me. Some of my men had, like Thomas, my son, begun families. If I could, then I would leave those at home. I finished the wine and went to bed. My wife was asleep and for that I was grateful. I had to leave Weedon by the end of the week but I needed two days with my grandchildren and my tenants. I did not mention the campaign to either Sir Richard or my sons. When I returned home there was silence from my wife and I knew that she was still angry that I might not be at the marriage.

I put the argument from my mind as I prepared for the campaign. I summoned my sons and Sir Richard and told them what the Prince wished. As I had expected all three of them said they would come.

"No, for you, Harry, have a wedding to plan and Thomas and Richard will be needed in case I do not return in time."

I saw that Harry was less than happy for he saw himself as the cause of this dilemma. "I wish I had never broached the subject of a marriage."

"Harry, you are a knight and need a lady at your side. Remember Sir Wilfred and his sacrifice. That was so that you could live, marry and father children. I need more grandchildren so that my blood continues into the future. Besides a siege is not a glorious thing. We will be sitting without the walls of Aberystwyth trying to starve them and reduce their walls while enduring hunger and cold ourselves. When the time comes to assault then it will be a hard battle and many men will die before they even set foot in the castle. No, this is for the best and when it is done then, hopefully, we shall have years of peace ahead of us."

They were not convinced but I was not only their father but their liege lord and they obeyed. I gave them a list of tasks which they needed to undertake while I was away for I knew that communication between Wales and Northampton would be almost impossible. Once we had the sea at our backs then we would, effectively, be cut off by the vastness of the Welsh mountains.

When they had left, I summoned my captains and we planned what we would need in terms of men, horses and weapons. I would not take Hawk for this was not a campaign for a warhorse. Once alone I prepared myself by choosing the clothes and the weapons I would take. It was as I was doing so that my wife entered the bedchamber.

I heard her before I knew that she was in the bed chamber, "This is the task of a wife!"

"And I thought that you no longer wished to be my wife for you have shunned me for some days."

"I was angry but I am over the anger now. I cannot fight a King and it would be folly to do so. I just have to accept that you may not be at the wedding." She began to pack for me and spoke quietly as she did so. "Just keep safe, eh? You have fought for two kings and for their purposes for thirty years or more and there is no end to it. It seems to me that they will only be happy when you are dead."

I knew that to be a lie for they needed me, father and son both, but I said nothing and smiled as she sniffed and then folded the clothes I would need.

When she had done, she kissed me hard on the lips. "And even as they lay me in my grave, I shall still wish to be your wife for you are the only man I ever want!"

I left as soon as the first fields had been sown and the spring lambs born. We were lucky to have both land and animals. They would sustain us if we had hard times ahead. Having visited the north I was keenly aware that we had a much easier life in the south and I could see why Red Ralph had raised hardy horses rather than cereal. In the north, it was barley bread and oatbread which were produced. Wheat was common in the south and explained why few knights were keen to be given a northern manor.

I had just twenty men with me and we headed for Shrewsbury. There we would meet Sir John Talbot and Sir John Oldcastle. Their retinues would join mine and we would await the arrival of the Earl of Arundel and the bulk of the men who would fight for the Prince to regain his land. As we waited the two border lords told me how much easier it had been since the isle of Anglesey had been conquered.

"The Welsh are trapped now. If it was not for their lands in the Gower then they would all have starved. Anglesey is their breadbasket and now that it is in our hands the Welsh are clinging on to their two captured castles as though their lives depended on it." Sir John Talbot kept an ear to the ground and knew more than any other man in the marches.

"And Mortimer and Glendower? What news of them?"

"The rumour is that they are in Harlech Castle for that is deemed to be impregnable but, in truth, we know not for none has heard of them for so long that there are rumours that they are dead."

Sir John Oldcastle topped up his wine, "If they were dead then the rebellion would have collapsed. The Welsh only fight because they see hope in Glendower. Mortimer...?" He shrugged, "The Welsh do not want him and we would hang him if we captured him. Mortimer is a dead man walking."

When Sir Thomas Fitzalan joined us, we held a council of war. "The Prince is in Bristol with his gunners and his engineers and they will be sailing for Aberystwyth by the end of the month. That means we leave as soon as we can. I am under no illusions, gentlemen, we may well have to fight our way across Wales but we have to be there to enable the Prince to land his men."

I knew what he meant. The Prince would have not only his master gunners but his other gunners as well as miners, carpenters, labourers, cordwainers and surgeons. He might even have fletchers for the bow was still our most powerful weapon. An army on the move did not need so many men who did not fight but a siege was different for we could be there for months.

He turned to me, "Sir William, I will be most reliant upon you for advice. No one knows war as you do and I am fully aware that you have forgotten more about war than I have yet learned. Have I missed anything out?"

I nodded, "I have not yet heard of the Welsh who will be fighting with us. The last time we fought we won two victories because of Dafydd Gam. Have you asked him and his brother to come?"

I saw realisation on his face and he shook his head, "I should have thought of that. I will send to them."

"And it may be that these two lords have loyal Welshmen who might aid us. The language and the land are as different from England as it is possible to be. We have archers who can scout but we need Welshmen who know the land. David of Welshpool and Owen the Welshman can scout but I would prefer someone with local knowledge."

The delay in securing the men we needed cost us another four days and when we left Shrewsbury, we were forced to move at a faster, more hurried pace than we might have liked. Sir Thomas Fitzalan was in command of the army but I placed myself and my men, along with Dafydd Gam and his brother at the fore. We would be the vanguard. My mounted archers and the Welshmen led by Dafydd gave us the best chance of avoiding an ambush.

David of Welshpool was our guide for the first thirty miles as he came from Welshpool and it was he who advised us on the route we should take. "Avoid Machynlleth, my lord, for the folk there are fanatical. The road further south will be a little harder but it will be safer."

There was little point in having a good scout if you did not heed his advice and he led us to his home town of Welshpool. His family were long gone but all of us were appalled at what we saw. The townsfolk were like skeletons. The war had caused major problems for them. With all English trade denied them and their men fighting a war they could not win the people were starving to death. As much as we wished to ease their suffering they were still rebels and were an incentive for us to win so that we could relieve their plight. The Earl of Arundel showed a thoughtful side and he sent men back to bring a wagon of food for them, from Shrewsbury. It showed intelligence too for by feeding them he ensured that they would be less likely to fight us. What we should have done was to fetch more food but our late departure meant we had no time to spare and we pushed on.

Our route was dictated by the River Severn and when we neared the mountains then our troubles began. The last place of any size through which we had passed had been Welshpool; indeed, some villages and hamlets had been abandoned or were inhabited by the dead but we had been aware that we were being watched. It was our own Welshmen who showed us the signs. They spotted the tell-tale footprints and smelled the fires that the rebels had used.

We were descending to the River Wye when the attack came. Had we not had Welsh scouts then they might have caught us unawares but Dafydd knew the land and had warned us that he thought we might be ambushed and our archers rode with bows which were strung and the rest of us with shields held ready to use. The Welshmen who attacked us were good and were well hidden on the slopes to our right. Their arrows showered down and they aimed, not at the knights but our mounted archers. I saw two of my men tumble from their saddles. We had prepared for such an attack and, drawing my sword, I turned to head up the slope and through the undergrowth. While we would be shortening the distance that their arrows would have to fly, a charging horse can unnerve an archer, especially a young one and many of the archers who remained in the rebel army were younger men for we had slain the veterans at Pwll Melyn and Grosmont. An arrow thudded into my shield from so close to me that it penetrated the wood. They were using bodkins! The archer was to my left and it was Stephen of Morpeth who made the archer pay the price for his boldness by hacking through his shoulder. Arrows were now flying from behind me as my archers released their arrows. I saw an archer rise from behind a rock and aim at Captain Edgar who led the men to my right. I veered Hart towards him and sliced down across his shoulder even as he drew back the bow. My blade grated off the bone and tore through sinew and muscle. Wheeling back up the slope I urged Hart on. Their attack thwarted, the Welshmen fled but it was in vain. It cost us a couple of hours but we hunted down and slew each and every one of them. There was little point in taking prisoners and my men were angry to be ambushed. When we returned it was too late to push on through the dark of an unknown land and so we camped.

We had lost archers. Dafydd had lost two as had I. Garth of Worksop and Will Straight Shaft had been with me for some years and both had been unlucky. Each had been hit by two arrows. Will had died when his head had struck a rock as he tumbled from his horse and Garth had been hit by an arrow in the neck. Others had been wounded but the wounds would not stop them being archers. The deaths of two veterans seemed to bring my men even closer together for it was rare for us to lose a man. We buried them on a flat piece of ground overlooking the river. The priests we had brought said the right words to send them to God but it was left to Alan of the Woods to speak the words that told of their skill. It was our way and the two men would be remembered with tales around campfires, long into the future.

As the last of the Welsh arrows, bows and bowstrings were collected I sat by the fire lost in my thoughts. My thoughts were on the men alongside whom I had fought. My father, Harry, Dick Long Sword and Long John were dead as was Red Ralph. That he had died in his bed did not diminish the memory of his courage. Old Tom might be dead; I had not had the opportunity to visit with him the last time I had been in Lincoln and Peter the Priest might still live and work in the alms house in York, I knew not. The memories stirred me. I owed it to both of them to see if they were still alive and to sit and talk of the past. When the Welsh were subdued, I would make time to visit with them. Neither man had children and both viewed me as a surrogate son. Wilfred's death had been a reminder not to forget my old comrades for we were bound together in blood.

Our archers were on either side of us and rode on the flanks to prevent a second attack but none materialised. We had slain more than eighty Welshmen. Not all had been archers but most were. Every Welsh archer we slew increased the Prince's chances of winning back his land for archers took years to train and the archer was the best weapon that the Welsh possessed.

We neared the mouth of the river and I was relieved to see that the Prince and his ships had not yet arrived. We turned a corner on the road which twisted through the mountains and saw the castle, town and the sea just six or seven miles away. I called the

Earl of Arundel forward so that he could view it. The castle of Aberystwyth, which I had seen a number of times, was on a promontory and rose above the town. Their defenders would enjoy height and we would not. Two sides were protected by the sea and the other two by the town. This was a mighty castle and King Edward had built well.

I pointed out the problems that the Prince would face when he did arrive. "As you can see there is nowhere which overlooks the castle. We can rain neither stones nor arrows at the walls. I have never used cannon and so, perhaps, they may be the answer. I know not." I pointed to the farms which lay between us and the town. Already folk were leaving them and heading for the castle. It showed their true colours. These were no friends to England. "We will find an empty town. Captain Alan, take your archers and stop those folks taking their animals."

"Do you wish them to be prisoners, lord?"

I shook my head, "Do not stop them from heading to the castle. Let the Welsh feed them. We need the food they have for us!"

As we continued our way down the steep and twisting road, I saw my archers gallop off. Sheep and cattle never move fast, unless they are running away from a farmer, and these were no exception. The farmers had a priority which was to get their families to safety and they abandoned their animals. By the time we had reached the flat valley bottom my archers had secured a sizeable flock of sheep and a herd of cattle. There were less than a hundred sheep and fewer than twenty cattle but, along with the pigs we found, we had food for several days and, more importantly, the Welsh did not!

We saw the town becoming abandoned as the townsfolk fled into the castle. The bridge became choked with the press of people passing over it. Dafydd and I led our men at a fast gallop towards the walls. The gates were slammed shut leaving twenty or so people trapped outside the walls. The townsfolk ran up the road which led to Aberdyfi. We let them go for we had ensured that little food had been taken into the town.

"Archers, make a defensive line so that none may enter or leave. Captain Edgar, go and find our quarters."

We had done this before and Edgar would leave one large house for the Earl but he would find the next best one and we would have a roof and shelter. By evening the castle was surrounded and the smell of Welsh mutton being cooked drifted towards the castle. Those inside were not yet hungry but the castellan, whoever it was, would need to ration food and the smell of cooking meat would make everyone hungrier. We would not dine so well every day but the Earl and I were making a point as we waited for the Prince, his ships and his cannon. We spent the time ensuring that none could leave the castle and we had a ditch to prevent us from being surprised by a sortie.

Prince Henry arrived a week later and his fleet anchored in the river. He stepped ashore first for it would take some time to unload the vessels. He went directly to the Earl of Arundel, "Well, Sir Thomas, have you asked them to surrender yet?"

The Earl smiled, "Not yet, Prince Henry, we thought to give you that pleasure."

"Good! There is no time like the present. Sir William, come with us."

We were all mailed and wore plate but, to show that we wished to speak peace we did not wear helmets and the Prince had his standard with him. The four of us strode to the gates. The nearest houses were more than a hundred paces from the walls but my archers were hidden on the rooves and would be watching for treachery.

The Prince stopped a hundred paces from the gate and, cupping his hands shouted, "I am Henry of Monmouth and Prince of Wales. You hold my castle against me and I demand that you surrender it to me. If you do so then I swear you will be treated leniently."

A Welsh knight appeared a moment or two later above the gatehouse, "I am Rhodri of Bangor and I command this castle for the true Prince of Wales, Owain Glyndŵr. I have to tell you, Henry of Monmouth, that we will not surrender for this is not your land."

The Prince turned to the Earl and me, "We had to try." He turned back to the walls, "Then it will go ill for you. I will try to control my men but you should know that the aftermath of a siege is never pretty. On your head be it!"

As we made our way back, he confided, "I expected nothing less but they have yet to be battered by cannon and I hope my new gunners and their fowlers can break their walls and their spirits." I learned that a fowler was a type of cannon. It was nine feet long and sent a rock the size of a man's head from its mouth.

If I thought there would be a rapid start to the siege I was mistaken. Sir John and I had already begun the trench around the castle walls and identified a place we could begin to mine. The four cannons took more than a week to assemble and to place in a position where they could begin to batter the walls. The cannons had been placed in a line where they could hit the same part of the wall. The Prince and his Dutch gunners chose the junction of the wall and the gatehouse which was on the eastern side of the outer wall. The castle was lozenge shaped and there was a huge barbican keep just inside the gatehouse. I would have attacked closer to the southern tower but the Prince and his gunners were confident that when the wall collapsed the gatehouse would follow. To me, that did not solve the problem as we would have the barbican keep to reduce.

When the guns were in place, I anticipated the beginning of an assault upon the walls but it did not materialise. The gunners took wagons to go to find rocks which they would shape as missiles. That took another week and I persuaded the Prince to have his miners begin to excavate close to the southern tower. A mine took a long time to dig but had we begun immediately then we would be closer to reducing one section of the wall. It gave me something to do and I went with Sir John Talbot and our archers who duelled with the Welsh archers while the miners erected their entrance to the mine. Until the mine was given a cover there would be danger and it took another week to get to the point where the miners could enter the mine and begin to dig. By that time the gunners were back with their missiles.

It was with great anticipation that we gathered to witness them being used for the first time. I had seen small cannons in Spain but they had been tiny tubes of metal. These were huge beasts and I stayed far enough away so that if there was an accident I would not be blown up. The fowler was as long as two men and was on a wooden stand. I was not certain if the stand would have to be replaced for, from what I had heard, the cannons moved and the stand had no wheels. The Master Gunner, Johann, knew his business for he chose the first rock himself and only when he was perfectly satisfied did he allow his gunners to load it. He repeated the procedure with all of the cannons. When the breech was secured, he moved his gunners away and then lit the fuse on the first gun. Apparently, it was his favourite and he had named it The King's Daughter in honour of King Henry's daughter. It was a long fuse and I saw the reason for he moved well away from the weapon. Fire belched from the end of the cannon and it did, indeed, move backwards. There was so much smoke that I thought a fog had descended and then I heard the crack as the stone hit the wall. The fact that the stone hit the wall at all appeared, to me, to be a remarkable achievement but when the smoke cleared, I saw little damage to the wall except for a black patch where the soot from the stone had been left on the wall. Of course, everyone cheered and the Master Gunner looked happy. He repeated the procedure with the other three guns. The fact that flames leapt from the end made us use the term fire when the cannon roared. The noise was terrifying and the smoke noxious. I did not know how the gunners could endure it. By the end of the day, the cannons had sent twelve stones at the wall. Eleven had struck and one had hit the earthen bank. There appeared to be little damage to the walls although one of the Dutch gunners kept pointing to the mortar shouting that there was a crack. There was not.

That evening as I sat with the other leaders and the Prince I said, "Prince Henry, with your permission, I would take my men on the morrow for a chevauchée to the north."

He looked disappointed, "Do you not wish to see the bombardment continue?"

I did not wish to hurt his feelings and so I did not speak the truth, "Prince Henry, Glendower and Mortimer are in Harlech. It would be too much to hope that they might bring an army to relieve this siege but they may have scouts out and we can deny them access to the land twixt Harlech and here. My men crave action and with the mine underway and the bombardment begun then they will become indolent."

"Very well but you will miss the spectacle of the walls falling soon."

I did not tell him that I did not anticipate an early end to the siege. From what I had seen the castle would be breached but at the rate the cannons fired and the results they achieved then it would be weeks rather than the days which Prince Henry hoped.

Chapter 13

My men were happy with the decision for a chevauchée meant not only the chance of action but also of booty. We headed north towards Machynlleth which I knew to be a centre of Welsh rebellion. We had been ambushed close to there before the Battle of Shrewsbury but I was confident that the bulk of the Welsh rebels would now be closer to Harlech. With Beaumaris and Anglesey back in English hands then the threat from Caernarfon and Chester increased.

We did not head up the coast but took the main road to Machynlleth as my Welsh archers and men at arms had assured me that there were no castles or defences along the road. The fifteen-mile journey could easily be done in one day. We would search out any rebels and rest and then return back to Aberystwyth and the siege. This was a land of small farms. Most of them grew a few crops but with the mountains so close and rocks lying beneath the surface then it was an animal-based economy. Sheep gave them wool and food while the few cattle they reared were kept for milk. I did not see much evidence of deer and other wild animals to hunt. This was a poor country and the people showed the hardship as we rode through their villages and hamlets. They barely looked up for there was little they could do to stop us and they were too weak from many years of a rebellion which had yielded them little except for a couple of victories and two captured castles. You cannot eat a victory and stone is hard to digest.

I was no fool and I sent Owen and David of Welshpool to scout out the town as I did not wish to be ambushed. It had been the first place which had declared for Glendower and I did not think that they would take kindly to us boldly riding into their town. It was as the main column neared the town that they both returned.

"They know that we are coming, lord, and they have made a barricade at the entrance to the town. They have archers and the menfolk are armed with pole weapons."

"How far is it to the barricade?"

"A mile or so. There is a bend not far ahead and the ground slopes up to the hills where there is a small wood."

"Could we use it to keep our horses safe?"

"Aye, Sir William. We saw neither horses nor knights in the town. They are farmers and burghers."

I had planned on simply riding in and using our armour and horses to intimidate them but now that they had defences then I changed my plans. "We will leave our horses in the woods." I still had a couple of archers who were not yet fully recovered from their wounds. They could wield a sword but not yet draw a bow. They could guard the horses. After leaving our animals with their guards I had my men at arms spread out in one line with the archers behind. I think we took them by surprise for they must have seen us in the distance on our horses and were expecting to see us riding down the road. The hedges hid us from view and that enabled us to march to within one hundred paces from the barrier before they saw us. Even then they panicked and arrows descended somewhat randomly. One lucky arrow hit the top of my helmet but when it clattered to the ground, I saw that it was a hunting arrow. If the men of Machynlleth had nothing better than hunting arrows then they would be as well to surrender now.

Captain Alan and my archers waited until they were all ready and then rained their war arrows on to the barricade. Few of the defenders had a helmet and fewer still had any mail. We kept marching although I raised my shield for protection. The Welsh should have aimed at our archers but mailed men at arms must have seemed like a better target and they wasted their arrows. Captain Alan thinned their ranks and when we were just forty paces from the barricade I shouted, "Charge!"

With Stephen of Morpeth on one side of me and Captain Edgar on the other, we ran at the hurriedly built barricade. Behind me, Abelard and three of my men at arms put their weight behind us and we crashed into the hurdles, carts and wicker baskets. With at least a third of the defenders incapacitated the barrier gave way so quickly that I almost lost my balance. I took two long strides to take me beyond the debris. One of the few mailed men at the barrier had retained his weapons and he swung his sword hard at me. It came at my shield and I easily deflected it. Even as my shield twisted his blade away to expose his middle, I brought my sword from on high to hack through his mail and into his left shoulder; he began to bleed out immediately. He was a brave man and he tried to stab me, a little weakly, with his sword. I punched him in the face with my shield and he fell to the ground.

The falling of the barrier and the death of the mailed man ended the fight. Those still close to us dropped to their knees and begged mercy. Those further away just ran. One or two were hit by the arrows of my men but most escaped.

"Captain Alan, go and fetch our horses. Captain Edgar, see to the Welsh. Did we lose any of our men or were any hurt?"

He laughed, "Had any man I led been wounded fighting these farmers then I would have dismissed him immediately."

Leaving my men to obey my commands I sheathed my sword and headed into the town with Abelard. I took off my helmet and let my coif slip down over my shoulders for it was a hot day and we had marched, mailed to battle. I remembered that there was a hall in the middle of the town and I headed for it. I was in no fear of being attacked for I saw just women and children, along with a couple of old men as I strode into the centre. When I reached the hall, the door was barred. Striding up to it I banged on it, "Open up in the name of Prince Henry, the Prince of Wales!"

I knew and accepted that they would plead ignorance of English but I was also confident that they would understand enough English to understand what I said. There was silence and when I looked around, I saw that the street had emptied. I banged again and repeated my words. Eventually, the door opened and a well-dressed woman stood there. "I am Sir William Strongstaff, Sherriff of Northampton." I pushed the door open and stepped beyond her. "Who is the mayor of Machynlleth?"

From a room to my left came a voice, "I am, Iago ap Gruffydd."

I entered the room and saw a man about my age. He was, like the woman, well dressed and it was in the English style.

"Why have you come here to disturb our peace?"

Taking off my gloves I placed them on the table, "You were the ones who made a barrier and you were the ones who loosed arrows at us. Who broke the peace?"

He glared at me, "We do not want you in our country! Leave!"

"This land belongs to Henry of Monmouth, the future King of England." I turned to the woman who had followed Abelard and myself in the room. "You are his wife?"

She nodded, "Myfanwy." She added a title but as it was in Welsh, I did not understand it.

"Pack your husband a bag for he comes with me to Aberystwyth."

The man said, "You have taken it?"

"Not yet but you shall meet Prince Henry and explain your actions to him. You will then be a hostage for the good behaviour of Machynlleth."

The man looked resigned but the woman shook her head and shouted, "You cannot do that!"

I smiled, "Ask your husband if we can or we cannot. Who will stop me?" She was silent. "I came to find out if there were rebels here in Machynlleth. Had there been none then I would have carried on to seek others. Your attack proves that there are rebels. Whichever fool decided to oppose us has cost your husband his freedom."

The looks they exchanged told me that it was him. When my men arrived, horses were found as well as papers with Glendower's seal upon them. We took those and a small chest of coins we found hidden in the Mayor's home. I wondered if we would have trouble leaving for the people had returned to the streets but they looked cowed. Captain Edgar had told me, as we ate, that nineteen men had died at the barricade. We had torn the heart from them and there was no fight left. That the place which had raised Glendower to power had now fallen to us gave me hope.

The Prince was delighted with my actions and, as he took me along the walls to show barely discernible scratches and chips, the result of the bombardment, he told me to continue my rides.

"I will ride in two days' time and cross the Dyfi. By then we will need more animals for food." We had managed to bring back a number of sheep. The men were eating better than they might have expected and it made up for the lack of progress on the walls.

That evening I spoke with Sir John Talbot. He was, like me, a veteran of the Black Prince's wars and I could talk to him for we shared a common language and experiences. "I had expected more from cannon, Sir William. To me, they are full of sound, fire and fury but they are slower than a trebuchet. I would have built a couple of trebuchets. They would have taken less time to build."

"I know that the progress is slow but we are all new to this and it is too early to judge success and failure. We have the whole summer to reduce the walls."

He shook his head, "The King's council which now rules for him, in his illness, are withholding funds. It is now thought that he has St Antony's fire." He crossed himself, "The man who told me of the illness also told me that the King's hold on power was slipping. I told the Prince when he arrived. He intends to return to London once the walls show signs of collapse."

I laughed, "Then he may have to endure the winter's seas. Still, it will be good for him to face the Council."

I was remembering when the Council of lords had thwarted King Richard. It had been the beginning of the end for the King. After he lost faith in them he had become more of a tyrant. Prince Henry had the opportunity to learn how to handle the senior lords of the land before he was the king. I had been close enough to the seat of power to see that it was difficult to hang on to power. A king needed allies and supporters.

I watched the cannons the next day and saw that they were now firing more regularly. They sent twenty stones in one day. Of course, that meant they would soon have to fetch more stones. It was then that Prince Henry took command. He sent other labourers to fetch the stones. We now knew what size they wanted and we had plenty of idle hands which could shape the stones. Until the fire in the mine was lit or until there was a crack in the walls then we just watched.

When my men and I rode out for our next raid we knew that we were heading into unknown territory. We had heard of a castle close by the river. Llewellyn the Great had held an assembly at Glandyfi Castle but that had been almost two hundred years earlier. The castle was a mile or so downstream from a ford. It was just a ten mile ride to the castle and, as we approached the river, I saw no sign of a stone building. What we found was a long-abandoned motte and bailey wooden castle. The mound was not particularly high but the site was a good one. If Prince Henry so chose then he could fortify it and defend the river and the northern approach to Aberystwyth. We rode along the river and crossed the ford which lay just a mile away. Beyond the river was Welsh territory for Harlech lay not far to the north. Part of my reason for venturing this far north was to test the Welsh resolve and their defences. Consequently, David of Welshpool and Owen the Welshmen were our scouts. We saw animals on the hillsides but as we neared each hamlet, we saw that the land did not support towns or villages and the inhabitants hid. We could have found them but I did not see the point.

Inevitably, we pushed too far. That was my fault for I was looking for their defences and we had seen none. I spied another deserted castle just half a mile ahead; we later learned it was called Cynfal, and I decided to investigate. This one had no wooden hall left at all and the palisades had begun to sprout! We were, probably, an hour past the time we should have turned and I had just dismounted to make water when Owen came galloping back down the road, "My lord, a column of Welsh warriors is coming down the road."

"How many?"

"I counted forty; there are some knights, squires and men at arms. David is watching them."

I had pushed our luck and I knew it. I looked at Hart. She was lathered and although a good horse, she needed some rest however brief that might be. "Did they see you?"

Owen looked offended, "Lord!"

"Captain Alan, we will ambush these Welshmen." The road was less than two hundred paces from us and the elevation of the mound meant that our archers would have the range."

"Aye, lord."

As the archers went to the edge of the mound and stuck their arrows in the soft earth close to the saplings and scrubby growth I shouted, "These Welsh are doing the same as we are; they are scouting. I intend to attack them with arrows and when their attention is on this old castle we will leave and head back to the river. I do not like to run from the Welsh but we need to tell Prince Henry of the potential danger from the north." They nodded, "Water your horses and let them rest."

David of Welshpool ghosted up the slope and he grinned when he saw the question on my face, "When I saw this, as we headed north to scout, I thought to use it should Owen and I be pursued and I had a feeling that you would be here, lord."

There are some things which cannot be easily explained and the affinity and understanding my men had for one another sometimes frightened me. I had seen it in the Blue Company and I thanked God for it now.

"Where are they?"

He pointed to the road, "You should hear them soon!"

I heard the hooves and, taking off my helmet I went to peer through the saplings. There were knights and men at arms. I recognised some Welsh liveries and also English ones. Mortimer's men were abroad and that was news indeed. It was confirmation that Glendower and Mortimer were in Harlech. It was hard to know where else they might be but if they were in Harlech then that would be our next target.

I turned to Alan of the Woods, "You choose your moment. We will be ready to ride when you tell us that they are committed to an attack."

"Aye, lord!"

I went back to my horse. Abelard had watered her and our horses grazed on a verdant patch of green. I used my cloak to wipe some of the sweat and lather from her.

"Do not mount until the archers do. We need the horses to have as much rest as they can get." I was counting on the fact that Harlech was as far from the Dyfi River as was Aberystwyth and that their horses would be tired too.

I could not see the road and I did not wish to risk moving closer and alerting them. I saw the archers pull back. It was always an inspiring sight and sound for you could hear the creak of the yew bows and see the strength it took to pull them back; their muscles knotted like young oaks. Then, without a command, they all released and the arrows soared. Each archer had a second arrow nocked even before their first had begun its downward trajectory. I heard the first arrows strike as the third flight took to the air. Some arrows hit metal but my archers used bodkins and the arrows would cause wounds. Some struck horses and I heard the screaming of animals injured by a missile which drove deep into their flesh. And I heard the cries of men who thought their plate and mail sufficient, it was not.

Captain Alan allowed two more flights before he shouted, "Back to the horses!"

They ran towards us and we mounted just as they did. Wheeling our horses, we left to the south and east away from the enemy who were to the north and west. They would have to climb the mound and then pursue us. The climb would weary their already tired mounts. Captain Alan rode next to me. "There are ten who are wounded, unhorsed or dead. The rest will follow."

"Then let us see who has the better horses and are the superior riders."

This was a matter of judgement as much as anything. If we went too quickly then we might lose them initially but when our horses tired, they would catch us and if we went too slowly then they could thrash their horses and catch us. To that end, Edgar and Harold of Derby rode at the rear. If we were being caught then they would tell us. Hart was one of the best horses we had and I rode her so that she was not exerting too much effort. She still had reserves of power she could use. The horses we had taken at Bramham Moor had been good ones and so most of my men had horses which had once been knight's horses but they were also big men. Welsh knights tended to be smaller and stockier. This would be a close call.

When we reached the road, I risked a look behind me and I saw the rebels. They were strung out as they raced across the open field we had just crossed and they were about four hundred paces behind us. I spurred Hart a little. I wanted a gap of at least six hundred paces when we forded the river to ensure that none of my men was caught. The afternoon was passing quickly and I doubted that we would reach the siege much before dark but to do that we had to lose the knights and men at arms. When we reached the river, we would have to head east and ride along its northern bank. It was there that I looked back again and saw that we had lengthened our lead and strung them out even more but none had been dropped. I saw that a couple of the horses of the men at arms were labouring. We had, however, kept our column tight and our column of twos meant that if we had to turn and fight, we would outnumber their first men and that could be vital.

I eased back ever so slightly. To those pursuing it would be imperceptible but to the two horses which were struggling it would be a slight relief. When a short time later we had almost reached the ford, which was now in sight, I saw that the enemy had closed to five hundred paces.

"When we reach the ford, Captain Alan, I want you to take your men across the river first and use your arrows from the southern bank. Leave us now and extend your lead."

"Aye Sir William! Ride!" Their horses, with a lighter load, began to stretch away from us.

"Men at arms, when we reach the wooded island in the middle of the river we stop, turn and bloody their noses. When I give the command to flee then do so! I want no heroes…Abelard!"

"Aye, lord!"

The ford had a twenty-five-pace swim followed by a long narrow island which was no more than fifteen paces wide but it was covered in shrubs and willows. When the enemy clambered out of the water they would be looking down at the bank to negotiate the passage.

I saw the ford and heard my archers splash through. The Welsh and the traitors had closed to within three hundred paces and were thrashing their weary horses in an attempt to stop us before we crossed. When we entered the water, it allowed the enemy to close with us. As I clambered on to the island, I saw that the leading Welshman was just twenty paces behind Edgar. Hart climbed wearily from the water and I rode just five paces, drew my sword and turned. I had just eight men in a line as the last of my riders struggled on to the island. We made a gap for them to pass through and then, as Captain Alan sent a shower of arrows at the men on the bank and in the water, I led my eight men at the riders who were struggling up the bank. The leading Welshman knew little about it for I lunged with my sword and it went directly into his nose, breaking it before entering his skull and killing him. My men at arms had varied success. Some of the enemy were wounded while others were either unhorsed or their weary horses baulked. I saw riderless horses in the river.

"Run!" I turned my horse and we crossed the last part of the ford which, thankfully, meant we did not have to swim. The bank was not as high and we were able to walk out.

Captain Alan said, "They have finally given up. A pity for there was some good plate there. We could be richer!"

I laughed, "We are alive and we have news. That will satisfy me. Let us dismount and walk our animals. We will sleep this night in the deserted castle at Glandyfi."

I hung my helmet on my saddle and led a weary Hart for the last mile to the castle. We had no food but we would eat well at the siege for I intended to pick up some of the hill sheep we had seen when we headed north. The banter in the camp, as men made hovels and tried to fashion comfortable beds, told me that they were all in good spirits. As I had learned in the Blue Company, silence was the worst of indicators! You wanted men talking, even if they were complaining. Silence meant that they were brooding and that was never good in a warrior. My father had been broody!

When we reached the siege, it was noon for we had risen late and, after capturing a few hill sheep, we had ridden back at a leisurely pace. Raiding a farmhouse, we found it deserted and we ate what they had before driving off the half dozen sheep that the farmer had failed to take with him. The last couple of miles were marked by the crack of the four fowlers as they continued their work.

The Prince was both relieved and pleased when we rode in. My news disturbed him a little but he took me to the walls and proudly showed me a crack which had appeared in the wall close to the gatehouse. To me, it did not look much but he was delighted.

Over the next days, we saw a second and then a third crack appear and when five days after our return the miners fired the mine, we saw the southern tower lurch and a crack appeared at the junction of the wall. The Prince was convinced that the castle would fall within the next week or so but then he received news which necessitated a change in plans. His brother, John of Lancaster, arrived by ship to tell him that he was needed in

London due to the Council and Parliament trying to take power from the King. Prince Henry was so confident that the castle would fall that he took me to one side and confided in me. "I will leave Sir Thomas here and he can finish the Welsh off. I will return to London and then we can turn our attention to Harlech. I know that your son is to be married. Take your men and ride home for the wedding and then return here."

"I do not need to, Prince Henry."

"I know but you and your men have done more of the fighting than any other. It is time that the Earl of Arundel earned his position as Lord of the Welsh Marches. I will see you back here by the end of October."

It was a generous offer but it was misguided for Sir Thomas Fitzalan, while an able administrator, was no general and I wondered what would have happened had I missed the wedding and stayed at the siege. That I shall never know.

The journey home, even though it was through the heartland of Wales, was without incident. It was late summer and the Welsh were busy with their animals and their fields. Another hard winter with tightened belts might prove to be fatal and they prepared to continue the fight. We did not know it but this was the start of the end of the rebellion. We still rode as though we might be attacked but we reached Shrewsbury without having to draw sword or nock an arrow. We still had a long way to go to reach Weedon but riding through the peaceful heart of England under summer skies was not a hardship.

It was the middle of August when we reached Weedon and I managed to surprise my wife. I think she had resigned herself to the fact that I would not attend and had grown used to the idea. My return made her weep as though she had heard the news of my death! Once she was over the shock she then began to fret and worry about my clothes and my appearance. When we had been given the manor of Dauentre the rich burghers there had looked down upon us and since then my wife was over sensitive about our appearance. She sent me to Northampton to a tailor who would make me clothes befitting a confidante of the future King.

While I was there, I spoke with my son Thomas, and told him of the siege and the cannon. "So, by the time that you return, the rebellion will be as good as over."

"I pray to God that it is for if not then the Welsh will cease to exist. I saw skeletons that had once been men tending the fields!"

"Aye, and then the Prince and his father will turn their attention to France."

I looked up from the excellent wine which my son's servants had given to me, "France?"

He smiled at me, "You have given me an easy life here in Northampton, father, and I do not waste my time. There are many visitors from far and wide who pass through the town and I speak with all of them. You know that King Charles of France is mad?"

"Aye, that is common knowledge but he is hale and hearty too."

"Yet he has but one son, the Dauphin, and the country is ruled by a council headed by his wife Queen Isabeau. It is she who rules the land and, it is said, the Duke of Burgundy, John the Fearless, is her lover." He shrugged, "That is immaterial but what you may not have heard is that John the Fearless had the King's brother, the Duke of Orleans and a potential King of France, murdered in the street by fifteen of his hired men. The new Duke of Orleans was so incensed that he sought the help of the Duke of Armagnac and now there is a civil war between Burgundy and Armagnac. The victor will rule France."

"And that is all very interesting but what has it to do with England and Prince Henry?"

"It was Louis of Orléans who took much of Gascony and it was he who supported the Welsh rebellion with knights."

"Then with his death, that threat is gone."

"Father, King Henry has a claim to France through his grandsire, King Edward and remember that Louis of Orléans challenged King Henry to single combat when King Richard died. There is bad blood between the house of Orléans and King Henry and his son. Much of Gascony is now French." He looked at me, "Surely you can see that Prince Henry is an ambitious king."

I suddenly realised that I had been so keen to protect Prince Henry that I had not looked beyond his charisma and personality. I confess I liked him and, perhaps, I had been blinded to his ambition. "It is no sin to wish to claim your inheritance."

My son spoke quietly, "You are right, father, but all that I am saying is that when Wales is subdued then the house of Lancaster will look to France and you, I fear, will not enjoy the peace of grandchildren for you will be needed to claim back Gascony and England's French lands."

I gave a rueful laugh, "I come home early and you greet me with such news!"

"I am my father's son and I do that which you would do; I speak the truth and I also know that such a venture would also result in Harry and me also going to war. I am an English knight and I will fight for my country but the thought of an extended war in France does not fill me with joy. I am not one of these knights who seek glory and booty. I am content with what we have."

I nodded, "And I thank you for your honesty. We will speak with Harry about this but not your mother. Let us not worry her."

"Harry and I have spoken of this. We have known for some time about this possibility but until the northern rebels were defeated and Wales reclaimed then there could not be another war. Now that Aberystwyth is almost ours, I thought you should know."

The news soured my preparation for the wedding of my son. What should have been a joyful time was marred by the prospect of a war in France. King Richard had been a king who sought peace and perhaps he had lost Gascony by his fears of a domestic rebellion but it would take a huge army to reclaim Gascony and that would incur such costs that Parliament might withhold the funds. Would the Earl of March, held in Windsor, be touted as a rival to the throne?

Fortunately, my wife drove all such thoughts from my head as she chivvied and chased me to ensure that when we rode north it would be in a manner befitting the Sherriff of Northampton and the man who had protected two kings of England!

Sir Humphrey Calthorpe was a rich and powerful man but he had no castle and that explained how the Sherriff of Nottingham had been able to make his life miserable. However, his hall was magnificent and large enough to accommodate all of my family. It was partly built of stone but there were elements of the original wooden hall. We were made more than welcome when we arrived for Sir Humphrey was grateful to me for the service I had performed and, I think, was pleased that his daughter was marrying into a family which held such power. For myself I did not make much of such matters but, as we rode north, my sons and son in law were at pains to point out the power I held.

"The King gave you Northampton, father, and that is the key to the defence of London from the north. That alone tells the rest of England the esteem in which he holds you."

"But, Thomas, I am just a Sherriff. There are dukes, earls and viscounts with more power than I have."

Harry laughed, "I have spoken with your men father, who did the King send to watch north? Who did Prince Henry entrust with the prosecution of the defence of the Marches? He has only left the young Earl of Arundel at Aberystwyth because the rebellion is almost over and he seeks to strengthen his position in London! Sir Humphrey knows this."

Perhaps I could not see that which was obvious to everyone else.

The celebrations and the ceremony lasted a fortnight. The two ladies were determined to make much of the marriage and Sir Humphrey was happy to spend his coin. For my part I found Elizabeth to be the perfect partner for my son Harry. He and Thomas were totally different. Harry was the lively one with a wicked sense of humour. His bride, Elizabeth, was clever, witty, but she was also quiet and thoughtful. The combination seemed to work. Added to that, the fact that they appeared to me to be totally in love with one another helped. That was not always true in such marriages.

One poignant part was that there was a spirit in the church and in the hall which none could see but my family felt. Mary was there. She and Harry had been close when they had been growing up and when Harry had first come to war with me it was he who was greeted first by his little sister. It was not just me who felt her presence. Eleanor spoke to me on the wedding night. She snuggled in to me and there were tears on my shoulder.

"Why the tears, wife? Surely this is a happy day!"

"The happiest and yet I felt sweet Mary in the chapel."

I shivered, "You felt her too? I thought it was just me."

"She is with God; I know that but this day was hers too. She would have loved Elizabeth and they would have been as sisters."

"Mary would have been wed herself by now."

"Yet she and Elizabeth would still have been close and all of the family would be happy."

It was October by the time we headed home and I was keenly aware that, having promised the Prince to return, I would have a day at home at the most for I had to return to Wales. I did not want to go but I was a man of my word and I would obey. My men had all had some time at home and they had made the most of it. All were now married, even the older ones. Each had a smallholding on my estate at Weedon and they, too, went reluctantly back to Wales. We were a quiet and sombre band of men who rode to Shrewsbury and prepared to ride to Aberystwyth. It was there we received the unwelcome news that far from reducing the walls of Aberystwyth the Earl of Arundel had been forced to fall back to Bristol. The Welsh had won. Sir John Talbot was back in Shrewsbury and he was bitter.

"Sir William, I wish that you had not returned to England! We might have won but Sir Thomas would not heed my advice nor that of Sir John Oldcastle! He knows numbers and can count but he is no general. We told him to assault the walls while we had the men but he did not and when some men deserted then others followed and our numbers became too few. He would not allow Sir John or me to do as you did and watch the north. When Glendower himself led men south we could not face them and the Earl took the cannons and the men back to Bristol and Sir John and I fought our way back here. I lost good men because of Arundel."

I felt as though I had been punched by a giant. I could barely breathe. We had been so close to victory and now it had all been taken from us. "And does the Prince know?"

"I sent him word as soon as we began to load the cannons. He will be here within a day or two. I am pleased that you are here for I would not face his wrath alone. I let him down."

The Prince had that effect on soldiers. You fought for the man as well as the title.

The Prince and his brother Thomas arrived at the start of November and his scarred face was as black as thunder. All else were dismissed and the two princes spoke to Sir John and to me. I was there, I suspect, as a witness to the words which would be spoken. Prince Henry did not enjoy berating a commander before a junior.

"So, Sir John, tell me all and leave nothing out. Know that I have spoken with the Earl of Arundel already and so I know what occurred. I seek the truth for I am angry."

Sir John might have been old enough to be the Prince's grandfather but he sweated as he recounted what he had already told me. The fact that not a word was changed told me that he had spoken the truth. I saw Prince Thomas nod once or twice and that seemed to confirm that the Earl of Arundel had been truthful.

When all was done Prince Henry nodded, "This is all my fault, or, perhaps the fault of the council, either way, I should never have left the siege before the end." He looked at me and gave me a wry smile. His scarred face made most of his smiles look strange. "And I hope the wedding went well for it has cost us dear." I was angry for it sounded to me like I was being blamed but the Prince must have sensed my anger for he then shook his head, "That was unfair of me. I sent you home because I thought that the Earl could complete what seemed to me a simple task. I was wrong. The Earl is a loyal knight but warfare is not his forte. He is now in London where he can organise the council and perhaps be Chancellor. That I know he can do and it means that I can stay here in Wales and end the rebellion once and for all."

We spent many hours with the two princes. It was from that time that Prince Thomas became his brother's aide, at least until they had a falling out but that was in the future. He was a loyal brother but a shadow of Prince Henry. I liked him for he would do anything for Prince Henry. We learned that the siege would be renewed in the spring. The Earl of Arundel's task was to weed out the members of the council who might oppose his plans so that we could bring a larger army to Wales. It was the start of an attempt by the Prince to marginalise his father. He was not usurping the throne but he was ensuring that England and the crown were safer.

I stayed for a month for the Prince wished me to help him inspect the border defences. While we rode, I learned that my son had been right. Prince Henry did have designs on France. When the rebellion was over, he would look across the Channel. "I believe, Sir William, that we can exploit the French divisions. I think that I will make overtures and form an alliance with Burgundy. They have no ambitions for England and it was Orléans which invaded Wales."

"But, Prince Henry, what of your father?"

"He is ill, Will, and I would take some of the burden from his shoulders."

I knew Henry Bolingbroke and I was not certain that his father would see it that way.

"And I am also strengthening the council with younger men who have vision. My uncles, the Beauforts, along with the Bishop of Durham and the Bishop of Bath and Wells have all shown that they are loyal to England and the House of Lancaster. With a strong council, we can neutralise Parliament and ensure we have monies for a foreign war. It will be an investment for Gascony and France are rich countries."

I started for he was no longer speaking of just reclaiming English land but the crown of France, "France, Your Highness?"

"My grandsire, King Edward III, was heir to the French throne through his mother, Isabella of France. He had more of a claim to the French crown than the man they gave it to, for Philip of Valois was a cousin of the King."

It struck me that they were looking back almost eighty years but there was little point in arguing with him for I was not learned enough to do so.

"I know that you will keep these confidences to yourself for first we must subdue the Welsh and this time you shall be my hammer to destroy my enemies. We will take both castles next year and then I shall return to London where I will begin my plans to conquer France and you, Strongstaff, will be at my side."

As my men and I headed home I was conflicted. I wished to serve my country and my King but I would, once again, be sent away from my family. More, my sons and son in law would be involved too. I had grandsons who would grow up without a father unless Prince Henry won a swift victory in France. All that I had learned would have to stay with me for I had been told in confidence. It was a burden I would bear alone.

Chapter 14

We returned in January through a bleak snow-covered land to muster with the rest of the army in Shrewsbury. Half of the army was already there and the rest would arrive soon. Once again, the Prince would sail from Bristol with his cannon. His younger brother had returned to Ireland and his place had been taken by Humphrey, another brother. I was not sure why Thomas had been sent away but then again, Prince Henry was increasingly a man of secrets. This time the Earl of Westmoreland, Sir Ralph Neville, was with us and that meant Red Ralph's son, Ralph, and his men were there too. It would be good to fight alongside the son of my mentor. He now had a family and a son to carry on the family name. In the tradition of his family he, too, was named Ralph.

We left for Aberystwyth at the end of January. I thought it too soon to travel for the roads would be appalling but the message came from the Prince and after the debacle of the previous year no one would gainsay him. In the end, the journey through the frozen heartland of Wales proved to be safer than when we had done the same journey the previous year. The ground was so frozen that even the land not traversed by roads was hard enough for wagons. We had carts with food, fodder and arrows and we were not attacked. Even better was the fact that there was neither snow nor frozen ground by the time we reached Aberystwyth and we occupied the town once more. The Welsh must have thought us beaten for they had neither repaired their castle walls nor removed our trenches. It was but a week's work to put back in place the defences around the castle.

Dafydd Gam was with us once more and we learned that it had been he who had advised the Prince to return so quickly. "I scouted the walls in December, Sir William, and saw that they had been lax. More, I knew that they had not replaced the food stores laid in for a siege."

I was curious, "How did you manage that?"

He grinned, "Why, we sneaked inside and pretended to be merchants. We bought some of the empty barrels in which they had stored their food and saw their cellars. They were empty as they had not yet replenished them. I had men watching and no wagons have brought food yet. We can starve them out."

We were standing at a window of the tallest house in Aberystwyth and looking towards the east gate when I pointed to the gatehouse, "Those cracks are worse than when I was here last and that may be down to the ice and frost. The gatehouse might fall soon enough."

"Aye, lord, you are right, nature came to the aid of the true Prince of Wales. The frost and ice enlarged the cracks which the cannons had begun. See, the mortar needs to be replaced for the early winter was harsh and they cannot make mortar when it is this cold."

This time, when the ships and the cannon arrived, I saw a change in both the gunners and the Prince. He had learned his lessons and they unloaded stone missiles to be used by the cannons. He had also brought more archers at his own expense. In addition, he brought three knights with horsed archers. I knew Thomas, Lord Camoys for I had fought alongside him before. He brought twenty men at arms and sixty horse archers. They were as good as my men. Sir Walter Hungerford was a knight who, like me, was an advocate of horsed archers. Unfortunately, he was also one of the bluntest men I knew and had a habit of speaking first and thinking later. It would bring him into conflict with the Prince. And then there was Thomas Chaucer, he was young and was an Esquire. He brought thirty horsed archers and five men at arms. I knew him a little for his father, who was a writer and served the King in London, Geoffrey Chaucer, had stayed at Weedon on his way to York. All in all, I was more confident.

The King sent a large number of his men, led by Sir John Talbot, to cut off Harlech. He gave strict instructions that Sir John was not to begin an attack until he arrived but he was to ensure that they received no supplies. They, too, would begin to starve.

The bombardment began in the middle of February when the snow still lay on the mountains to the east. We did not bother with a mine for we had a breached wall already but the Prince wished to make a two-fold attack. We had spent many hours devising the plan. When the gatehouse wall was breached then we would attack the two breaches with men at arms. Once the southern tower was in our hands then we would use our superiority in archers to rain arrows on the defenders of the inner wall whilst attacking the barbican keep with all of our men at arms.

Each day I went with the Prince and Lord Camoys to view the cannons and this time I saw that they were effective. The gunners had improved and they now concentrated their rocks on the same spot. Their first volley would be with all four fowlers at the same time. The combined noise was terrifying to hear but the collective strike of four heavy rocks which had taken two men to load began to take effect. Then the cannons would be fired individually to hit the same spot. The result was that after a week the cracks in the wall were clear for all to see. The Prince was so confident that we could soon attack that he sent half of the men at arms and the archers to the southern tower by the river and told us to prepare to follow him into the breach.

This time the gunners began to batter the wall at the point just above the earthen rampart. Above it, the walls had serious cracks and we had heard the defenders shoring them up with wood. The first four rocks struck stones in the wall which had yet to be hit. The effect was staggering. A huge section of crenulated wall tumbled into the ditch and the cracks became wider. Instead of employing the same technique as previously the Master Gunner ordered all four cannons to be reloaded and to fire at the same time. The process was still no quicker and almost an hour elapsed between firing. I understood the reason. The barrels were washed out so that when more gunpowder was placed in them they did not ignite. The second volley was even more successful and a huge section of the upper wall cascaded into the ditch thereby making a bridge. Even as they loaded the cannons again there was a rumble and a crack and more of the wall fell into the ditch. We could now see the shoring and the barbican keep. More importantly, we could see the inner gates were open. Prince Henry showed, that day, how much he had learned. He raised his sword and shouted, "God, for England, St. George and King Henry!" He led us towards the breach. Sir John Oldcastle was waiting at the southern tower and, raising his sword, he led the other half towards the damaged wall.

I stayed as close to the Prince as I could manage. The Earl of Westmoreland was on the other side of him and Sir Ralph of Middleham Tyas was close to my side. We had caught the Welsh unawares. They had been expecting a longer bombardment and half of the defenders were busy trying to repair the damage. The walls on either side of the breach were unmanned and neither arrows nor bolts came our way. We scrambled over the fallen masonry and then clambered over the remains of the wall. It was then that we should have been exposed and subject to attacks from the defenders but men who are repairing walls might wear mail and plate but their hands are filled not with weapons but tools. The speed of our attack took them by surprise and they raced for the barbican keep within. I heard Welsh voices shouting as a few arrows and bolts came belatedly from the barbican keep but the Prince and we bore a charmed life. The Welsh were trying to close the gates to the barbican keep. One brave Welshman swung at me with his mattock but Ralph remembered his time with me as a squire and took the man's arm with one swipe of his sword. I knew as we neared them that even if they closed them then more than a third of their defenders would still be trapped outside their walls for Sir John had trapped many men on the south-eastern wall.

I already knew the Prince to be both brave and fearless but that day showed that he had taken those attributes to a different level. Even though the gates were closing he hacked and slashed at the Welsh who were still trying to get inside. I managed to use my long arms and long sword to bring it down and split the head and back of a huge Welsh blacksmith who was trying to swing his hammer at the Prince. He had no mail and I laid his flesh open to the bone. More importantly, his bulk filled the gap and the Prince stepped lithely through followed by my former squire, Ralph.

Shouting, "Save the Prince!" I threw myself through.

Rather than waiting for help the Prince and Ralph were racing after the fleeing Welsh to the second gate. I did not look around and I just prayed that the Earl of Westmoreland and the rest were securing the first gate behind me. As it was, we had to take the second gate or risk being trapped between the two gates and I knew that there were many murder holes both above us and to the side. The Prince and Ralph had been held up by four men who were blocking the gates which were slowly closing behind them.

Behind me, I heard Abelard shout, "I am with you, lord!"

I shouted to the Prince and Ralph, "The Strongstaff comes!"

I ran at the two young warriors who had fought at my side and I counted on the fact that they would push to the sides and allow a gap for me to step into it. I had no intention of doing so. Instead, I would become a human missile. Holding my sword in two hands I hurled myself at the tiny gap between Prince Henry and Ralph. I knocked both of them and the men they were fighting to the side. I hoped Abelard had my back and I struck the two Welshmen standing in the narrowing gap with my sword and shield. Abelard was pushing behind me and the strength he had accrued training with his father propelled the two of us through the gap. My sword caught under the Welshman's breastplate and entered his body. Abelard's charge pushed me forward and I lost my grip on my sword. I leapt to my feet and drew my rondel dagger.

The men who had been pushing closed the gates now turned their attention to me. One grabbed a spear and ran at me. I had my mail gauntlets and I deflected the spear but it tore through the leather strap on my shield. It fell from my arm while the man ran into my dagger which tore into his throat. Still holding the dagger, I grabbed his spear and swashed it before me. When they fell back a little, I reversed it so that I was pointing the metal head at them. Abelard's backplate touched mine and the two of us faced the defenders as the Prince and the others pushed at the gates to attempt to secure the entry of the rest of our men. My spearhead caught one Welshman in the eye and I then lunged at his fellow. I caught him in the shoulder between metal plates and, as he fell backwards, he dragged the spear from my hands.

Seeing his chance, a Welsh Esquire wearing a mail hauberk ran at me with his sword and buckler shield. I held my dagger in my right hand and with my left grabbed the blade. My strength surprised him; I saw it in his eyes. I hooked my right leg around his left and pushed, using his shield to help me. He tumbled backwards and I used my right foot to stamp on his face. He was rendered unconscious. I ran at the two men who were still pushing on the opening gate. I stabbed one in the side and the other fled through the door into the keep. Suddenly the gates burst open and the Earl of Westmoreland led our men at arms and knights to flood into the inner bailey.

Turning I saw that the Prince, Ralph and Abelard were alive and unhurt, I grabbed my sword and looked for enemies. There were none and I saw the door to the southern part of the barbican keep was open. The man who had fled from me had been so frightened that he had forgotten to close it. I shouted, "Follow me!" and ran inside the door and up the spiral staircase. I was lucky that the last man had been so afraid. Had he had the courage then he could have stopped me from ascending. As it was, I found no-one until I reached the first floor. I knew that I had pushed my luck already and so I stood, panting to catch my breath while my men raced up.

Captain Edgar and Stephen of Morpeth were the first through the door. My Captain shook his head, "My lord we have others who can risk their lives!"

I laughed but I was too out of breath to speak. There were twelve men before us but, somehow, our bloody weapons and my surcoat covered in gore and blood seemed to intimidate them. The Prince stepped into the chamber followed by the Earl of Westmoreland.

"Throw down your weapons and I will let you live." I had never heard such command in a voice that was not mine. They hesitated and the Prince shouted, "Do it!" The weapons clattered to the wooden floor. He then shouted, "Those who are above us, you have a choice, surrender or I will burn down the keep with you within it!"

It was draconian and meant that the barbican keep would have to be rebuilt before we could use it.

A Welsh voice from above shouted, "Do your worst! English bastard!"

The Prince said, quite calmly, "Earl, have men fetch kindling and torches."

"Aye, lord. Fetch kindling and torches." Some of the earl's men left us

One of the men who had surrendered shouted to their comrades above, "He means to do it! The castle is lost!"

The Welsh voice shouted back down, "It matters not, we will fight to the end."

We heard an argument break out above us as the earl's men began to pile kindling at the bottom of the ladder leading to the upper floors of the keep. We understood not a word for it was in Welsh but then we heard the clash of steel and a cry before a body crashed down on to the kindling. The belligerent warrior had been silenced by his peers.

"We surrender and we will come down."

And so the siege was ended. The Prince was not as pleased as one might have expected because this would have been the result the previous year if his orders had been obeyed and if it had been better led.

The townsfolk returned to their homes but there was precious little food for them. The Earl of Westmoreland and I persuaded the Prince that it was in his interests to feed them. He did so, albeit reluctantly. He had the men who had surrendered manacled and told them that although he would keep his word and let them live, before he would grant them their freedom they had to repair the damage to the castle. The work was well underway by the time we prepared to head north to Harlech, the last bastion of the Welsh rebels and the place where Sir Edmund Mortimer and Owain Glendower had taken refuge. It was becoming a little warmer when we did so. It was still a cold and inhospitable land through which we travelled but the lengthening days promised warmer weather to come. Messengers had been sent to alert the garrison at Caernarfon and to raise the levy of Cheshire to bring their archers to our aid. The cannons were sent by ship and they would land close to the camp of Sir John Talbot. The Prince was leaving nothing to chance.

The same problems which had beset Aberystwyth now beset Harlech. Trapped inside their castle the defenders had not had time to lay in supplies of food. Added to that their numbers were swollen by the arrival of refugees and they would already be on short rations.

After joining Sir John and the men who were surrounding the castle, the Prince went to speak with the besieged. This time he took a delegation with him, including Dafydd Gam who had become an integral part of the Prince's retinue since this campaign had begun. The Prince had us ride horses for he wished to be closer to their eye level. The two rebels appeared with armed and mailed knights close to them. I recognised some of the English ones and they glared daggers at us. Mortimer did not look a well man. He was thin and emaciated while Glendower looked little different from the last time I had seen him.

The Prince took charge and that was another difference I had noticed since he had returned from London. He seemed driven and yet in perfect control of himself. "I am here to demand your surrender. Aberystwyth has fallen and I showed mercy to the defenders. Surrender and I will afford the same to you."

Glendower laughed but Sir Edmund Mortimer asked, "All of us?" Glendower flashed him a look of pure scorn.

The Prince shook his head, "No, Sir Edmund. You and Glendower will be tried by a jury of your peers for the crime of treason."

Glendower jabbed a finger at the Prince, "How can I be tried for treason? I have done nothing against the rightful ruler of my land for that is me."

Mortimer looked angry too, "And where are my nephews? Where is the Earl of March? Are they safe?"

"They are safe and neither have any desire to become King of England. In fact, when I attain the crown, I shall release them for I believe they are both loyal subjects and they are kept as guests and not as prisoners."

"And my son and family?"

"Are treated well, too, Glendower, but they are closely guarded for unlike Edmund and Roger Mortimer they are not to be trusted."

"Then my answer is that we will not surrender."

"Will you allow the women to leave the castle?"

Sir Edmund said, "My wife is the only woman within these walls and she swears that she will stay by side."

As she was not present, I found that hard to believe. He was making an assumption.

"Then there is no more to be said. May God have mercy on your souls."

We headed back to our camp which was in the tiny town of Harlech.

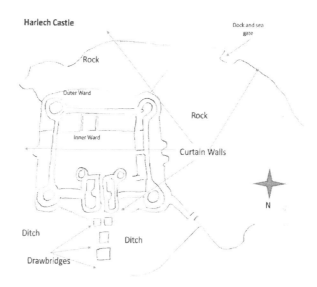

The gunners had a problem for the castle was built upon solid rock and the only places we could attack were on the south and the east curtain walls. Even when we battered them into submission, we could not then use our cannons to take on their formidable walls. That would have to be an assault by men and it would be costly.

Once again, the gunners showed that they had learned from the sieges of Aberystwyth and the guns were in position and firing within a day. We had no reason to raid and so we watched each day as the stone balls battered holes in the curtain walls. It took just three days to make inroads and then disaster struck. The gun they called The King's Daughter exploded, much to the delight of the defenders who cheered as though the siege had been relieved. One of the master gunners and eight gunners died. It was lucky that neither the Prince nor any other leader was hurt for we would normally have been close but as a ship had arrived with messages from Bristol we were by the shore. With only three guns to fire and a slower rate due to the caution the remaining gunners took progress was slow but, by the end of the second week, the curtain wall was destroyed and the gate had been hit a number of times. This time the gunners had aimed at the smaller gatehouses and the gates.

I spent many hours watching the men on the walls. I took the Prince to one side one morning and pointed out the men on the walls. "Prince Henry, what do you notice about the men on the walls?"

He was short-tempered because of the accident with the gun and he was curt, "They are on the walls! That is what I notice and we have not taken the castle!"

I sighed, "Firstly, Your Highness, there are fewer of them today than there were yesterday and if you notice, even at this distance they look thin and in need of a good meal."

He looked at them again, "You may be right. What does this portend? Are they protecting their men for they do not think we will assault?"

"I think that the siege is beginning to bite, Prince Henry."

"Should we make an assault?"

I did not want to say yes for men would die but the professional in me thought that this was a good time.

"Perhaps we make an evening assault for they will not expect it. We could make a feint on one side and then use ladders and bridges to cross the ditches." The castle had a double drawbridge but the defences there had been destroyed by the cannons and the obstacle that would hurt us was the ditch. We would need bridges.

"Then have the bridges built now and we will attack tomorrow at dusk. Have the work completed away from the camp so that they do not know what is afoot."

The men enjoyed having something to do and the bridges were completed before nightfall. The next day our men rested during the hours of daylight although the rest was not sleep for the guns kept up a constant bombardment on the gate and gatehouse all day. In hindsight, the lack of men on duty could have warned them of our impending attack. When darkness fell, the curtain wall remained intact but it was a small low wall and men with shields could easily scale it. We had our men prepare to attack. Sir John Talbot and his men were ready for an attack on the south wall. They would begin the attack to draw the defenders thence. While that attack began, we would put our bridges into place and then attack silently. Our archers would try to pick off men on the walls. It was as good a plan as we could manage and I lined up with the Prince again. He refused to go in the second wave and that meant that I would go with him.

As we lined up with the men at arms holding the bridges and ladders, I saw that Sir Ralph was closer to me than his liege lord, the Earl of Westmoreland and that my men at arms had placed themselves immediately behind me. They were not taking any chances this time! We heard the sound of battle as Sir John and his men sneaked close to the wall and then used archers to slay the sentries. There was a single cry and then, from within Harlech came the sound of the alarm. Then we heard the clash of steel as men fought. Sir John had strict orders not to risk his men. He was to draw attention and that was all.

The Prince waited; I think he was counting in his head and then he stood and raised his sword. Silently the men at arms picked up the bridges and the ladders and we headed across the open ground to the ditches which lay between us and the castle. There were two of them. Our archers followed and when I heard the twang of a bowstring and heard the whoosh of the arrow then I knew a sentry had seen us. He fell without a cry but his body fell on to the roof of a building below the fighting platform. That another sentry would see us soon was obvious and it added urgency to our pace. The first two bridges were laid across and the Prince led men over one and I the other. We then held up our shields as we waited for the second bridges to be brought. There was a strangled cry from the wall as a second sentry was slain but this cry would bring more men and when the second bridge was across, I ran as soon as it struck the stone next to the wall of the gatehouse. The gates had been destroyed and my reckless run ensured that I beat the Prince and ran towards the huge barbican which was the real entrance to the castle.

Some of the stones had struck the main gate but as it had metal strips it was largely undamaged. The men at arms with the ladders made their way down the wall. Once we had created a hole in the gate they would ascend and attack the inner wall. The Prince and I stayed at the gate where we had twelve men at arms with axes and as more defenders arrived at the barbican they began to hack and hew at the wooden gate. Axes were blunted by the metal strips but we had spares and the men hacked and chopped until they were too weary to continue and another would take over.

Stones were dropped upon us but our archers limited their efficacy. I could hear the defenders bracing the gate. Then the first sliver of light could be seen as a lump of the gate fell.

The Prince shouted, "Ladders away!"

The sound of the eight ladders hitting the walls gave the axemen hope for it meant we were splitting the attention of the garrison in three directions. As soon as the men reached the wall, we would have a chance and the axemen switched with fresh men and axes and renewed their attack.

Sir John Oldcastle was with us and he shouted, "Let us rush at the gate for I can see that the bar is damaged." We all nodded. He grinned at Prince Henry, "I think, my lord, that we use the men with larger bellies for this, eh Strongstaff?"

I was not insulted and I nodded, "Aye. Let us go on three!" I locked my shield with his and Lord Camoys joined us with six other large men. We stepped back a few paces and I shouted, "One, two, three!" On three we ran and hit the gate. There was still some resistance but our weight did it and the gate cracked asunder. We poured into the castle.

The Prince shouted, "Sound the horn!" It was the signal for Sir John Talbot to withdraw his men and support our attack.

As we raced into the castle men threw themselves at us to try to slow down our progress. Archers sent arrows at us and if I had not held my shield up then the bodkin arrow sent at me would have pierced my breastplate and mail rather than just my shield. As I blocked a blow from a small Welshman with an axe the Welsh arrow embedded in my shield hit him in the eye. Gouging out the orb should have slowed him down but it did not and he hacked at me. I blocked his blow and rammed my sword up under his arm and into his neck.

The door to the guardhouse was open and that guarded the stairs to the barbican. Shouting, "To me, Weedon!" I ran towards it. As I burst in men were descending from the fighting platform to clear the entrance to the castle. The first Welshman died because he had not seen me appear and I thrust upwards when he was on the staircase just ahead of me. His momentum took him over my shoulder and I rammed my shield with the embedded arrow towards the next man. He saw it and he jumped to the side of me where Abelard thrust his sword into his side between back and breastplate. The four who were still on the stairs ran back up. We now had the guardhouse and I had eight of my men with me. I headed for the stairs where, as I ascended, I kept my shoulder to the wall. Any Welshman coming down the staircase would have an advantage but their lack of numbers had undone them. I was moving as fast as the men I was pursuing and when I reached the first floor of the barbican I discovered a huge room. This was a great hall and I saw the Welshmen disappearing through a door to the next floor.

That they were weak became obvious when I caught up with one who should have been able to outrun a knight who had seen over fifty summers. I slashed across the back of his leg where there was no protection and ripped through the tendons. As his knee collapsed, I pressed into the side and shouted, "Ware below!" as he tumbled down the spiral staircase. The chamber at the top of the barbican was empty and the door to the fighting platform was ajar. I was not a fool and I was out of breath and so, once more, I waited for my men. Captain Edgar and Stephen of Morpeth were the first with me and I nodded to the door. Stephen held his shield before him and faced the opening as Captain Edgar kicked it in. The arrow which came at Stephen of Morpeth drove halfway through his shield and almost touched his helmet. My northern warrior did not hesitate but raced through before the bowman could nock another arrow. I heard a cry as the archer died and then Captain Edgar led my men through to the platform. I heard his stentorian tones as he shouted, "Lay down your weapons you miserable apologies for men or we will butcher you where you stand!"

As I stepped through to the top of the barbican and the fighting platform, I heard swords, spears and bows fall to the floor. We had the barbican and as I went to the edge to view the inner bailey, I saw the Prince's men flooding across to take the Great Hall and the chambers to the west. We had won but had we ended the rebellion and captured Glendower and Mortimer?

By the time we had cleared the walls and collected the prisoners then a chilly dawn was breaking. The Prince and the Earl of Westmoreland were in the Great Hall. I looked at the Prince, "Glendower and Mortimer?"

He pointed to a door which led to a staircase. "Mortimer and his lady are dead. It looks like they starved to death."

I shook my head, "And yet others who were lowlier did not."

"I cannot explain it but their bodies are laid out upon their bed."

I could explain it. King Richard had done the same thing; he had purposely not eaten to die of starvation. It was not suicide and so they would not be denied heaven. As soon as Aberystwyth had fallen then they would have known that there was no hope and that the rebellion was over. All of the major castles in the north, east and south-east were now in English hands and the road to the Gower was barred. They would surrender without a siege.

"And Glendower?"

The Prince looked annoyed, "I have men searching the bodies for him. I assume he was not in the barbican?"

"No, Prince Henry, there were few knights or men of breeding there."

Just then Sir John Talbot entered with an archer, "Prince Henry, you should hear this man."

"Speak."

"My lord, I was on watch at the south-west tower awaiting the orders to begin the attack. Almost as soon as the attack began, I saw a small boat push off from the dock and head north."

I saw the Prince clench and unclench his fists. Glendower was as slippery as an eel and had a sense of self-preservation which I had to admire.

Sir John said, "We attacked as commanded and then Robert here told us when the horn sounded. We investigated the dock and saw signs of a hurried departure. From the footprints which led from the castle, there were half a dozen men."

There were some purses on the table and the Prince, smiling ruefully, threw one to the archer, "You have done well, for now we know the worst." The grateful archer left and the Prince said, "And I thought the rebellion was over."

I said, "And it is. True, Glendower is at large, Prince Henry, but did you not hear the words of the archer? Glendower went north. Your ships were to the south and he could not go there. He has to go to the Clwyd for that is the only river which is not guarded by a castle. He cannot get to the south. When word of the defeat gets out then the castles in the south-west will have to surrender. His knights and nobles are dead or they have left him. We killed all that were loyal here and at Aberystwyth."

"Are you just telling me what I wish to hear so that you may go home, Strongstaff?"

"I have served King Richard and your father. I have served you. Tell me, Prince Henry, when have I ever done that?"

"You are right and to speak truthfully, in my heart I know that you are right but I wished to try and then hang the traitor!"

"And sometimes, Prince Henry, we cannot have that which we most want."

"Then I shall take my ships and head to the Gower. When they are in my hands I shall return to London. All those who are here shall be rewarded. Mortimer's lands are forfeit and he and his wife brought their treasure with them. Glendower also left his monies. Every man will be richer. Following the white swan is worthwhile, eh?"

Chapter 15

The rebellion was indeed over. As we headed home, I began to anticipate a period of peace. I had done all that King Henry had asked of me and helped his son to regain his birthright. I wondered if I could persuade the King to allow my son to become Sherriff of Northampton for he had done the work since Shrewsbury five years since. I was the titular Sherriff and that was all. I looked forward to spending time with my family and especially my four grandchildren.

We reached home by the start of summer which was a green and verdant time in this rich part of England. In contrast to the stark rock and snow-covered peaks of Wales, this was a land filled with growing crops and fields full of grazing, well fed animals. There might have been war in the north and the west but the southern part of the land had enjoyed peace since before Shrewsbury. The nearest that war had come had been Bramham Moor. The men I had sent on ahead had warned my wife of my arrival so that I was greeted by my sons, son in law, Mary and Alice, not to mention my grandchildren. Weedon was not London but it felt like that as I rode past the village green to be greeted by cheering family and tenants. Normally I would arrive home almost apologetically but the victory had been proclaimed by the Prince's men in every town in England. He had won and he wanted the land to know. When we had travelled east, we had heard church bells ringing in celebration and we had been feted in every town and castle but they were as nothing compared with the welcome when I reached my home.

The extensions to the hall were completed and so we dined in a Great Hall which was almost as large as the one in King Richard's favourite home, Eltham Palace. As I walked through the hallway the manor house was filled with laughter and squeals from all. The grandchildren were vociferous and I could barely hear my wife as she first kissed and hugged me and then whispered in my ear, "Welcome home, my hero, tonight we celebrate and the children will stay a week." She pulled away and laughing, shouted, "We may not hear ourselves think but what of that? We have you home and the family are together."

And I enjoyed peace if not the quiet. For the first time, I had a whole year without being called upon to fight or to go to war. I enjoyed the birth of my third grandson, Humphrey, named after his other grandfather and I saw my daughter and daughters in law all become pregnant in that year of peace. I took over the role of Sherriff and enjoyed not only the company of my family but also my tenants. My men at arms and my archers all prospered and their families grew. Abelard had been one of the first to join my service but now there were others who would, within the next year or two become archers and men at arms. My retinue was made up of men who had the income of a gentleman. The wars in which we had fought had been good for us and for that I thanked God. I knew that most men did not enjoy as many riches from such conflict.

I even managed to visit with Old Tom and Peter the Priest as well as Mistress Mary. In Old Tom's case, it was to visit his grave for he had died, peacefully in his bed. He had died without family but his standing was such that the priest told me the church was so full that most of the mourners were without. I knelt and told Old Tom of my family knowing that he would be listening in heaven for he had been a good man and had lived a good life.

Peter the Priest was still alive but now was infirm and was enjoying the benefits of the alms house. I sent a stipend once a year for its upkeep and Peter was the one who benefitted the most. It was hard to look at the old man who appeared to have shrunk. I still remembered the mighty warrior from Spain. He still had his memory and his eyes still sparkled when I told him of our campaigns.

"Here in York, we have many travellers and I still frequent *'The Saddle'*. The landlord keeps me informed of all that goes on in the world and I have heard of your deeds and your young Prince. I heard that you saved the day at Bramham Moor."

I shook my head, "Peter, you know that no one man saves the day. I led good men and used all that you and the others taught me. The victory that day was as much down to you as to me."

"You do yourself a disservice. Old Tom, Red Ralph and I all saw, in you, something that was special. Perhaps you are like a fine sword. You needed the tempering of your father and his temper to make you the man you have become and I am proud to call you a friend." I had told him that Tom had died and he said, "Soon you will be the last of the Blue Company. You should know that while you live the company lives too."

I said, "It will live on for my sons know the tale and when I am too old to war and sit entertaining my grandchildren, I shall enliven their lives with tales of the Blue Company."

When I left, after three days, I did not know that it would be the last time I would see him but we had said all that needed to be said and I was content.

Of course, when I was at home I learned of the wider world and of the in-fighting between the Royals for it was not just the King and his sons. There was the extended family, the Beauforts, the Mortimers, the Beauchamps and the Hollands. Prince Henry and his brother fell out because Prince Thomas married Margaret Holland, the widow of John Beaufort, his uncle. That was not a major problem but when Prince Thomas tried to claim the estates it brought him into conflict with Henry Beaufort, the Bishop of Winchester. The Prince of Wales and his uncle were close and the Bishop was a staunch ally of Henry. It meant that Thomas was driven to side with his father in the internal squabbles of the Lancasters. Prince Henry was, in effect, running England for his father was still ill and something of a recluse. My year and more of peace ended when King Henry sent for me and I travelled, with a handful of men, to Windsor where, for the first time in over two years, I met with the King of England.

I expected to see a shell of a man for he had rarely been seen in public and, I confess, that as I headed towards Windsor I wondered if this might be the preface for an announcement of abdication. Prince Henry ruled England and, as he was now twenty-three, he was a man who could rule the Kingdom. I was in for a shock.

The man who greeted me seemed to have healthier skin than even five years earlier. He was also more alert and had bright eyes which bored into me. This was Henry Bolingbroke reborn. I was never much of a dissembler and the King laughed, "Will Strongstaff, I have missed you and your honest face. Aye, I am somewhat recovered. The doctors say it may not last but while I am in better health, I thought to take my Kingdom back!"

It was as blunt a statement as I could have expected. I looked around and saw that we were completely alone in his chamber. He waved me to a seat and poured us both a goblet of wine. "You do look better than you did the last time I saw you, Your Majesty, but what mean you, take back your Kingdom? Has Prince Henry usurped you?"

He laughed, "As blunt as ever. No, he has not usurped me but the Council is now made up of those who support him. I languish here without an ally on the Council"

"And do you need one?"

"It is my Kingdom." He sipped his wine and I saw him self-consciously touch the skin which, while not completely healed, was far less angry than it had been the last time, I had seen him. He smiled at me, "You are above politics and still the one man I trust more than any other in the whole Kingdom. I say this for I know you are close to my son, Henry."

"And that was at your command, King Henry. It was you asked me to help him recover his lands."

"To the point and as true as ever. Yet now he makes decisions and determines policies which should be mine to make. I did not ask you here as a politician but as a soldier." My heart sank for my year and more of peace was ending. "You know that there is discord in France?" I nodded. "There are two factions: the Burgundians led by John the Fearless and the Armagnacs and the Duke of Orléans who support the Dauphin. I have decided to throw England's hat into the ring."

I took a draught of wine. It was, as I had expected, the best. I was not surprised for I still kept an ear to the ground and I had heard whispers of the Prince's plans. "And Prince Henry wishes to support the Burgundians."

"There you have it. I would prefer to see which leader gives us a better offer. Our longbows, as you have so ably shown in the past, can defeat any enemy. Whoever we support will win. To that end, I intend to lead the army which will travel to France in September myself."

"Will the council grant you the funds you need?"

He gave me a smile which I had seen regularly when he was Henry Bolingbroke and sought the crown. It was the schemer reborn. "I have, as commanders of the army, Arundel, Warwick and Bishop Henry Chichele." It became clear what he planned. "They are all allies of my son. I will not say which side we will support for that should be secret anyway and then, when we land, will give our support to the one who comes to us with the best offer. I will regain Gascony, hopefully, without losing a man!"

I saw it all clearly and I slumped back in my seat, "And the last appointment will be William Strongstaff who is seen as the Prince's right hand."

"Clever as ever. I know that you are loyal and with you as my chief adviser then we will defeat whichever faction we fight and when I return with the same sort of success which my son enjoyed in Wales, I will reclaim my throne and replace the Council with my own men."

I did not like being used but it was a clever plan. However, if I was the one making the decision then I would have sided with the Duke of Burgundy. As usual, this would not be my decision. "And when do you need me?"

"Bring your men and knights to Dover by August. I will meet you there and we shall sail in *'Trinité Royale'*, my new ship. When we land in Calais I shall send for the emissaries of both armies. With luck we shall not even need to draw sword for our army will sway the balance of power!"

When I left, two days later, I had spoken with him at length and I knew the King's mind and saw a Henry Bolingbroke reborn. I had sworn an oath and I would keep my word. At least I would not have to fight Prince Henry and fighting Frenchmen was never a problem for an Englishman. I had fought them in Spain when I had been in the Blue Company and in Wales too. I just wondered if I was getting too old.

I had some months before I needed to begin preparations in earnest but I sent for my knights, Sir John of Dauentre, Sir Henry of Stratford, Sir Richard of Kislingbury and my two sons. They were each expected to bring men at arms and archers. I knew that Sir Henry had not been to war for some time and he might have allowed his numbers to fall. I summoned them to Northampton where I told them that we would be sailing to Calais but no more than that. In truth, I could not tell them more for I did not yet know with whom we would be fighting. Sir John would be taking his two sons as squires and Sir Henry of Stratford would be taking his son. I knew that my elder grandsons, even though far too young to be even considered as pages, would be distraught that they were being left at home.

Sir Henry of Stratford had been with me the longest and was almost forty years old. He had been with me on the early campaigns and knew King Henry well. It was he voiced the worries that they would all be feeling. "So, Sir William, we go to France, prepared to fight a war but we will not know whom we fight?"

I nodded, weakly.

My son, Thomas said, "Then we may not need to fight at all?"

"There is that possibility."

"So, who bears the expense of the venture?"

"I confess, Thomas, that we did not discuss that but as I am the one who agreed to support the King, I will guarantee that none of you are out of pocket."

Harry shook his head, "That is not right, father! You have done more than enough for the house of Lancaster!"

I banged my hands on the table for the talk was becoming rebellious, "And I will continue to do so for none of us would be in the position we are but for King Henry and his cousin. They were the ones who gave me my manors and good ones they were. You have all travelled north and seen how hard is the life in Yorkshire and Northumberland and would any of you even consider a manor in Wales? Whatever I have I owe to the King and I have given you all that I can. That is an end to the matter." I saw the shock on their faces.

John, Henry and Richard were all older than my sons. They were aware of my journey but my sons had been born the sons of a rich and prosperous man. I think that meeting was the first time they understood how privileged they were. Once I had cleared the air then we got to the serious meat of the matter. We had to work out how many men, horses, arrows and spare weapons we would need. As we would be in Calais at first the provender would come from the King and if we went to war then we would take from whichever enemies the King chose. It was easier from that moment on as they all understood how to prepare for war.

My knights all stayed the night and we enjoyed a fine feast with venison which had hung for a month. I used my best wine. If we were going to war in France then it could be easily replaced even if we took it from the cellars of our enemies.

Harry felt bad about his outburst and he came to speak with me as we ate some fine, aged cheese, "I am sorry for my words, father. Young Humphrey does not sleep well and …"

I smiled and patted the back of his hand, "And I was not offended. If you cannot speak that which is in your heart then my table is badly run. What you do not know, Harry, is that the Prince paid us well for the sieges. He used punitive fines for all those who rebelled and he took land from them. The money I may have to spend is not that which we have saved for it was given to me as a reward for what we did for him."

He nodded, "And Glendower?"

"He hides somewhere. The rebellion is over and the fact that he has not been seen leads some to believe that he is dead. I doubt that for the man has more lives than a cat but he can do nothing from his hidey-hole in the vastness of the Welsh mountains. He can rule that part of Wales for there is nothing there worth fighting for. Let him listen to his Welsh songs of Llewellyn the Great for that is all that they have, memories."

After they had left the hall felt empty and I did too. It had been some time since I had had all of my knights together. All had been squires and I knew each of them as well as any man. That set me to thinking about my men at arms and archers. I had no more manors to give but I had the power to raise them. I decided to make my captains, Esquires. It was more than I had been given by King Richard but they had been both patient and loyal. A week before we were due to leave, I gave them the papers the clerk in Northampton had made up for me. They were titles which could be passed on to their sons and they gave them status. It also meant that they would no longer command my men and they would have to find their own men.

Captain Alan's eyes narrowed, "Does this mean we will not be coming with you to France, my lord?"

"It does."

"Then I refuse the title!"

I smiled, "You cannot but hear me out. It is no secret that Prince Henry has designs on France. He sees it as his birthright. When he becomes King, he will need to go to war and you have until he becomes King to raise your own retinues. I will follow his banner and you will follow mine. Who knows, Master Alan, by then Abelard may well be a knight and have men and archers of his own. I am planning for the future for I know I am old and that I have been lucky to live this long. When Thomas, inherits my lands and titles, he will need men to follow his banner. Now, do you see?"

They both nodded and Alan said, "We do, my lord. You are wise. Forgive me."

"There is nothing to forgive. I should have explained all to you without the questions."

I had had more than a year at home and with another grandchild and the prospect of more I knew that I would not be missed. In fact, my sons and son in law had more tears than were shed for me as we left for Dover. We would stay in London on our way south. I knew enough lords who owed me favours to be granted chambers for us all. We only stayed one night but the word of my presence spread and I was visited by Prince Henry who strode into the hall as though he owned it. He grabbed me by the shoulders and hugged me. That it was a genuine hug was not to be doubted.

"Why did you not tell me that you were coming? This is not the residence for you. Come with me! Abelard, fetch Sir William's gear." He grinned at my son, Thomas, the two had played together as adolescents. "Tom, I will fetch your father back on the morrow! I need to catch up with this hero who has shunned me for more than a year! Come, old friend!"

I did not wish to go but I knew I had no choice. I did not wish to alienate the Prince nor did I wish to humiliate him and so I went. We did not have far to go. His father had given him a residence called Cold Harbour although originally it had been called the Pulteney Inn. As soon as I walked in, I felt ancient. It was filled with the young bloods of Prince Henry's acquaintance. I saw knights alongside whom I had fought but they were all Thomas' age. I saw Humphrey and John there too, Henry's brothers. Both looked worse for wear. This was obviously Henry's centre while in London. It was not a castle nor was it a hall and I knew why he made it his home. It would endear him to the common soldier and the people of London. As we had walked to the old inn the Prince had been greeted almost as a friend. None of them would ever have called Henry Bolingbroke a friend.

The Prince, however, was both sober and serious as he sat me at a table in what looked like it had been a small room in the old inn. He said, "Abelard, my man will show you your room and then enjoy yourself, there are young doxies here and they will show you a good time!" My squire left us. A servant brought us wine and then stood so that the two of us could speak privately.

"Here's to you, the protector of the crown and of England! Thank God we have you!"

I downed the wine and then said, "And to you, Prince Henry, but you did not bring me here to flatter me, my lord. Speak what is in your head."

He frowned briefly and then smiled, "My father said that you would say that!"

"You have spoken to your father recently?"

"Do you mean since he asked you to go to France with him? Aye. Do not believe everything that you hear. I am not disloyal but my father is ill and sometimes his judgement is flawed." He quaffed some wine and sighed, "I will not insult you by asking you to remain silent for I know that you are like the confessional. What I say stays in your head. I would have the King's army fight for the Burgundians."

I nodded and sipped my wine, "But your father will lead the army!"

"He will not. Men will say that he is unwell and, in truth, he has relapsed since you saw him but the real reason is strategy. We fight against the Duke of Orléans so that when we defeat him the King of France will fear us. I intend to ask for the hand of King Charles' daughter, Katherine. We can change sides from the Burgundians and I will have the throne of France in my hands."

This was a complicated plot but I saw the hands of Henry Bolingbroke all over it. He had ever been the master of chess when he and Richard had played together. "And who will lead the army in France?"

"The leader, officially, will be Thomas Fitzalan, the Earl of Arundel, but you and the Earl of Warwick will make all of the military decisions. We just need the Armagnacs to be defeated and we can leave the rest for later." He saw the doubt on my face. "Will, would my father have made me the Captain of the Pale of Calais if he did not support me?" The Captain of the Pale of Calais was the effective ruler of the port which contributed one-third of all the taxes England collected. It confirmed what my gut told me, the King and the Prince had colluded to deceive their enemies.

"And you will be in England as will the King so that if we fail then the blame will be on Arundel."

The Prince shrugged, "Sir Thomas has been well rewarded for his service. If he fails, again, he can bear the humiliation. My father and I cannot."

I emptied my goblet and filled it again. I said, to no-one in particular, "I grow weary of games and yearn for the days of the Blue Company."

The Prince looked hurt and leaned forward, "Do not say that, my old friend. What we do is for England. We will be stronger and with France as my kingdom too then no-one will ever threaten us again!"

"Prince Henry, if there is one thing I have learned it is that there is always someone bigger and stronger somewhere but I will do as you ask because I promised the Black Prince." He beamed a smile at me. "Do the other leaders know of this arrangement?"

He nodded. "I have spoken with them all. There are four of you who will be seen by the army and the French as the leaders and, in public, you will all defer to Sir Thomas but he knows his shortcoming and he is in awe of you. He will do all that you ask of him. The Earl of Warwick is also a good man."

I knew that the Beauchamps were well connected and an important family. I had fought alongside the earl, Richard Beauchamp and knew him to be a steady warrior. I could work with him. "Then I will do all that I can to ensure an English victory but I will not be profligate with the men I lead for I take my family and they are more precious to me, Prince Henry, than any king or prince."

If I had slapped him, I could not have expected more shock but he smiled and nodded, "And that is what makes you the man you are. I am content, Will."

The next day I led my men to Dover. We stayed at Canterbury so that we could all pray in the cathedral at the site of the murder of the martyr and then we reached Dover where the harbour was filled with ships. Even though we were a relatively small force, less than two thousand men, we each had two horses and that took many ships. I was just grateful that the voyage would be less than twenty-five miles and we would not have to sleep aboard the ships. I did not sail aboard the royal flagship for I wished to sail with my knights and men.

When we reached Calais then the real campaign would begin. I was in France for the battles and the two earls and the Bishop were the ones who would make political overtures to John the Fearless. The Bishop, with armed men, rode ahead to meet with the Duke of Burgundy for the negotiations which would bring us to war with the Duke of Orléans. This war would be a different war for us. We would not have to scout, at least not yet, for we not only did not know with whom we would fight but also where. It could be anywhere from Calais to the borders of the lands of the Germans. It gave us the chance to let our horses recover. It might have been a short journey but horses were sensitive creatures and they needed rest. I had only brought one horse, Hawk, for Hart was getting old and it made me realise that I too was getting old. Would this be my last campaign?

Chapter 16

The negotiations did not take long, Duke John of Burgundy was called the Fearless for a reason. He was not only without fear he was quick thinking and the opportunity to have reinforcements and from England was not an opportunity to be spurned. The Duke had an army of, it was rumoured, 60,000 men. I doubted that but whatever the true numbers it was a large army and they were heading for Paris. We were a very small army but the Duke, it appeared, valued us.

We would have to make the long journey without the aid of the Burgundians and so we moved as though in enemy territory with scouts out and a strong guard for our baggage train. The thousands of arrows we had brought could not be replaced and they would be as valuable as our horses. As we moved towards the French capital, we met bands of Écorcheurs. These were bands of bandits who were using the civil war to rob any who used the roads and had been created by Bernard, the Duke of Armagnac, as a way of destabilising the Kingdom. They stripped their victims of everything leaving the naked bodies to litter the highways of France. One band was both large enough and bold enough to attack us.

We were passing through a forest close to Beauvais when my archer scouts spotted the waiting bandits. They were bold men and most of them had served either Burgundy or Orléans before going into business for themselves. They just did that which they had learned from the high and the mighty. They had not, however, met English archers. It had been almost seventy years since the Battle of Crécy where the French had learned of the skill of the English longbows. When my archers turned tail and ran for the main column, they just saw lightly armed hobilars. They did not see their leather-covered bows. I was in the van and when the archers galloped towards us, I ordered the knights and men at arms to form a half-circle of spears and lances. Alan of the Woods was no longer with us but Owen the Welshman was an equally skilled captain and he led the archer scouts behind us to join the rest of our bowmen who were already stringing their bows.

As a battle, it was nothing for it was won with the first flight of two hundred arrows. The mob, for that was what they were, came at us en masse and despite their mail and helmets, they had little defence against the two hundred bodkin tipped missiles which plunged down amongst them. As Captain Owen and the advance guard added to the aerial attack so the casualties amongst the Écorcheurs increased. I did not even have to order the charge for when more than eighty of their number lay dead or dying, the rest fled. The attack merely delayed our arrival at Duke John's camp by half a day. We had had to clear the bodies from the road. Unable and unwilling to bury them we burned their bodies and the pall of smoke was a warning for other such brigands to leave our small column of men alone. The Bishop warned us that there were much larger bands closer to Paris and that they supported the Duke of Orléans and the Armagnac faction. We would be fighting with them again.

The Burgundian camp was close to St. Cloud which was a short distance from Paris and spread over a large area but Duke John knew our worth both as soldiers and as potential allies. Space had been left close to the hall he had commandeered for our camp and while our squires saw to our horses and erected our own tents, I went along with the other three leaders to meet with the Duke in the dining chamber in the hall. I guessed that the hall had belonged to a supporter of the Armagnac faction who must have fled when the Duke and his army arrived. We were given a warm welcome by the Duke and his leaders. While the food was brought to us, he told us of his plans and of the opposition we would face. He spoke in French and although I could speak the language, I had to concentrate to understand each word. The longer I was in France then the better was my understanding and by the time I left France, I was fluent once more.

The Duke was a plain-spoken man and he explained his choice of battlefield first and he did so simply, "The Bretons are in Paris and that is why we have withdrawn here for I wish to draw them from the streets of Paris. I have the support of the burghers and merchants of Paris and I would not lose their support by fighting a war in their streets. I wish to fight them here. Bernard, Count of Armagnac, brings his rabble, the Écorcheurs, to fight with as well as the knights of Orléans and Armagnac. He relies on the sheer numbers of his mob and he thinks he has us for he outnumbers us but with your archers, we will teach him that he is wrong."

I saw him examining our faces as he spoke. The other three had been sent by the Prince and his father for disparate and varied reasons. They could each fight but I was the one who would lead the army and it must have shown on my face for Duke John suddenly said, "You are the one they call the Strongstaff!" He used the English word and I nodded. "I like the name and it suits you for you have the look of one who can endure blows in a battle and not run! I can see that you are the warrior here." If he thought to insult the other three then he was wrong for they had each already told me that they bowed to my military prowess. I do not think, however, he was insulting them. He was a plain-speaking man which explained how he had won the support of the ordinary people of France. "If you were in command of this army then how would you win the battle?"

I was speaking French and so I considered each word before I spoke it. "We met these Écorcheurs on the way here, my lord, and they were reckless, wild and we sent them packing in less than a handful of heartbeats. I would draw them on to our bows. We have over 500 archers and they can send 5000 arrows before enemy horseman can cover four hundred paces. When their attack is broken then I would use your horsemen, knights and men at arms to scatter them."

He laughed, "And it is almost as though you are reading my mind, Strongstaff. My plan was close to that. I had intended to draw them onto my swords, lances and shields. They say I killed Louis of Orléans and they hate me with a passion. When they see my banner, they will come for me. I will incorporate your plan into mine, for it is a good one."

I nodded, "And did you have this man killed?"

I saw shock on the faces of the two earls and heard the sharp intake of breath from the Bishop but the Duke merely smiled. "Some men deserve to die and do not deserve the honour of death in battle! Louis was a violator of women and worse, he cuckolded the King. He was attacked and killed when he left the Queen's bedchamber." He raised his goblet, "You are not afraid to speak what is in your mind and I like that. I would have when we fight, you and your retinue be with my bodyguards. There the fighting will be the fiercest and I will be happier knowing that I have your arm to protect me." He had not given me a direct answer but his eyes told me that he had ordered the assassination. Duke John was a ruthless man and for all of his plain speaking, he would get his own way.

"King Henry sent me here to serve him and England. My men and I will be honoured to act as your bodyguard." This meant that we would be in the heart of the battle and the thick of the fighting. Duke John had killed a prince of France and they would try to kill him. King Henry and his son had put my men in extreme danger.

The Duke was a soldier through and through. He spent the rest of the feast explaining his dispositions and his choice of ground. His words gave me confidence for he knew what he was talking about. Before he retired, he came to speak to me, "When your Bishop approached me about an alliance, I was wary for it is known that your King seeks France for his son." He held up a hand. "There is little point in denial and besides I do not care. I am ruthless and I know that he is too. He does what he does for England. I do what I do for Burgundy and France. The battle between England and France is not yet here. When that day comes it will be an interesting battle." His eyes bored into me. I used the same technique for it helped to see into a man's soul. "I need you and your men to win me this battle. I will not need you after."

"And if we lose?"

He laughed so loudly that nobles turned to look, "Neither of us believes that. Your war bows are renowned as you showed on the way here and I have the better knights. Orléans is a weak man and not a warrior to be feared. If you were commanding the opposition or your young Prince Henry then it might be different." He grinned, "I would still win but it might take me longer and I might lose more men. Fight well and you shall be rewarded."

It was my turn to smile, "I always fight well; I have been doing so for more than forty years and there is no other way to fight. Those who do not do so lie in unmarked graves!"

He clapped a bear-like arm around me, "Good fellow! You will do for me!"

As with all such battles the two forces camped across from each other with their forces arranged traditionally. The wings were protected by horsemen and the ranks were arrayed in successive lines. Both sides would use missiles to weaken the enemy before mounted men and men on foot clashed to settle the battle. The difference was a small but crucial one in the battle of St. Cloud for we had archers and Owen the Welshman had stakes cut behind which the archers stood. The fact that we had hundreds rather than thousands meant that, on this battlefield, they appeared to be an insignificant number. I knew that they would have an effect which was out of proportion to their numbers. We had brought many arrows and each archer had a bundle of forty arrows which he could use. There were more arrows than the enemy had warriors! The French and the Burgundians liked to fight on horseback when they could and so I lined up close to Duke John. We were not directly behind our archers; instead, before us was a force of almost a thousand crossbows. Each had a large pavise behind which they sheltered. When the enemy attack was spent, they would pick up their pavise and move to the side. These were mercenaries. They came from many different nations. Some had the windlass type crossbow which was wound back while others had one which required a foot and a strong back. Each man had no more than twenty quarrels, or bolts for it was unlikely that they would have the opportunity to use more than half of that number.

While Duke John rode down the line exhorting his men to deeds of great valour, I spoke to my familia. In my case, it was almost entirely made up of my family. Sir John and Sir Henry of Stratford had both been my squires and so they felt like family. "Remember that we do not need ransom. I suspect that when this battle is done then, whatever the outcome, we shall return to England." That had been the gist of my conversation with the Duke.

Sir John frowned, "Then why are we here at all?"

212

"Prince Henry believes that France is his by right and he has more claim to it than either King Charles or his son. One day he will need to come and claim his birthright. We are here to test the strength of the foes he will face."

"Then we are not here at the command of King Henry?"

I smiled at Sir Richard, "I have been involved with the Kings of England since before the time of the Peasants' Revolt. Both kings that I have served have been clever men and they play chess with real people. You have all played chess and know that it is a game of deception, traps and sacrifices. King Henry would have his son King of France. That is all that I will say."

My knights understood the reality of keeping a crown and winning another.

When the Duke returned, we all knelt while we were blessed by the Archbishop of Rheims. The enemy did the same for many thousands might die this day and each of us wanted to ascend to heaven. The blessing done, we mounted our horses.

Both sides had some cannons which were fired to begin the battle. Most men were able to move away from the missiles as the stones seemed to move more slowly than an arrow. You saw the smoke and were able to watch the rock's flight and only a couple of careless men were killed. In my opinion, all that it did was to frighten the horses and make the air smell foul! Then their crossbows advanced and began a duel with our crossbows. The pavise behind which the Burgundians sheltered won that battle for us and the exchange did not last long. The enemy outnumbered us and the Écorcheurs, along with the knights of Armagnac led the wild charge. I saw that the Bretons and the men of Orléans waited and would be the second wave.

Owen the Welshman looked to me and I nodded. I heard his voice sound above the thundering hooves of the men who were galloping towards us. "Draw!"

The front ranks of the enemy were made up of horsemen whose horses had caparisons and some even had mailed heads. The riders were armoured in plate and mail and they were followed by men on foot who were also armoured. It was like a steel snake racing to gobble us up.

"Release!"

His next command would be lost for the arrows soared towards the enemy and the sound of the enemy horses, combined with the sounds of the bows would hide his words from us. I heard the cracks of crossbows as they sent bolts towards the enemy too. The difference was that while the crossbows were being reloaded the archers had sent a second, third, fourth and fifth flight towards the horsemen. Both the bolts and arrows cut a swathe through the enemy who charged at us but it was clear that the ones attacking the hedgehog of stakes and the successive flights of arrows had suffered more casualties. The enemy visibly slowed for there were many bodies to negotiate. I saw that some of the arrows had fallen amongst the men who followed the horsemen while the bolts had only slowed the front rank. The rest were intact.

The Duke turned to me and smiled, "I should have archers! They are like machines!"

"Yet they are men, my lord, and while you can train a man to use a crossbow in a month or so it takes a lifetime to become an archer! The men I lead began training when they were less than ten summers old."

The crossbows managed a ragged second volley before they were struck by the horsemen. Some managed to flee while others were butchered. The attack on the archers had faltered for the horses had to slow to negotiate the stakes. Some of the archers raced amongst the ones who made it to the stakes; hamstringing the horses, pulling the riders from their backs and slaying them through their eyeholes using bodkin daggers.

It was clear that the attack on the archers had failed but the main attack had cleared a thousand crossbowmen and we had to react or take a charge at the halt. The Duke shouted, "For Burgundy and France!"

His standard-bearer sounded the horn and we began to trot towards the enemy. The few remaining crossbowmen were caught between the hooves of the men of Armagnac and our horses. Some must have survived but most were either speared or trampled. The difference to us was that our spears and lances were unbroken while some of the enemy had had theirs shattered spearing crossbowmen. Abelard and the other squires were two ranks behind us and for that, I was grateful. None would have to fetch us spare horses. If we were unhorsed then we would simply fight on foot.

I had done this so many times that, even though we were still more than a hundred paces apart, I knew which knight I would fight. He had a full-faced bascinet with a boar's snout. He had a shield with ten gold and blue horizontal stripes. I vaguely recollected that such a livery belonged to the knights of Grandpre. He had a lance and I still used my spear which meant he would have a longer reach and would strike me first. Neither group of knights would be riding at full tilt for the field between us was littered with the bodies and equipment of the crossbowmen. That suited me and I did not push my horse. The Frenchman, however, was spurring his mount and urging him on. Horses are brave creatures but in obeying his master the horse was slipping and sliding on the bloody, muddy ground. The knight did not have a stable platform and I did.

Duke John was rightly named for he rode ahead of all of us and he, too, was riding as hard as he could. My familia was to the left of me and they kept a perfectly straight line. We all hit the enemy as one. The French lance wavered so much as it came towards me that the knight would be lucky to hit anything at all. As luck would have it his horse slipped as he neared me and his lance struck the poleyn protecting my knee. It hurt and I would ache for weeks but it neither stopped nor slowed me and the wooden head shattered. I thrust hard with my spear. My knee prevented me from standing but the slip from the Frenchman's horse meant that the knight was unbalanced and had to use his left arm to stop himself from falling to the ground. My spear struck his breastplate beneath his surcoat. His momentum and my powerful arm drove it up and under the besagew to pierce his aketon and tear through his shoulder and into his neck. I think he was dead, even as he fell to earth. He fell away from me and I was able to tear my spear from the body. I still had my weapon and I saw that it was needed.

My familia was still intact and to my left. The Duke and his standard-bearer had become isolated and were surrounded by the men of Armagnac. If the standard fell then the battle was lost. Duke John was not only fearless, but he was also reckless. I shouted in English, "To me! To me!" My familia would hear my words and follow.

I rode at the Frenchman whose back was to me and who was raising his war axe to hack into the Duke. I rammed my spear as hard as I could. There was no besagew at the rear of the knight's armour and I was travelling slowly enough to be able to aim accurately. It slid into his mail and tore open a hole to allow the broadest part of the spearhead to punch a hole as wide as my hand in his back. This time his falling body took my spear with it.

Thomas, Harry and the rest of my knights tore into the huddle of surprised French knights as I drew my sword and stood in my saddle. My knee screamed in pain but I bore it as I brought down my sword to break the arm of the Frenchman who was trying to take the standard from the mortally wounded standard-bearer. As the Frenchman withdrew the standard began to fall. Stretching out my left hand I managed to grab it. The top dipped but I pulled it up and braced the bottom against my sabaton. A sudden wind made it flap and snap above my head. I saw the Duke turn and smile for, like me, he had an open-faced helmet.

I was suddenly the target for the men of Armagnac as it was I who now held the standard of Burgundy. My shield protected the standard but I could no longer move. The Duke and I, along with my familia, were an island in a sea of Frenchmen trying to kill us. I heard Thomas shout, "Shield wall!" It was an old-fashioned formation but it would work. As my men at arms raced to join us my knights turned their horses to face the enemy and make a barrier of horses, shields and steel. It protected the left side of the Duke and I. The knights of Armagnac could attack our right but the Duke's own men were rushing to his aid and the Duke and I could use our swords.

I hacked, chopped and slashed at all who came near to me. Forty years of fighting had taught me how to survive. I was older than all of the men I fought and I was tiring but the same spirit which had made my father so hard to kill came to my aid and I found reserves of strength I did not know I had.

Even so, things might have gone ill with us had not Owen the Welshman, seeing that there were no more foes before them, turned the archers to loose them into the knights who were fighting us. I had never been so close to bodkin arrows striking plate armour and it terrified me. It was though the steel was parchment. The accuracy of the English longbow was such that a red and white fletched arrow went into the side of the helmet of the knight fighting the Duke. The sudden savage rain of death broke the already weakened men of Armagnac and the Écorcheurs. They turned and rode away.

Duke John shouted, "After them!"

I had to ride with him, despite my injury for I had the Burgundian standard. We faced no foe for their backs were to us. The Écorcheurs were all slain for most wore just mail. Some of the knights of Armagnac surrendered while others were slain. Duke John stopped only when we reached their tents for the enemy had all fled. The army had simply disintegrated.

We reined in and Duke John shouted, "Surrender or die!" The handful of men in the camp threw their weapons to the ground. We had won for the ordinary warriors and the mob were either dead or fled and, taking off his helmet he turned to me, "Sir William, I am in your debt. You not only saved my life but the battle and the honour of Burgundy! I shall reward you."

I smiled, "My lord, I have been protecting kings since I first became a warrior. It is in my blood."

He nodded, "And your archers. I wish I knew who was the archer who struck that knight for I would reward him."

I pointed to the archers who were moving over the battlefield relieving the dead knights of their plate and their treasure. "It was a man called Owen the Welshman, lord."

He looked stunned, "How could you possibly know that?"

"I recognised the arrow. Owen makes and fletches his own arrows and the red and white fletch is his. I could identify, perhaps six of my archers' arrows." I shrugged. "They are like my family."

He pointed to my familia who were still unhurt and had gathered behind me, "And your own family are as brave and fearless a group as any. Tonight, you and your men will dine with me for I would speak to each of you." He rode off to speak to his lieutenants.

My archers and men at arms had joined us as well as the rest of the English contingent. The three leaders looked as though they had not even used their weapons. The Bishop's mace hung from his saddle and had no marks of war upon it.

The Earl of Arundel nodded, "You did well, Sir William, and I am guessing that your act of bravery will have earned respect as well as reward from the Duke."

"Yes, Sir Thomas, although I suspect that the Duke expects more from me and, perhaps the rest of you, for my men and I are to dine with him this evening."

"Better and better. This has worked out well for both the King and the Prince." Sir Thomas was a good man but he was a politician. He saw the victory differently from me.

I looked around the battlefield and saw the many dead who littered it. We had been lucky. My men had skill and training and that had helped but it could, so easily, have ended in disaster. I had lost few men and for that I would give thanks to God. We headed back, once we had taken all that there was to take from the tents and the baggage of the Armagnacs to our own camp. Of course, my men were more laden than the others for we had been the first into battle and as such they had had the first pick. Our squires had managed to capture loose horses and I saw that eight of them had chamfron fitted. Such metal headgear for horses was expensive and meant we would all be better protected next time we went to war. The archers and men at arms who had followed me had also gained treasure.

Owen the Welshman was riding a warhorse and was grinning. "Like a proper lord, eh Sir William?"

"Yes indeed, and when we return to England you shall be elevated to a gentleman for your arrow saved the Duke's life and earned the English his undying gratitude."

"I was just doing my duty, Sir William, but I confess that this is preferable to fighting my countrymen. I do not mind killing rebel Welshmen but they are poor as church mice. These French lords go to war with more treasure upon their fingers than an archer might earn in a lifetime."

As we made our weary way back to our camp the same sentiment was expressed by many more of my men. If they were going to risk their lives then it might as well be for great rewards. I know that when we reached home, they told all and sundry of the benefits of war with France.

We were so close to Paris that Duke John was able to send for food and wine from the best shops in that great city. He also sent for cooks who were eager to ingratiate themselves with the victors. Abelard did his best to clean the houppelande I had brought but I had not been careful whilst wearing it in Calais. I now saw that I should have brought more such garments. I had not anticipated great feasts and assumed that it would be like an English campaign! However, I later learned that Duke John did not worry about such matters. To him, it was not the garment but the man who wore it.

I was seated at his right hand and my knights were spread along the table. Our squires would serve us. The Duke began by praising us, once again, and telling the assembled nobility of Burgundy that the English were his friends. He did not go so far as to call us his allies for to do that would have meant alienating some of his other allies. He told the assembled knights that his bodyguard, by which he meant us, would all receive gold taken from the ransoms for the knights of Armagnac and Orléans. He then hinted at more rewards later.

When he sat then the food was brought in and for a short while we were all busy eating. Having risen before dawn and fought for most of the morning then this was our first opportunity to eat well and we did. When we had finished the meat and the cheese was brought in, he turned to speak with me, "Sir William, I would like to make you Count of Arles and I will give to you the city for your own. What say you?"

It was the equivalent of being given the city of York to rule and I would be lying if I said I was not tempted but I was also wary. "And that is a great honour, Duke John, but I am not certain if I could continue to run my own manors and Arles."

He laughed, "If a man rules Arles then he needs nothing else for the city is a rich one."

"And how would I continue to serve King Henry?"

He stopped mid-bite, "You would not! You would serve me."

I shook my head, aware that I could be undoing all the good work we had done thus far. Talking before the meal with the Bishop I had realised that the whole point of our involvement was to make Duke John a friend who would help us to fight the French. It was obvious that he was now willing to do so. "I am sorry, my lord, but many years ago I swore an oath and I have to protect the offspring of King Edward. I know that I am throwing away the chance for riches and great power but an oath is an oath."

He stared at me and then put an enormous bear-like paw around my shoulders, "And you are a true knight. You are a throwback to the knights of old. Your king is lucky to have such loyalty." He glowered at some of his own nobles, "Would that I had such loyalty! Then, instead, I grant you the manor of Sunderda which is in Brabant. It is yours to keep and there are no ties of fealty attached to it. It is small but profitable and by giving it to you I hope that, if I need you, there may be times when you can serve me."

"And you would have that without the manor, my lord, for we have fought together and shared the dangers of battle. That makes you a brother in arms."

He stood and banged the table to get silence. He pointed at me, "Let all here know that the English are now our friends and Sir William Strongstaff is an honorary knight of Burgundy!"

To my great surprise, all the nobles stood and banged the table. I was embarrassed for I had done little enough but it seemed that the Prince's plan had worked. We had seen war could be won by the longbow and we had a friend in the Duke.

It was left to the Earl of Arundel to make our excuses and for us to head back to Calais, laden with French booty. The Duke did not seem to mind for we had done that which he had wished. We had destroyed the enemies of Burgundy although he was disappointed that my men and I would not be with him as he drove towards Berry and Orléans where he hoped to end the civil war.

As we rode west my knights told me of the conversations that they had had around the table. Both our archers and my familia, as well as myself, had surprised the Burgundians. I think that when they had met the earls and their men, they thought that we would be the same. The respect we enjoyed was also reinforced by the first instalments of the ransoms which we would take back. The two earls and the Bishop, not to mention their men did not enjoy the same financial reward. The Burgundians believed in paying those who took the greatest risks and that was my men!

Epilogue

We reached England just a week before Christmas. As we had
to pass through London on our way north, I went to speak with
King Henry at Windsor. I sent my knights home to their families
and I went to see if I had done that which the King intended.

He looked as though he had had a relapse in more ways than
one. His skin had become angry again and he appeared tired,
almost to the point of collapse. However, he appeared to be
pleased with my actions. I made a point of telling him about the
offer of Arles for I did not want another to tell him. Sometimes
Henry Bolingbroke could be petty. He was not surprised that I
had been offered the city but he was amazed that I had turned it
down.

"You really are a strange fish, Strongstaff. Had I been in your
position then I would have grasped it with both hands. You will
not receive such a title from me, you know!"

"And I have been handsomely rewarded by you and your son. I
am content but, while we are alone, King Henry, I have to ask you
something which has been bothering me since I visited with your
son. Were you happy for me to do what I did?"

He smiled, "Of course I was happy! Do you believe that I
would do anything to harm my son? These are games that we play
to deceive our enemies and, sometimes, our friends. I am sorry
that you were deceived for you deserve better. The kingdom
which King Edward made was almost destroyed by my cousin
and that snake, de Vere. You are a warrior and fight your way. I
am not a warrior and I fight my way but we both have the same
end. We seek to make England great once more."

With that, I left but I called in at Cold Harbour to speak with
the Prince. He was even more delighted and his reasons were
more personal. "You have done all that I hoped and more. Now
my father and I can send embassies to France to ask for the hand
of Katherine of France. They will be more likely to listen to the
request now that they have seen what a handful of Englishmen
can do and you have exceeded my expectations in terms of the
Burgundians. The Bishop told me how impressed he was with
you. You are the best of fellows! And now go home and be with

221

your family. You have earned this rest. When I go to take back my birthright, it will be with your knights behind me and then they will be richly rewarded. This is the start of an adventure which will reclaim France for the English crown and we owe it to you, Will Strongstaff!"

The End

Glossary

Abermaw-Barmouth

Aketon- padded garment worn beneath the armour

Ballock dagger or knife- a blade with two swellings next to the blade

Barbican-a gatehouse which can be defended like a castle

Bastard Sword- two handed sword

Besagew- a circular metal plate to protect the armpit

Bodkin dagger- a long thin dagger like a stiletto used to penetrate mail links

Brigandine- padded jacket worn by archers, sometimes studded with metal

Chevauchée- a raid by mounted men

Cordwainers- shoemakers

Cuisse- metal greave

Dauentre-Daventry

Dunbarre- Dunbar

Esquire- a man of higher social rank, above a gentleman but below a knight

Familia – the bodyguard of a knight (in the case of a king these may well be knights themselves)

Fowler- a nine-foot-long breech-loading cannon

Galoches- Clogs

Houppelande -a lord's gown

Horsed archers-archers who rode to war on horses but did not fight from horseback

Hovel- a simple bivouac, used when no tents were available

Medeltone Mowbray -Melton Mowbray

Mêlée- a medieval fight between knights

Poleyn- a metal plate to protect the knee

Pursuivant- the rank below a herald

Rondel dagger- a narrow-bladed dagger with a disc at the end of the hilt to protect the hand

Sallet basinet- medieval helmet of the simplest type: round with a neck protector

Sennight- Seven nights (a week)

The Pale- the land around Dublin. It belonged to the King of England.
Wolveren Hampton- Wolverhampton

Historical Notes

Warkworth Castle (Author's Photographs)

For the English maps, I have used the original Ordnance Survey maps. Produced by the army in the 19th century they show England before modern developments and, in most cases, are pre-industrial revolution. Produced by Cassini they are a useful tool for a historian. I also discovered a good website http: orbis.stanford.edu. This allows a reader to plot any two places in the Roman world and if you input the mode of transport you wish to use and the time of year it will calculate how long it would take you to travel the route. I have used it for all of my books up to the eighteenth century as the transportation system was roughly the same. The Romans would have travelled more quickly!

The King's Illness

King Henry's illness was very real and no one knows exactly what it was. It was partially a skin complaint and St. Anthony's fire or venereal disease might have explained that but he also had fits. The common people, especially those in the north blamed it on the fact that he had the Archbishop of York executed. In terms of the plot, it did keep him from the public's gaze and thrust the Prince into the limelight.

Grosmont

Grosmont was a very prosperous town with almost two hundred houses. There was a castle there but when the Welsh came, they tore the heart out of the town and it never recovered. However, they were caught by English knights, archers and men at arms and important captives taken.

Battle of Pwll Melyn

After Grosmont the Welsh thought that they were close to victory and Usk castle had been allowed to fall into disrepair. Unbeknown to them it had been not only repaired but also reinforced and when the sons of Glendower came, they were chased, not west, but northeast towards a large pond where the majority were slain and Owain Glendower's eldest, captured. It was almost the end of the rebellion.

Battle of Bramham Moor

The last battle of the rebellion which began at Shrewsbury took place close to Wetherby. The Earl of Northumberland did not have a large army. It was made up of the sweepings of the borders. What I found hard to understand was why the battle was fought there. The Earl and Lord Bardolf were heading for York but Bramham Moor is south of York! It was Sir Thomas Rokeby and his Yorkshire knights and the levy who destroyed the threat. This was the end of the Percy family until they were reborn many years later. The dead were hanged drawn and quartered and their parts displayed around the country. Lady Bardolf pleaded with the King for the return of her husband's parts so that he could be buried. The King agreed.

The sieges of Aberystwyth and Harlech

Cannons and artillery were used at Aberystwyth and, for some reason, Prince Henry thought the siege almost over and returned to London. When he left the siege was lifted. He returned and both Harlech and Aberystwyth were besieged at the same time. For the purposes of the narrative I have changed the events slightly but Mortimer and his wife did die of starvation and Glendower did escape. However, he was never seen in public again and was rumoured to have died some four or five years later. Harlech marked the end of the rebellion.

Duke John the Fearless

Duke John is a larger than life character and deserves a whole book to himself. He openly admitted ordering the murder of his rival and, at the battle of St. Cloud, he had a bodyguard of 1000 Englishmen. The English contingent only fought in one battle and then returned to England. Historians still debate the actual motivations of the King and his son. What you have here are my answers to those motives.

The next book will take us to the time of King Henry V[th]. It will cover the Battle of Agincourt which won, (along with the French princess, Katherine,) France for Henry and England.

Books used in the research:
- The Tower of London -Lapper and Parnell (Osprey)
- English Medieval Knight 1300-1400-Gravett
- The Castles of Edward 1 in Wales- Gravett
- Norman Stone Castles- Gravett
- The Armies of Crécy and Poitiers- Rothero
- The Armies of Agincourt- Rothero
- The Scottish and Welsh Wars 1250-1400
- Henry V and the conquest of France- Knight and Turner
- Chronicles in the Age of Chivalry-Ed. Eliz Hallam
- English Longbowman 1330-1515- Bartlett
- Northumberland at War-Derek Dodds
- Henry V -Teresa Cole

- The Longbow- Mike Loades
- The Scandinavian Baltic Crusades 1100-1500
- Crusader Castles of the Teutonic Knights (1)- Turnbull and Dennis
- Crusader Castles of the Teutonic Knights (2)- Turnbull and Dennis
- Teutonic Knight 1190-1561- Nicolle and Turner
- Warkworth Castle and Hermitage- John Goodall
- Shrewsbury 1403- Dickon Whitehead
- Agincourt 1415- Matthew Bennett
- Ordnance Survey Original series map #81 1864-1869

For more information on all of the books then please visit the author's web site at http://www.griffhosker.com where there is a link to contact him.

Griff Hosker
December 2019

Other books
by
Griff Hosker

If you enjoyed reading this book, then why not read another one by the author?

Ancient History

The Sword of Cartimandua Series (Germania and Britannia 50 A.D. – 128 A.D.)
Ulpius Felix- Roman Warrior (prequel)
The Sword of Cartimandua
The Horse Warriors
Invasion Caledonia
Roman Retreat
Revolt of the Red Witch
Druid's Gold
Trajan's Hunters
The Last Frontier
Hero of Rome
Roman Hawk
Roman Treachery
Roman Wall
Roman Courage

The Wolf Warrior series
(Britain in the late 6th Century)
Saxon Dawn
Saxon Revenge
Saxon England
Saxon Blood
Saxon Slayer
Saxon Slaughter
Saxon Bane
Saxon Fall: Rise of the Warlord
Saxon Throne

The Road to Agincourt

Saxon Sword

Medieval History

The Dragon Heart Series
Viking Slave
Viking Warrior
Viking Jarl
Viking Kingdom
Viking Wolf
Viking War
Viking Sword
Viking Wrath
Viking Raid
Viking Legend
Viking Vengeance
Viking Dragon
Viking Treasure
Viking Enemy
Viking Witch
Viking Blood
Viking Weregeld
Viking Storm
Viking Warband
Viking Shadow
Viking Legacy
Viking Clan
Viking Bravery

The Norman Genesis Series
Hrolf the Viking
Horseman
The Battle for a Home
Revenge of the Franks
The Land of the Northmen
Ragnvald Hrolfsson
Brothers in Blood

Lord of Rouen
Drekar in the Seine
Duke of Normandy
The Duke and the King

New World Series
Blood on the Blade
Across the Seas
The Savage Wilderness

The Reconquista Chronicles
Castilian Knight
El Campeador

The Aelfraed Series
(Britain and Byzantium 1050 A.D. - 1085 A.D.)
Housecarl
Outlaw
Varangian

**The Anarchy Series England
1120-1180**
English Knight
Knight of the Empress
Northern Knight
Baron of the North
Earl
King Henry's Champion
The King is Dead
Warlord of the North
Enemy at the Gate
The Fallen Crown
Warlord's War
Kingmaker
Henry II
Crusader
The Welsh Marches
Irish War
Poisonous Plots

The Road to Agincourt

The Princes' Revolt
Earl Marshal

**Border Knight
1182-1300**
Sword for Hire
Return of the Knight
Baron's War
Magna Carta
Welsh Wars
Henry III
The Bloody Border
Baron's Crusade

Lord Edward's Archer
Lord Edward's Archer
King in Waiting (December 2019)

**Struggle for a Crown
1360- 1485**
Blood on the Crown
To Murder A King
The Throne
King Henry IV
The Road to Agincourt

Modern History

The Napoleonic Horseman Series
Chasseur a Cheval
Napoleon's Guard
British Light Dragoon
Soldier Spy
1808: The Road to Coruña
Talavera
The Lines of Torres Vedras

The Lucky Jack American Civil War series
Rebel Raiders
Confederate Rangers
The Road to Gettysburg

The British Ace Series
1914
1915 Fokker Scourge
1916 Angels over the Somme
1917 Eagles Fall
1918 We will remember them
From Arctic Snow to Desert Sand
Wings over Persia

Combined Operations series
1940-1945
Commando
Raider
Behind Enemy Lines
Dieppe
Toehold in Europe
Sword Beach
Breakout
The Battle for Antwerp
King Tiger
Beyond the Rhine
Korea
Korean Winter

Other Books
Great Granny's Ghost (Aimed at 9-14-year-old young people)

For more information on all of the books then please visit the
author's web site at www.griffhosker.com where there is a link to
contact him.

Printed in Poland
by Amazon Fulfillment
Poland Sp. z o.o., Wrocław

55128525R00141